LIQUID
STEELE

A Daggers & Steele Mystery

ALEX P. BERG

BATDOG PRESS
KNOXVILLE, TN

Batdog Press
www.batdogpress.com

Publisher's Note: This is a work of fiction. Names, characters, places, and incidents portrayed in this novel are a product of the author's imagination.

Cover Art: Damon Za
Book Layout: ©2013 BookDesignTemplates.com

Liquid Steele / Alex P. Berg — 1st ed.
ISBN 978-1-942274-27-8

1

I stood in front of the door to apartment three fifteen, feeling like anyone but myself in a tailored gray suit, a white shirt, and even a tie, for gods' sakes. My stomach felt like it might turn and run for the hills if only it could battle its way past my other internal organs and through my suddenly narrow windpipe, and the slab of gray matter between my ears briefly weighed whether that was the best choice. But neither my brain nor my gut nor my most masculine of organs won control of the rest of me. That honor, at least for now, belonged to my heart.

I reached out and knocked on the hardwood.

I shifted my weight as I waited for an answer. The painted wood stared me in the face, questioning my commitment. Had I remembered the apartment number correctly? Or worse, had I arrived at the wrong building? That was just the sort of stupid mistake I'd make, taking the second left turn instead of the third right, or arriving at Gustafson Street thinking it was Gustavsson Street. All the old New Welwic apartment complexes looked the same anyway, having been constructed by some unscrupulous builder who spent the lion's share of his profits greasing the palms of city council members, most likely. Maybe I mistook the building for the one across the avenue. Maybe...

I heard footsteps, and the door creaked open. A smiling face greeted me. "Jake. You made it."

My half-elven partner in crime, Shay Steele, stood in the doorway, tall and elegant and as breathtaking as ever. A hair clip kept her long chocolate locks bunched at the back of her head, though a few strands had escaped and now floated lazily over her shoulders like mischievous will-o-wisps. She wore a diaphanous blouse, almost identical in color to her azure eyes, over a white undershirt, all of which she'd paired with a checkered knee-length skirt and—gasp!—strappy heels. That wasn't the accessory that really surprised me, though.

"An apron?" I said. "You're not going all domestic on me, are you?"

"I'm helping in the kitchen. You know I like to cook."

"You like to eat. There's a difference."

"I'm learning. It's a valuable life skill, something I'd think you'd be ecstatic about." She nodded toward my hands. "What's that?"

Unless she was going blind, it was a perfunctory question. "A bottle of wine. I've been told it's not polite to visit without a gift, although I can't vouch for the quality. You know me and fermented grapes have a longstanding feud."

"Is that what you're calling it these days?"

"Today, anyway. The word that appropriately describes my distaste for the drink hasn't been invented yet."

Something flashed in my peripheral vision, a bicolored blur near the floor. It emitted a banshee-like wail as it slunk toward my shoes, or maybe it was more of a mewl. Same difference.

I looked down. A tabby had escaped the apartment and begun rubbing its musk over the hems of my expensive pants.

I glanced at Shay. "You neglected to mention the feline terrorist."

She shrugged. "Barnabus, though we call him Barney. Would you have come if I'd said anything?"

I hesitated. "Of course."

A dainty snort. "Liar. Come on in."

She took the bottle of wine and stepped aside, waving me in. I took a deep breath and crossed the threshold into the apartment, but nothing crackled through the heavens, breaking through the stories above me to strike me down. Even the butterflies in my stomach had all found places to roost.

Shay closed the door, but not before allowing the demon-possessed sack of claws and fur back inside. The tabby purred as he meandered through the entry hall past me.

"There's a coat rack on the left, at the entry to the living room," said Shay.

"You know me all too well." I stripped off my jacket while Shay continued to talk.

"I'll set the wine on the table, then I'll need to get back to the kitchen. I'm in charge of the yams, and they're close to done. Make yourself at home. Nobody bites, not even Barney. *Oh.* Speaking of which. Jake? This is my dad. Stephen Steele."

I looked up as I hung my jacket on a hook, the butterflies momentarily fluttering. A tall middle-aged elven gentleman had joined Steele where the hallway flared into the living room, dressed in a checkered shirt, a vest, and khakis. He held two fingers of brandy in his left hand.

"Jake Daggers," he said in a welcoming voice. "I've heard so much about you. Nice to finally meet you." He extended a hand.

Shay wasn't exactly his spitting image—the man's hair was lighter in color and salted with grey, and his eyes couldn't decide if they were green or more of a bluish-gray—but the fundamental structure of the face was all there. A sharp nose, arched eyebrows, and ears only slightly more pointed than Shay's.

I shook his hand. "Nice to meet you as well, Mr. Steele. Stephen. Steve?"

"Mr. Steele is fine."

"Right. Of course."

Shay motioned toward an open doorway, one through which delectable smells wafted. The aforementioned yams, and something of the more meaty variety. Maybe a ham. "Kitchen. I'll be back."

She skedaddled, leaving me alone with her father. He clapped me on the back. "Come on in, Jake. Did you have a nice walk over?"

"It didn't rain or snow, and I wasn't mugged, so as nice as can be expected, I guess."

"Good, good."

He led me into the living room to a set of couches and a matching club chair already inhabited by a pair of young men who looked more familiar than not. They stood as we approached.

"Jake," said Mr. Steele. "This is my oldest, Samuel."

"Sam," he said.

"And his younger brother, Shawn."

The young men extended their hands. The elder, who according to Shay was a year or two shy of my age, sported a crop of wavy, chestnut colored hair, while the younger had a shorter, more traditional cut, the kind you'd see on well-dressed kids who went to fancy colleges and took debate. They were both tall like their father, about my height, although more slender than me and with more angular features. Inescapable carryovers of their father's elven blood, no doubt—not that anyone had every complained about inheriting either of those traits.

I shook my way through the extended limbs. "Samuel. And Shawn? Good to meet you. And Stephen?"

"Mr. Steele," said Shay's father again. "Call me old-fashioned, but I prefer a bit of formality now and again."

"Right. Sorry. That's a lot of s's."

"That's my fault," said Mr. Steele. "My wife, Melody, isn't as fond of alliteration as I am. I think she prefers assonance."

"I'm a bit of an assonance man, myself." I grimaced, regretting the joke the instant it left my lips.

Mr. Steele gave me an odd sort of look. "Of course. Please, have a seat."

I did as indicated, as did the cohort of Steeles around me.

Mr. Steele took a sip of his drink. "So, Jake. Tell us about yourself."

It wasn't a request. "Oh. Well, ah...I'm sure Shay has already related most of what there is to tell."

"Of course she has," said Mr. Steele. "But I'd like to hear it from you. Besides, Samuel and Shawn don't have my daughter's ear quite the same way I do."

I glanced at Shay's brothers. They sat on opposite sides of the couch, eyeing me, legs crossed, leaning back, engaged but not welcoming. "Well, where should I start? I'm a homicide detective, obviously. Shay's partner at the precinct. Been doing that for, oh...what? Twelve years now, give or take. Hard to believe it's been that long, or that the Captain was willing to put me on homicide at such a tender age."

"It sounds like thrilling work, if Shay's stories are accurate," said Shawn, his voice not quite conveying the sense of thrill he spoke of.

"Well, it can be. Some of the time, anyway. Obviously, there's a learning curve, not just with the investigative aspects but the emotional ones. Even with the physiological responses. Training yourself not to get queasy when you see some of the victims. That's more experience than anything else. Dulls the senses."

"So you've been a detective for twelve years?" said Samuel.

I nodded. "That's right."

"And how old are you exactly?"

"Ah...thirty-three. Ish."

"*Ish?*" Samuel lifted an eyebrow. Apparently Shay's whole family was as good at that trick as she was.

"Well, it's hard to remember sometimes. Not because I'm getting prematurely old, I assure you. One of the perils of the job. You take a lot of beatings from ogres and the like. I've been telling the department they need to take concussions more seriously, but nobody listens."

I smiled, but nobody else did, so I packed my grin away and saved it for later.

Samuel cocked his eyebrow again. "And I assume you're taking steps to protect Shay from these *vicious ogres?*"

I snorted. "As if she needed my help. I'm sure you're all aware, Shay's quite capable of handling herself, both mentally and physically. She's not afraid of anyone. Liars, thieves, crazed criminals—"

Samuel's facial expression hadn't gone anywhere. If anything, it had hardened.

"But...yeah. To answer your question, I'm taking most of the lumps myself. I'm taking good care of her. *Very good.*"

That last bit hadn't come across as sexual, had it? I sure hoped not.

"Hey, Jake?" Shay's voice rang across the living room, mercifully providing me an exit. She waved from the mouth of the kitchen.

"Just a moment." I rose and joined her.

She glanced at me curiously and spoke in a low voice. "Everything okay?"

"What? Sure. Why not?"

"You seem tense."

"It's nothing. Jitters. I don't think your older brother likes me very much."

"Sam? Nonsense. You're overreacting, same as always. He's protective of me, nothing else."

I glanced back at the trio, still sitting on the couch. It wasn't just Samuel. Shawn's body language hadn't been any warmer, and Steele's father, while superficially pleasant, seemed as if he was playing a role.

I kept that to myself. "I'm sure you're right."

I heard another meow. Looking down, I discovered Barnabus was back. Apparently, he'd taken a liking to my pants. My expensive, virgin to cat pee and claws pants.

A new figure came around the corner from the direction of the kitchen: a middle-aged woman, a good five inches shorter than Shay with hair the same color as hers that fell to the shoulders, dressed in an immaculate white dress that reached to just below her knees. Her azure eyes sparkled almost as brightly as her daughter's. All told, she was quite attractive for a woman of her age, which I took as a good sign for Shay—and me.

"Mrs. Steele," I said. "A pleasure to meet you."

"Yes. Welcome."

I'd expected a "Please, Jake, call me Melody," or something of that nature, but *nope.* Like husband, like wife, I supposed.

"I must say, dear, you have good timing," continued Mrs. Steele. "The food is about ready."

"Johnny on the spot, that's me. It's why I waited ten minutes at the door before knocking."

"Pardon?"

Another joke, fallen flatter than a pancake trampled by a herd of stampeding buffalo. "Never mind."

"Well, don't bother yourself over it. Shay? Could you show Jake to the dining table? Stephen? Boys? Dinner's ready."

Shay touched me on the elbow and gave me a nod, leading me through the kitchen to the dining table beyond. There, I found a spread worthy of kings. Not just the ham and yams my nose had alerted me to, but fresh baked buttered rolls, peas sautéed with bacon, some sort of braised greens, maybe beet or collard, and a mysterious gelatinous mass with pieces of fruit suspended in it—probably something that would be passed off as a desert despite its distinct lack of chocolate, whipped cream, or fried dough. Dishes large and small choked the white lace table cloth underneath, joined as they were by pitchers of water, highball glasses, wine glasses, neatly folded napkins, and more pieces of silverware than you could shake an oyster fork at.

Shay showed me toward a seat in the middle while everyone else filed in, making remarks about how delectable the dinner smelled and giving thanks.

"Jake? Perhaps you could serve everyone the wine you brought?" Shay's mother gestured toward the bottle, which Shay had placed at the center of the table.

And make a buffoon of myself in the process, showing everyone that I didn't know the foggiest thing about wine or how to pour it? "Of course. I'd love to."

Shay took her seat. "Everyone here partakes, except you of course."

Mr. Steele looked up as he scooted his chair in at the head of the table. "You don't drink, Jake?"

I removed the wax from the top of the bottle and fumbled with the corkscrew. "Well, not wine."

"Ah."

One word, two letters, and yet the man managed to make it sound judgmental. Was he disappointed I didn't drink wine, or that I drank anything but?

The cork came loose with a loud *pop*. Rather than shred it attempting to loosen it from the screw, I handed the whole kit and caboodle to Shay. I poured her glass first, hoping her family might start portioning the food, but they all sat there, waiting patiently and staring at me.

"So, Jake," said Mrs. Steele. "Shay's told us quite a bit about your adventures. Kept us abreast of the cases you've solved. From what she tells us, it seems the two of you get yourselves into the oddest of situations."

"It's not by choice, Mom," said Shay. "We investigate every murder that comes across our desks. Sometimes they're mundane, a stabbing or a bar fight gone wrong. Other times they're convoluted webs of felonies and deceits."

"Isn't that the truth," I said, moving the wine bottle to the next glass in line, Shay's father's. "We've solved cases where the impossible turned out to be possible, and others where the impossible was, in fact, impossible, just a ruse to throw us off. Technology masquerading as magic, magic used to cover deceits, fantastical creatures. We've just about seen it all, and in less than a year working together, amazingly enough. I think that says something about the city we live in..."

I thought Mrs. Steele might inquire about the cases, but she seemed more focused on the latter part of my reply. "Well, regardless, we're very proud of our little Shay. To have achieved what she has in so little time.

It's remarkable. How long have you been a detective, Jake?"

I finished with Mr. Steele's glass and moved on, grabbing Samuel's. "Well, as I told Samuel here—"

"Sam," he said.

"Right. Sam. As I told him, about twelve years. I was a young pup when I started."

"About the age of our Shay," said Mr. Steele. He eyed me, swirling his glass of wine. Somewhere under the table, Barnabus meowed.

"She's a little older than I was when I started. A few years, at least." I set Samuel's glass down and moved to Shawn's.

"Shay's told us precious little about your family, though," said Mrs. Steele.

"Well, it's, ah...not something I talk about much. If I'm being honest, I'm not particularly close to my folks."

Shay's father's eyes narrowed. "That's a shame."

I felt something rub against my leg. Barney, no doubt. What in the world did the cat think he was going to get out of me? Couldn't he sense I'd as soon pet him as throw him off a cliff? I shook my leg to clear him away, but not so much as to slosh the wine.

"It's probably not what you think. My mother was murdered when I was young. It was difficult. Like it or not, it drove a wedge between my brother, my father, and me. It was one of the motivating factors behind my career choice."

"Oh, I'm terribly sorry to hear that," said Mrs. Steele. "We had no idea."

Finally, a little sympathy. I set Shawn's glass down and moved to Melody's.

"But I wasn't asking about your parents," she continued. "We understand you have a son. From a previous marriage?"

I hesitated as I reached for her stemware. I felt my cheeks warm. Deep inside, the butterflies had fled, replaced instead with a wasp's nest—which Shay's mother had apparently decided to poke with a stick. The damn cat kept purring and rubbing against my leg.

"Mother..." said Shay.

"No, it's alright," I said, lifting her glass. "Yes, I do. His name is Tommy. He's about five and a half. A wonderful age."

"It's a great responsibility, being a father, isn't it, Jake?" said Mr. Steele.

Barney kept making love to my leg. I shook him off, trying to keep the rest of my body still as I poured the wine but probably looking like I was suffering from degeneration of my nervous system. "Ah. Yes. It...it is. Very."

"Well," said Melody. "I hope you're able to give him the attention he needs. At that age, children need a strong guiding hand. Without a father by his side, a boy—"

Pain lanced through me as claws and teeth sunk into my shin. I swore and lashed out, kicking my leg.

The table shook. Glasses tipped. Barnabus soared, mewling in panic before slamming into the wall with a thump. I tumbled and fell. Wine flew.

A chorus of voiced cried out.

"Good gods! Barney!"

"The table!"

"My gown!"

I scrambled to my feet, searching for words. "I...uh..."

Mrs. Steele glared at me, her white dress soaked through the bodice and sprayed with a hundred tiny droplets of red. Samuel and Shawn glared at me as more wine soaked through the tablecloth and dripped onto the floor. Mr. Steele glared at me, the pitiful whining form of Barnabus cradled in his arms.

And there stood Shay, a look of horror frozen onto her face.

I swallowed. *Hard.*

2

I turned the corner from Schumacher Avenue onto 5th, the morning breeze cool but the sun already warm on my back. The summer solstice was a few weeks away, but it seemed as if the season might arrive early this year.

In front of me, the massive seal of justice hung over the precinct's front doors, the carved granite depictions of soaring eagle wings and balanced scales glittering in the early morning sunlight.

Well, maybe not *early* morning.

I yanked on the front doors and let myself in, relishing in the cool air that greeted me. I reveled less in the stale smell, a mixture of burnt coffee, old wood, and cigarettes impudent beat cops had hastily puffed in the hallways when no one was looking. Still, it was a familiar smell, one that had soaked into my skin over the years and would soon claim the piece of cowhide I wore over my shoulders. I'd picked up a new one a few months ago, but eventually the tanning chemicals would fade, leaving Eau de Precinct in its wake.

An unfamiliar face manned the welcome desk, one belonging to a dark elf breed who looked as if he'd spent the entire night there and then some. I gave him a halfhearted wave and wove my way around the edge of the tangled morass of cubicles and workstations we lovingly referred to as the pit. Luckily, my workspace was at the swamp's edge.

Shay's desk butted up against my own, facing away from the precinct's entrance. My partner sat there, wearing a bright yellow blazer and dark slacks, her chocolate brown hair held in a bun by a pair of crossed sticks. Her head was buried in a pile of papers.

I sighed.

Through I wasn't close enough for Shay to pick up on my breathy expression of sorrow, someone else was. Quinto turned and shot me a glance. "Daggers. You made it."

The big guy filled his chair with his bulk, all three hundred odd pounds of it, and though in his current state he only measured about five feet, he'd be quite a bit taller if he stood. His thick skin was a pale gray in the morning light, a byproduct of his alleged trollish heritage, something which was well agreed upon but which to my knowledge Quinto had never admitted to.

I understand why. Despite recent education efforts, New Welwic still suffered from its fair share of race relation problems, and trolls got a worse rap than most. All it took was a single lunatic who killed a half-dozen people and tried to eat them for the whole race to get negatively profiled for another decade.

I gave the one man goon squad a nod. "You sound surprised, almost as if I hadn't established a long history of coming into work late."

I thought I heard a sniff from the direction of Shay's desk, but my partner didn't turn.

"Oh, I know," said Quinto, flashing me a smile full of mismatched buckteeth. "And it's not even that late. Not for you, anyway. It's that you'd actually started arriving at a decent hour and kept it up for a couple months. I thought you'd turned a new leaf."

"I had."

"And?"

"The leaf blew away." I nodded at the desk opposite Quinto's. "Where's your perpetually cheery partner?"

Quinto's smile broadened. "Rodgers got randomly selected for compliance training. He'll be stuck in meetings and seminars for three days."

"A plight you seem particularly empathetic to."

"Hey, I remember when you got selected a few years ago. The bitching took weeks to subside."

"Which means you'll be subjected to the same when Rodgers returns, so I don't know what you're so happy about."

"You mistake my smile," he said. "I'm glad I wasn't the one selected. Besides, Rodgers isn't the grouch you are. I'll deal with the aftermath for a day, tops."

I nodded, tapping my fingers against the edge of his desk. "Gotcha."

Quinto turned back toward his reading materials.

I lingered.

He looked up. "Something wrong?"

"Huh? No. Wooden leg syndrome. Better than wasps in the stomach."

Quinto's brow furrowed, but I left before he could grill me over it. I crossed to my desk, pulled out my chair, and dropped into it.

Shay held a pencil in her hand, her eyes darting between a case file and a form. After a few scribbles she looked up. "Hey."

"Hey," I said.

She glanced at the window. "Quinto's right. You're late."

"It's all relative. If you consider the last month, I'm here forty-five minutes late. If your frame of reference is a year ago, I'm an hour early."

Shay snorted and shook her head.

"Hey, I didn't sleep well, okay? It was hard enough forcing myself out of bed to get here at this hour."

"And you think you're the only one who didn't sleep well? Give me a break. As if I would've slept like a baby after last night."

"Hey, I don't know. Maybe. There are a lot of things that don't seem to bother you."

Shay narrowed an eye. "What's that supposed to mean?"

"Just that it took an act of dramatic tragedy to get a rise out of you last night. Sure, when the wine goes flying and I get savaged by a feral cat, you show some emotion, but when I'm getting attacked by your parents and brother, it falls on deaf ears."

"*Excuse me?*" Shay's cheeks darkened. "Daggers, you ruined my mother's dress, not to mention the table-cloth. A half dozen glasses and dishes are broken! Who knows if Barnabus is going to pull through after you drop kicked him into the wall, and you're concerned that *I'm not standing up for you enough?*"

"Hey, guys?" Quinto had left his chair and sidled up next to us. "Is everything okay?"

Perhaps we were being louder than I'd thought. "It's fine."

"No, Daggers, everything is not *fine*," said Shay. "My parent's cat is on the verge of death thanks to you."

"*What?*" said Quinto.

I snorted. "Now who's prone to exaggeration?"

Shay turned to Quinto. "While meeting my parents last night, Daggers punted the family cat into the wall, probably fracturing half his rib cage based on how he's been acting since. He also spilled a bottle of wine onto my mother's bosom, something he still hasn't apologized for."

"What are you talking about?" I said. "I apologized profusely last night."

"For curb stomping Barney, sure."

"No. I apologized about the wine. I never apologized about the cat. That little hellion tore into my leg like a savage goblin, and at the worst possible time. He knew what he was up to. Speaking of which, I should probably get tested for rabies..."

Shay turned to Quinto. "Are you hearing this?"

The big guy gave me a glum look. "Look, Daggers. We all know about you and cats. *Tore into your leg?* Come on, man."

"You want to see the scars?" I said. "He came out of nowhere. I was totally blindsided. And lest Shay trick you into generating too much sympathy for her cat, let's not gloss over how the more sentient members of her family treated me."

Shay looked exasperated. "Daggers, what are you talking about?"

"I told you, everyone there was ganging up on me. Your dad held me at arm's length, your brothers clearly thought I was nothing more than a human shield to protect you while at work, and your mother was far more interested in harassing me over my previous marriage than she was in getting to know me."

"That is *so* not true," said Shay.

"Guys," said Quinto, holding up his hands. "It's possible you're both right, at least in your interpretations of the night's events. Daggers, obviously you injured their cat, maybe not on purpose, but you have to admit your attitude toward those animals makes you far from a reliable witness on the matter. And Steele, even though you feel your family might've been welcoming to Daggers, you have to consider how he might've perceived the situation. After all, meeting a girl's parents—"

Shay shot him a withering glance.

"—is, uh...well, it's none of my business, is what it is. In fact, I think I'll get back to work now that I mention it."

A new voice emerged, a hard, measured, feminine one. "Not so fast, Detective Quinto."

I turned toward the voice. Captain Beverley Knox stood outside her office, her arms crossed and her face set with a perpetually stern expression. She regarded us with cool grey eyes, eyes that somehow managed to combine all the best and worst elements of an irate father, a disappointed grandmother, and a teacher who believes you can do anything if you simply put your mind to it. She may have only stood tall enough to provide my elbows a convenient resting spot and weighed barely more than Quinto's left leg, but the aura she projected was anything but small. I suspected her spirit animal was an elephant or a kraken or an aurochs on steroids.

Quinto nodded. "Captain."

Steele and I nodded, too. We'd been louder than I'd thought, no doubt about it.

Knox unfolded her arms and approached our desks. She surveyed Shay and me with a careful glance. "Everything under control here, detectives?"

Shay and I answered at almost the same time. "Yes, Captain."

Knox swept those omniscient eyes of hers over us before responding. "Good. Because I have a suspicious death for the three of you that needs looking into."

Quinto lifted an eyebrow. "Is it related to the runner who dropped by first thing this morning? You know I'd have been happy to get the investigation started."

"You know the rules, Detective," said Knox. "We work in pairs, at a minimum. As long as Detective Rodgers is busy in his compliance training, you're in the company of Detectives Daggers and Steele, the former of which is *finally* here."

Captain Knox shot me another look. I'd bet she could deflate balloons with her eyes.

"Sorry, Captain," I said. "I'll be on time tomorrow."

"I hope so," she said. "But in this case, your tardiness may not make much of a difference. It doesn't appear as if time is particularly of the essence in this case."

The venom had left Steele. She tilted her head in question. "What do you mean by that?"

"A body washed ashore," said Knox. "Down at the shipyards, at a place by the name of A&G Shipbuilding Limited. I don't have all the details, but it sounds as if the corpse has been at sea for at least a week, maybe more."

I grimaced.

Knox noticed. "Exactly. So take Coroner Moonshadow with you. I suspect you'll need her expertise."

We all sat there for a moment until Knox gave us one of those nods with an implied, "What are you waiting for?" in it. Then we scattered like ants.

3

A&G Shipbuilding was on the east side of the city, across the bridge that spanned the Earl River and quite a ways from the precinct, so we took rickshaws. I'd thought Shay's anger had faded upon the arrival of Captain Knox at our desks, but perhaps not, as she chose to ride with Quinto instead of me.

That left me to ride with our coroner, Cairny Moonshadow, who happened to be Quinto's girlfriend. I can't imagine she or her beefy beau were particularly pleased about the arrangement. Then again, Cairny was Shay's best friend, and they'd developed almost a psychic connection during my partner's stint at the precinct— psychic in the mundane, we glance at each other and giggle and know exactly what the other is thinking sort of way. In any case, if anyone would understand Shay's desire for privacy, it was probably her.

Cairny's long black hair fluttered in the cool breeze that whistled off the Wel Sea and up the Earl as we crossed the bridge, smacking me in the face with its wispy tendrils. She stared at the water as our driver slapped his feet against the pavement, paying me the same heed as she would the machinations of kings or the threat of the world suddenly imploding. I didn't take it personally. She'd always been a daydreamer, seemingly finding death to be the most interesting part of life, which explained her career choice. Quinto had managed to bring her out of her shell, as had Shay, but her more vivacious personality quirks only came out when we all spent time together, along with Rodgers and occasionally his wife Allison.

Come to think of it, despite all the years I'd spent alongside Cairny at work, I could count on one hand the number of times she and I had been alone together. Usually when I consulted with her it was alongside my partner, now Shay and before her Griggs, rest his soul. I didn't start spending time with her outside of work until after Shay's appearance. One of the many ways my partner had changed me, I guess.

I cleared my throat as we clattered off the far end of the bridge and delved into the dock district. "So, Cairny. How've you been lately?"

She turned and blinked at me with those huge, saucer-like eyes of hers, the only part of her that really screamed fairy. "How have I been?"

"Yeah. You know. How's life?"

"It's the state of living. The antithesis of death, but not of being undead. That's an entirely different state altogether, one I'm still woefully uninformed about. What did you want to know about zombies?"

"I didn't ask about zombies."

"Oh. Right. So the opposite of zombies? Those are the living, aren't they? Or were you referring to something else? Some construct maybe? What was the question, again?"

I sighed, remembering why I didn't spend a lot of alone time with Cairny. Luckily, we were nearing our destination.

I pointed down the harbor, toward a collection of brightly-colored warehouses that stood along the shore like a set of toy blocks belonging to the world's largest baby. "That's Cornwall Heavy Industries, isn't it? Remember when we found that man there? What was his name? Barrett, I think. I know that case was only five or six months ago, but it feels as if it's been ages."

Cairny surprised me with her answer. "We've undergone quite a few changes since then, haven't we? It was during that case that my relationship with Quinto started to blossom, and I believe the same could be said of your relationship with Steele. We lost the Captain to that case, among others. I'm sorry about Griggs, by the way. I'm not sure if I ever adequately expressed that to you."

I blinked. Cairny's dispassionate personality made me suspect she didn't possess the same capacity for compassion most people did. It was nice to see I was wrong. "Thanks."

Cairny kept me enthralled with her eyes. "Speaking of relationships, what's the matter between you and Shay?"

"A difference of opinion. Or perhaps a difference of perceived reality."

"I see."

Our rickshaw pulled up in front of A&G Shipbuilding, a much smaller shipyard than the aforementioned

Cornwall Heavy Industries. A thick-necked bluecoat lounged at the entrance, an officer by the name of Poundstone who was good at lifting heavy objects, eating doughnuts, and little else. At his side stood a fisherman or dock worker of some sort, an assumption I made based on his thick beard, flannel shirt, and woolen cap.

I reached into my wallet for some coins to pay the driver. Behind us, I heard the clatter of Shay and Quinto's rickshaw as it arrived.

"Daggers?" said Cairny.

I looked up. "Yes?"

"I know you, better than you think I do. Don't be an idiot. With Steele, I mean."

"I'll try."

We stepped down from the hand cart and approached Poundstone, almost simultaneously with Steele and Quinto. I gave the beat cop a nod. "Poundstone. Who's your friend?"

"Harris," said the flannel-swathed one. "Danny Harris. I work here at A&G."

"You're the one who found the body?" asked Quinto.

"One of them anyway," he said. "Me and my mates Frederick and Tolliver chanced across him first thing this morning."

"Well, what are we waiting for?" I said. "Show us the way."

Poundstone grunted and turned into the shipyard, tailed closely by his new best pal Harris. Following in their footsteps, we trekked through the maze of structures at the water's edge, past flimsy metal buildings belching smoke from tall chimneys and past huge dry docks, some with the skeletons of boats within and some without, under tall cranes and past hulking piles of lumber, sheet metal, coiled rope, and steel pipes. Though the buildings at A&G weren't quite the size of those further down the street, the steady progress of the industry was on full display, as even the smallest ships under construction would've dwarfed those of a decade ago.

We reached a quay with a flimsy staircase that led down to a narrow beach. There in the sand, amid bits of discarded trash that had floated ashore on the tides, lay a still form.

Sand crunched underfoot as I left the safety of the stairs. Waves lapped the shore about eight feet from the edge of the body, the water seeping through to keep the sand under the corpse damp but not saturated.

I gave Harris a nod. "Did you or anyone else touch the body?"

"Didn't have to," said the dock worker. "Tide's going out. Will be for another couple hours. Besides, none of us wanted any part of touching *that*."

I understood what Harris meant as I closed to within sniffing range. The dude was *ripe,* like a dumpster behind a sushi restaurant on the hottest day of summer. He wore similar garb to Harris: a woolen sweater underneath a wine-colored jacket, a thick woolen cap of the same hue, grey canvas pants, but no shoes. He was also only barely discernable as a 'he.' The beard gave his gender away, but the other fleshy parts of him were a horrifying mess. Birds, fish, and crabs had eaten their fill of the man, pecking at his eyes and cheeks and lips. Bits of bone, teeth, and gristle peeked through holes in his face, the majority of which had turned a shade of bluish-green.

I swallowed hard and looked away, keeping the contents of my stomach in place only through sheer force of will.

Steele shook her head, giving me a disappointed look. "And to think you gave me a hard time for getting queasy during our early cases."

"Hey, gore I can handle," I said. "Decay is another matter. Cairny? You're up."

Cairny pulled a pair of delicate white gloves from the pockets of the jacket she wore and donned them before kneeling next to the body. She trailed her eyes across the mangled corpse, touching an ear, tilting the head, pulling on the edge of the jacket or the hem of the pants, her lips pressed tightly together all the while.

I gave Harris another nod. "Tell us everything you know."

"There's not much to tell," he said. "Already told you how me and Frederick and Tolliver ran across the body this morning. Around eight I'd say. We sent for the police. Your man arrived within the hour. We've been waiting for you ever since."

"And I'm assuming you didn't see any signs of activity around the beach this morning? Mysterious individuals loitering about, footsteps in the sand, anything of that nature?"

The dock worker gave me a cockeyed look. "Look, mate, I'm no expert, but I'm pretty sure he washed ashore."

"Just checking," I said. "It's possible someone left him here, intending for you to find him, looking like he'd been brought in by the tides. I've encountered weirder things in my time."

Harris shook his head. "Well, I didn't see anything like that. Just the body, that's it."

I turned back to the mangled corpse. Shay and Quinto had joined Cairny and the flies within buzzing range. I tied my stomach down and joined them.

"So, Cairny," I said. "What are we dealing with? A death, or a murder?"

"Oh, definitely the latter," she said without looking up. "Check out the feet."

I grimaced. "Do I have to?"

"The man's skin has been picked apart by wildlife," said Cairny, "but if you look at his ankles, you'll see more than that. The flesh has sloughed off, a result of ropes cutting into his muscle and ultimately slipping off after a number of days of decomposition. I'd say somewhere between seven and ten."

"So someone tied weights to his ankles and pushed him off the edge of a boat?" asked Shay.

Cairny nodded. "I'd assume as much."

"Could be a mob hit, except for the shoddy knot work." I rubbed my chin. "Was he dead when he hit the water, or did he drown?"

"Hard to tell," said Cairny. "As you can see, he's in rough shape. I'll need to get him back to the morgue before I make any guesses as to the manner of his demise."

"Well, I'm sure you'll figure out what did him in sooner or later," said Shay. "The bigger problem, I think, is going to be figuring out *who* this guy is."

Quinto nodded grimly. "Yeah. Every last scrap of Boatreng's artistic ability isn't going to help us if the sketch he produces looks like something out of a nightmare. I'm not even sure if one of this guy's next of kin will be able to identify him given the state he's in."

I thought that was a bit of an exaggeration, but Quinto was right about the sketch. We wouldn't be able to figure out his identity showing that around. All we'd accomplish would be to give people the shakes.

I shrugged. "We haven't checked his pockets. We might get lucky."

Shay shot me a glance. "I don't see you volunteering."

"Damn right you don't."

Quinto sighed. "And to think you two get paid more than me."

The big guy knelt, rolled up his sleeves, and starting patting down the corpse's coat. He lifted the flaps and checked the interior pockets, then moved on to the pants. He shook his head, wiping the sand from his knees as he stood.

"Nothing," he said. "Looks like his assailants cleaned him out before leaving him to the fishies. Unless the crabs stole his wallet..."

"Unlikely," said Cairny. "To my knowledge, crabs aren't one of the species that exhibit symptoms of kleptomania. Many animals are thieves, but only when it comes to food or other natural resources that grant a tangible benefit to survival. A wallet wouldn't. A bowerbird, on the other hand, might've taken it, but there's none of those in these climes."

"A what bird?" said Quinto.

Cairny looked up from the corpse. "A bowerbird. The males of the species build mating lairs out of sticks and decorate them with all sorts of gaudy trinkets to attract females. In the wild, they use brightly colored objects such as stones and fruit, but bowerbirds living in proximity to urban environments have been found to use trash of all kinds as decorations. But that's not even the most intriguing fact about bowerbirds. Did you know they employ the physical principle of forced perspective while crafting their bowers? Ornithologists suspect they do so to make themselves appear larger and more attractive to prospective females."

Quinto scratched the buzzed hair on the top of his head. "Really, I was just making a joke..."

"More on topic, though," said Shay as she gazed at the dead guy. "I think we might be able to identify the victim via other means."

"Such as?" I asked.

Shay gave me a sharp look, one that either indicated disappointment in me for not noticing the same clue she had or one that meant she was still steamed at me for other reasons. "The man's coat is monogrammed. Over the right breast. NFC. Could be his initials. Or given that his coat and hat are matching in color, his clothing could be part of a uniform. It's possible NFC are the initials of the company he worked for."

I hadn't noticed the lettering initially, probably because the coat was so tattered. The crabs and fish may not have stolen the man's clothing, but they'd certainly tried to eat it. There were at least a hundred small rips, tears, and pockmarks in the fabric, as there were in the stiff's pants and, presumably, his cap and sweater. Those were knit, which made it harder to tell.

I turned to Harris, who stood by the edge of the wooden steps with Poundstone. "NFC mean anything to you?"

The dock worker shook his head. "Sorry. But I'm only familiar with the shipbuilding and transportation businesses here in the district, east of the Earl."

"Meaning what, exactly?" I said.

Harris pointed into the water. "Currents flow west to east. Do all along the shoreline, for hundreds of miles until the transverse thermals break the trend. If this guy got dumped at sea, he probably floated here from someplace to the west. No way to know where, though. He could've been dumped five miles out or a hundred."

"A hundred miles?"

"Or more."

I sighed, turning back to my crew. "I think this case is going to redefine the term legwork."

"Not for me," said Cairny. "I need to get this body to the lab to start a more thorough analysis. Canvassing the surrounding areas lies on the wrong side of the line separating mortuary and detective work."

"Lucky you," I said.

"You could help me transport the body first," said Cairny. "I'm sure Captain Knox wouldn't object."

My nose wrinkled as I took another look at the corpse. "On second thought, I could use the exercise. Quinto? Steele? Let's hoof it."

4

I walked down a rickety dock, the salt- and spray-weakened boards under me clattering against their loosened nails with each of my steps. A fisherman wearing a set of suspenders and with his arms bare coiled rope on the deck of his boat, a modest vessel with a green hull and the name *The Drag Queen* painted in stenciled letters across the bow.

I waved as I got close. "Ahoy there. Nice ship you've got." I made sure not to call the vessel a boat. I'd made that mistake more than once already.

The fisherman looked up. "Ahoy there, yerself. An' the *Queen* accepts yer praise with a knowin' but humble thanks. She's one of the best trawlers in the Wel Sea, an' she darn well knows it."

Was the fisherman speaking on behalf of his ship? I'd met some oddballs on my morning's travails, but none *that* odd. "A *troller?*"

"Get the wax outta yer ears," said the fisherman. "Do ya see any outriggers? She's a trawler, not a troller."

I had no idea what he was talking about. "Right. My mistake."

The man kept coiling rope. "Ya need something?"

I felt a sense of déjà vu as I launched into my spiel, probably because I'd gone through the same set of questions about fifty times already over the past hour and a half.

"I do, actually. The name's Jake Daggers, NWPD. We found a body washed ashore this morning a few miles from here, over at A&G Shipbuilding. The guy'd been lost at sea, probably for a week or two based on our best guess. We're trying to figure out who he is. He was wearing a jacket with the letters NFC stitched over the right chest. I don't suppose that acronym means anything to you?"

The fisherman barely looked at me as he finished with one massive coil and moved onto the next. "You be supposin' right. Them letters aren't ringin' any of me bells."

"They could be the man's initials," I said. "Or an abbreviation of his company."

"Or an abbreviation of his ship's moniker."

I perked. "You think?"

"Probably not. Never heard of any bloke who put his ship's initials on his jacket, but there's all kinds o' odd folk out at sea."

I held my tongue. "So can you think of any ships with names that start with the letters NFC?"

The fisherman stood and scratched his temple. "Well, let's see now... The *Naomi Francone*? No, that would just be NF, wouldn't it? Well, if not her... Oh!

I've got it. The *Knack Fer Catchin.'* I've seen her out in the bay a few times. I'd guess she's local."

"Wouldn't that be KFC?"

The fisherman frowned. "Would it? Eh, I suppose so..."

I suppressed a sigh. "What about a uniform? Do you know any seafaring companies or organizations where the employees wear maroon jackets and knit caps?"

"Not sounding familiar, there. Sorry."

I gave the man a halfhearted wave. "Not a problem. Thanks for your time."

I headed back up the dock toward the main wharf, where I saw Steele and Quinto approaching from the far side. Upon reaching solid ground, I rested my backside against the concrete railing and waited, letting the cool sea breeze tickle the back of my neck.

I tried not to let a sour mood overtake me, but my feet were already complaining from all the walking. Canvassing was unequivocally my least favorite part of detective work, and I couldn't help but simmer over the fact that Steele had once again chosen to head off with Quinto rather than stay with me. Not that we were working together, exactly. We'd all split up upon arrival at the wharf to be able to talk to as many fishermen as possible, but my eyes didn't deceive me. Shay had chosen to head over to Quinto's side of the pier each and every time before branching out on her own.

I gave the pair a nod once they broke into hailing range. "I sure hope you had better luck than I did."

"By the tone of your voice, I'd guess not," said Quinto. "Not a man I talked to had ever heard the initials NFC, much less knew what they stood for."

"Man or *woman*," corrected Steele.

Quinto gave her a dubious look. "I'm all for political correctness, but I'll be honest, I didn't meet a single female working any of those vessels. Did you?"

"Yes, actually," said Steele. "At least, I think so. She was an ogre. It was hard to tell."

"Gender confusions aside, I'll bet your outings fared better than mine," I said. "This last guy I talked to thought his boat had a mind of its own, and he mistook the letter N for the letter K."

"Like in the word knot?" asked Shay.

"Knack, actually, but yeah."

Quinto sighed. "Normally, I don't mind legwork, not on nice days like today, but it could take us days to canvass all the marinas in New Welwic—and weeks longer if we have to expand our search outside the city."

"Think the dockworker at A&G was giving an accurate estimate of a hundred miles as our target radius?"

Quinto shrugged. "Might be, but I'd suspect it's what we'd normally call a WAG."

"Wives and girlfriends?" I said.

Quinto snorted. "The other meaning. Steele, you noticed the monogram in the first place. You have any better ideas for identifying the stiff than our current spray and pray method?"

Shay cocked an eyebrow. "Well—"

"Fishy," I interrupted.

Steele and Quinto both shot me odd looks.

"The corpse needed a name. I like Fishy. It humanizes him. Makes him more than an odious pile of rotting flesh. And how come you automatically assumed Steele would have a better idea about how to proceed than me, Quinto? I noticed the monogram, too, you know."

Quinto frowned. "I asked her because she has good ideas. And it doesn't matter if you noticed the lettering. This isn't a competition."

"Good thing, too," I muttered. "Otherwise I'd get picked last every time."

Shay crossed her arms. "Excuse me?"

"Nothing," I said. "Just seems like no one wants to ride in rickshaws with me. No one wants to canvass the piers with me. Either I smell worse than Fishy or I'm really bad at dodgeball."

Quinto held up his hands. "This isn't my fight. You two do whatever you want. I'm heading to Public Records. They should have information on individuals and corporations with the initials NFC. It's a scattershot approach, but it's sure to be better than this. I'll see you back at the precinct."

Quinto shook his head as he stomped off between the seaside warehouses and back toward the main thoroughfare. Shay stood there, her arms still crossed and a piqued look on her face. "Well?"

"Well, what?"

"We're here. Alone, more or less. Would you care to talk things over, perhaps in a more reasoned manner this time?"

I took a deep breath. "Yes. I'd like that very much."

"Great. You can start by apologizing."

I sputtered as I pushed myself off the concrete railing. "What? *Apologize*? For what?"

One of Shay's eyebrows shot up. "You seriously can't think of anything?"

"Hey, I've gotten to a point now where I can admit mistakes. I fully agree the crap hit the proverbial fan last night, but I don't see how any of it was my fault."

"Okay. Let me count the ways." Shay ticked items off on her fingers. "You deliberately stepped on and nearly killed my parent's cat. You spilled wine all over the table. You spilled wine all over my mother. You accused my family of badgering and needling you incessantly, and you acted like a huge ass about all of the above in the aftermath. Need I go on?"

"See, this is what I'm talking about," I said. "I didn't *intentionally* kick Barnabus. He bit me. I lashed out. It was instinctual, and everything else was a logical extension thereof. The wine went flying because I lost my balance. And I'm telling you, I already apologized about kicking the little feline agitator when it happened."

"You said you apologized about the wine, not the cat."

"Whatever. Same difference. It was all connected."

"And my family?"

"What about them?"

"Do you plan on apologizing about the way you treated them?"

I sputtered some more, my eyes bulging. "Are you kidding? They're the ones who should apologize to *me*."

Shay scoffed. "About *what*?"

"Look," I said, holding up my hands. "I've told you why. I've explained how they *welcomed* me. At some point you're going to have to make a decision to trust me or them. It's not always going to work both ways."

Shay sighed and rolled her eyes. "Fine. Clearly you're not ready to deal with this like an adult. Let's just...go back to the station. Maybe the Captain will have some suggestions about what to do next."

Shay set off along the same path Quinto had taken. Part of me wanted to hang back and sulk, to stew in my sorrowful, masculine juices, but I couldn't. Shay was my partner. Even though I might be upset with her, I couldn't let that get in the way of our work. The captain wouldn't forgive me for it, nor would I in the long run. Besides, two separate rickshaw rides back to HQ weren't in the budget, and I didn't feel like walking.

5

My ride back to the precinct was roughly the same as the one out to A&G, containing slightly less conversation and equal amounts of breeze-driven hair slapping me in the face. I didn't think any of it boded well for my immediate future, and I fully expected to return to my desk to sit down and begin an extended period of brooding interspersed only by the occasional piercing stare from my partner or a dressing-down from the captain.

Thankfully, a note circumvented that most unpleasant of possible futures. I picked it up as I reached my workspace, scanning my eyes across the neat calligraphy.

"Well?" said Shay. "Who's it from?"

Apparently, my partner *hadn't* come down with a debilitating case of laryngitis during the ride. "Cairny. She says she's already got something for us."

We headed for the stairs and followed them into the station's basement. Though often referred to as the dungeon, over time I'd come to the conclusion that the station's bowels had never been used as a den of torment and suffering. Despite having gotten lost in the maze of subterranean passages, once for so long I wish I'd brought a snack along with me, I'd never chanced across any rusted shackles, stocks, or iron maidens. Besides, despite their dark, dank, unsettling aura, none of the chambers below harbored that ancient stink of death—all except one.

The cool, subterranean air greeted us as we descended into the morgue proper, mostly free of that distinctive scent of decay but this time with a familiar fishy tang to it. I recognized it immediately, although the other scent that hung in the air caught me off guard. Something acidic with an overtone of oranges. *A new cleaner?* Normally the janitor used a lemon-scented one.

Regardless of what had been used, someone had gone through the space recently, intent upon keeping the chamber tidy. The cadaver vaults on the far side of the room gleamed, their stainless steel faces and handles polished to a shine. Exam tables dotted the room, each adorned with neatly folded stacks of white linens, pairs of gloves, an assortment of surgical tools, and empty clipboards. One of them, however, contained something more. A human-like shape poked from underneath a linen draped over the exam table in the furthest corner. Unless my nose deceived me, it was the source of the fishy tang.

Cairny sat nearby, scribbling upon a clipboard, this one with a sheaf of papers clipped into it. She looked up at the sound of Shay's and my footsteps, blinking several times as she took us in. "Oh. You're here."

Shay shot a thumb toward the entrance. "You did leave a note for us, right?"

The corner nodded. "I did. It's just...I only went up there a few minutes ago. I thought you'd be gone longer. No big deal."

I gave her a nod. "You're already writing your report? That was fast."

Cairny snorted. "Please, Daggers. I'm not a miracle worker. I'm not anywhere close to being done. I'm merely jotting down notes to ensure I don't forget anything. I have a tendency to forgot things in the heat of the moment."

"You don't say."

Shay glared at me before turning a more pleasant gaze on Cairny. "So you haven't finished your analysis, but you must have found something important. You wouldn't have left the note otherwise."

"Correct, as always, bestie." Cairny punctuated her statement with a stab of her pencil in Shay's direction. "Seeing how little information we had to go on this morning when we found the body, I figured any knowledge might be helpful in getting the investigation going. No sense in waiting until the final verdict when the preliminary guess is likely to be sufficient. And the piece of information I have for you might be revealing. I believe I've discovered the man's death wound."

"Really?" said Shay. "Where?"

Cairny stood, setting her clipboard aside. "Come. I'll show you."

She sauntered over to the occupied exam table, rounding to the far side while Shay and I squeezed together on the other. Cairny grabbed the edge of the white linen over the still form and started to lift it. A wave of decaying fish funk crept out from under the cloth.

I stopped her with an outstretched hand, trying not to breath.

Cairny looked at me with puzzled eyes. "Is something wrong, Detective?"

I didn't blame her. She really didn't get it most of the time. It was as if she was born without an aversion to death and decay.

I squawked out a reply, feeling my lungs slowly run out of air with which to express myself. "You know, I've found a good description...can be just as effective...as a visual...demonstration."

I might've hacked and coughed a bit at the end of my appeal. Cairny shared a concerned look with Shay, who didn't express a lot of empathy. I think her stomach and olfactory system agreed with me, however.

"To be fair, Daggers makes a decent point," said Shay, grimacing in the general direction of the linen.

Cairny lay the sheet back down, smothering to a certain degree the rotting fish funk. "I understand. The body is mangled anyway, which I find *fascinating*, but not everyone shares the same passions I do. Still, I'd rather let you come to your own conclusions..." Cairny tapped her chin. "Here. I have an idea."

A metal cart had been rolled next to the table, whereupon the surgical tools and towels and other items had been relocated. Cairny bent down and rummaged around the bottom of it. When she stood back up, it was with Fishy's tattered jacket and sweater in hand.

"Daggers, if you don't mind," she said, "could you snag that empty coat rack and bring it over to this table?"

I wasn't sure where she was going, but I agreed anyway. "Sure."

I crossed the room, snagged the rack, and brought it over to the empty exam table in question, upon which Cairny had already spread the maroon jacket. As I set the coat rack in place, Cairny approached with the sweater.

"You're taller than I am, so if you could help me with this..."

I eyed the sweater with distaste, knowing full well where it had been. "Help you with what, exactly?"

"I'd like to drape the sweater over the rack so we can get a good view of the front. There's a spare pair of gloves on the table if you need them."

I grabbed them and slipped them on, noting Shay's amused look. "Don't judge me. I'm all about hygiene."

With the gloves in place, I did as Cairny asked, draping the sweater over the rack such that its collar snagged upon the hooks at the top.

When done, I stepped back. "Alright. Now we've got a foul-smelling sweater hanging from a coat rack. All we need is a tattered hat and some straw and we'll have ourselves a reasonable scarecrow facsimile. It should kept the ravens away, no problem."

"Believe it or not, Detective Daggers, I don't suffer from overaggressive bird attacks in the morgue."

Shay snickered. She waved at the coat and jacket. "You mentioned a death wound, Cairny. I'm guessing it was inflicted on the man's torso?"

"Correct again, Detective," she said. "It was difficult to see at first because of the condition of the man's jacket, as well as the coarse knit of his sweater. But if you look carefully you can see part of it here."

Cairny pointed at the jacket, to a rough circular tear over the right breast near the monogrammed lettering. With emphasis drawn to it, it did appear both larger and more jagged than the majority of the other crab- and fish-inflicted rips.

"So, what?" I said. "He was murdered with an ice pick, or something a bit more nautical? A spear?"

"I said you could see *part* of it on the jacket, not all." Cairny moved to the sweater I'd draped from the coat rack. "Again, it's hard to see because of the sweater's loose weave, but if you look closely, *here* is where the weapon that struck the jacket pushed through, and here to the *left* are two other nearly identical tears in the fabric. I suspect the jacket must've flapped open as he was struck."

I moved closer to the sweater, ignoring its fragrant perfume of barnacles and rotting flesh, and inspected the points Cairny had drawn attention to. Based on the location of the tear in the jacket, I found the looser, stretched fabric and torn yarn on the matching spot on the sweater. If I hadn't known what I was looking for I would've easily missed the two similar, evenly spaced spots to the left.

"Three entry wounds, all in a row?"

Cairny nodded.

Shay, with her superior eyesight, hadn't needed to close the gap to observe the torn fabric. "Because of the way they line up, I'm guessing they were inflicted upon our victim at the same time. But with what? A pitchfork?"

Cairny frowned and cocked her head. "I doubt it. Pitchforks generally have five tines, not three. Besides, the cloth is torn, and pitchforks have smooth tines."

"So what then?"

Cairny pursed her lips. "Well, based on the tearing pattern in the cloth, and in the resulting decayed flesh underneath, I'm confident whatever pierced the victim had notched heads. Because there were three such wounds in a row, and given the nautical nature of the deceased, I think it's reasonable to assume he was murdered...with a trident."

I stepped back, removing my gloves and placing them on the exam table. "You mean, like a god of the oceans sort of trident?"

"Spear fishermen use them, too, Daggers," said Steele.

"Yes. In the shallows. But our guy was murdered at sea."

"His body was *disposed of* at sea," corrected Steele. "We have no idea where he was murdered."

"Fair enough." I gave Cairny a nod. "So is that all you've got for us?"

The fae-blooded coroner blinked. "Isn't that enough? How quickly do you expect me to work?"

"Don't mind him," said Shay. "He has all sorts of unrealistic expectations. Thanks for the update. Come get us if you find anything else intriguing."

Steele turned toward the stairs, and I followed her, wondering what exactly she meant by that. *Unrealistic expectations?* Was that another jab at how her family had treated me, or *not treated me,* in her eyes? I thought I'd progressed to a point where I could simply ask Shay to clarify a statement, even one made in anger, and the logical portion of me told me I could, even now, but my heart said otherwise. It told me to wait a little longer to bring it up, at least until I'd fully cooled and Shay had done likewise, and to sure as hell not bring it up in a snarky tone.

The beating organ at the center of me didn't always know what it was doing, but in this instance, I decided to trust it.

6

Sometimes I think if the tables were turned and I were the one being interrogated by a hard-boiled, graying cop with a multitude of scars and the threat of the law behind him, I'd crack like an eggshell under the pressure. Certainly, I wouldn't be able to lie effectively, spinning a convincing tale out of thin air without giving myself away. Even if I somehow managed to slip my deception under the eye of the grizzled veteran, I'd never manage to pull the wool over the eyes of his preternaturally aware, smoking hot elven sidekick.

Shay elbowed me as we returned to our desks. "What's on your mind?"

I blinked, pushing back the fog of memories and internal relationship discussions and what-ifs. "Huh?"

"You're doing that thing again, with the vacant stare and the lip chewing and the only barely metaphorical gears churning up top."

I lied, but only by omission. "You really think Fishy was killed with a trident?"

Shay shrugged as she sat down. "Why not?"

I took my seat, too. "It's just an...odd weapon, that's all."

Shay lifted an eyebrow. "Really? We've come across individuals murdered with swords and spears and stilettos filled with refrigerated liquid. Beaten to death with two by fours and frying pans. Strangled with belts or with pairs of pants. Orange corduroy pants, if I remember correctly. A trident really seems that weird to you?"

"It's not a common tool, is all."

"It is among spear fishermen."

"Something you already pointed out," I said. "But how many of those are left? You saw those ships in the harbor this morning, the trollers and trawlers and whatchamacallits. Fishing's big business. I can't image many people do it by hand anymore. Not in these parts."

Shay shrugged again. "Well, if Cairny stakes her reputation on it, that's good enough for me. She's rarely wrong about what killed someone. Besides, her explanation fits the evidence as I see it. As odd as it might be, it's the best guess we have right now. On the bright side, the stranger the weapon, the easier it will be to connect it to the murder when we actually find it."

"Assuming we find it. It could be at the bottom of the ocean for all we know."

"Are you going to be a pessimist all day, or do you plan on turning a corner at some point?"

I opened my mouth to reply, but the sight of Quinto waltzing through the front doors with a sheaf of papers in hand kept me from digging my own grave.

I shot a finger toward Shay and flicked it in the direction of the doors to make sure she knew I wasn't ignoring her. When Quinto arrived, I gave the big guy a sly smile. "I don't know where you went, but it certainly wasn't a government office."

"I know, right?" said Quinto. "There was a new kid at Public Records. Couldn't have been on the job for more than a couple weeks, maybe only a day or two. Anyway, when I introduced myself and showed him my badge, he shot out of his chair like a bolt out of a crossbow. I don't think I've ever seen a public servant move so fast. I couldn't have been at the records office more than fifteen minutes before the guy emerged from the stacks in back with this folder full of papers." Quinto waved it for emphasis. "According to him, this is every individual in the city with the initials NFC, which a quick perusal suggests is about a hundred and fifty. He didn't even make a copy first. Said our police work was *too important,* that I should take the files and bring them back when I was done."

I would've whistled if I could. Instead I settled for a forceful, breathy blow. "Well, he'll learn, even if it takes a few tongue-lashings from his boss. Rule number one of public service. If you can move slower, do. Speed creates unsustainable expectations."

"And rule number two is never convenience another government agency without securing concessions first," said Quinto.

Shay shook her head. "How did you two get so cynical?"

"You've only been here a year. Give it time." Quinto fanned the file again. "The good news is—better than the speed with which I secured the information—is that the city has far fewer corporations with the initials NFC than it does inhabitants. According to the records the young retriever secured for me, there's only two dozen entities within the greater New Welwic area that fit the bill, and I was already able to sort through them on my trip back here. Of the twenty-five, a mere three seem to be nautical in nature. Norman Family Charters, located in southeastern New Welwic, Nicchi Fishing and Crabbing, located far to the west in Aragosto, and Newtown Fishing Corporation, far to the east in, of all places, Newtown."

Shay lifted a brow. "Aragosto and Newtown are both pretty far from here. Companies filed for incorporation in those towns show up in our public records office?"

Quinto nodded. "I think it's a cost cutting measure. A lot of New Welwic suburbs use municipal services like Public Records and Taxation and Revenue instead of running their own offices. It's not particularly efficient for them to do it themselves. Though they operate their own police and fire departments. Sanitation, schools, and libraries, too, assuming they have any of the latter."

Apparently I wasn't the only one who'd trained an eye on the front door. Captain Knox appeared in her doorway, motioning for us to come to her rather than vice versa. "Detectives?"

I stood and joined her at the base of her office, as did Steele and Quinto.

Knox didn't waste any time. "Let's hear your updates."

"We located the body and transported it back to the morgue," said Shay. "Cairny's working on her report as we speak, though she's already shared some preliminary findings. Due to the condition of the deceased, we haven't been able to identify him based on physical characteristics. He also lacked any personal identifying information, but we're following other leads that seem promising."

"Such as?"

Quinto lifted the file. "The man was wearing a monogrammed jacket and a matching cap. We think it might've been a uniform. These are from Public Records. Names of individuals with initials to match, as well as businesses. We suspect the latter is probably a better avenue to pursue. Certainly, it's a narrower one. I've already trimmed the list down to three potential enterprises at which the deceased might've worked."

"And they are?" asked Knox.

Quinto gave her the rundown. She nodded.

"Detective Steele? You mentioned Coroner Moonshadow had delivered some early results?"

Shay nodded. "On site, she came to the conclusion the man had been dumped into the ocean based on the marks left by ropes used to secure weights to his ankles. After a more thorough search, she's come to the conclusion the man was stabbed with a trident before being disposed of."

"A *trident*?" For some reason, Captain Knox affixed *me* with a stare as she said that.

"It seems plausible, based on the physical evidence," I said. "Admittedly, anyone could've been disposed of at sea, but the man's clothing suggested he was a sailor or dockworker of some sort. If so, that would make slightly more sense."

"Fair enough," said Knox. "Have you considered your next steps?"

"I figured we'd start with the NFC businesses," said Quinto. "Probably Norman Family Charters."

"Because it's in New Welwic?"

"Well...yeah," said Quinto. "Reach for the low-hanging fruit first."

"Good," said Knox. "Detective Daggers? Accompany Detective Quinto to the travel company. See if you can get an ID on our John Doe."

Shay's eyebrows drew together. "What about me, Captain?"

I'm pretty sure Knox smiled, but the shadow that crossed the corner of her lips might've been from a passing cloud. "I'd rather you stayed. I have a few matters I'd like to discuss, and I suspect Detective Daggers and Quinto will fare fine on their own."

Shay gave me a sideways look and a tiny shrug before entering the captain's office, but she didn't look bent out of shape by the sudden change of plans. Knox gave us the sort of look used to shoo flies. Quinto clapped me on the back, and the pair of us meatheads headed toward the exit, Quinto's mind undoubtedly focused on the task at hand and mine anything but.

7

Our rickshaw driver panted heavily under Quinto's and my combined weight, though should the poor sap keel over under the mid-day sun's bright rays, I'd know who to blame. While I'd slimmed down to a svelte one-ninety under Shay's watchful eye, I don't think Quinto had shed a single pound since starting to date Cairny. Perhaps she preferred him that way. Some ladies liked their men large and in charge, accepting the fat along with the muscle, although despite Quinto's relative lack of activity, he certainly seemed to carry more of the former than the latter. Darn unfair genetics...

A cool sea breeze whistled past our rickshaw as we veered back into a section of prime, oceanside real estate. We'd left the dock district in the dust of our handcart's wheels and kept on going, heading toward the address of Norman Family Charters, which according to the minimal information Quinto had on hand was the 'premier destination for family cruises and sea adventures in and around New Welwic.' Though some might find a certain appeal in the sales pitch, I found it dull, and life had taught me that rarely did situations which initially presented themselves as dull actually hide more interesting layers, like gangs of trident-wielding murderers who dumped bodies into the bay by the light of the moon.

Still, it wasn't as if I would've been able to focus on our destination even if it sported a more salacious tagline. I couldn't stop thinking about what the captain wanted with my partner. Surely they were going to talk about me, which I didn't say out of sheer egotism. Knox tended to let us work problems out on our own, at least work related ones, asking only for updates as she had today and providing the occasional kick in the pants or vote of confidence. Rarely did she pull either of us aside—even more rarely once I'd learned her ways and stopped acting in a manner that annoyed her.

Quinto's low rumble sounded beside me. "You okay?"

I blinked and focused. Apparently, I'd been staring into the distance. If I'd had long hair, I'm sure it would've slapped Quinto in the face as had happened to me twice already. "More or less."

"That's not very convincing," said Quinto, his brow ever so slightly creased.

"Well, I'm a terrible liar. What do you expect?"

Quinto snorted.

I shifted in my seat, turning inward. "You mind if I ask you something? About you and Cairny?"

Quinto shrugged as best he could in the confines of the rickshaw. "Shoot."

"How do you deal with fights?"

"We don't."

"Seriously?" I lifted a brow. "You ignore them, as if nothing ever happened?"

"No, I mean we don't have them."

I snorted. "Come on."

"I'm serious," said Quinto. "I mean, we have disagreements, don't get me wrong. No two people are going to agree on everything all the time. But the stuff we butt heads over is largely immaterial. Where to eat or whether we agreed to hang out on Tuesday or on Wednesday or if a laceration was caused by a piece of old, hardened steel or a blade that had more recently been sharpened."

I scrunched my face.

"She uses me as a sounding board. She doesn't actually care about my answer most of the time. Don't tell me Steele doesn't talk shop with you when you're off duty?"

I didn't deny it. "Admittedly, Cairny's a special case. She doesn't exhibit many of the same foibles other females do."

Quinto smiled. "Don't I know it. I'm a lucky man, Daggers."

As long as you don't mind playing second fiddle to a rotting corpse on occasion, I thought. "Still, you have to have had at least a few disagreements that turned into something more. Say...when meeting her family?"

"Sorry, Daggers. I wish I could commiserate, but the fact of the matter is, her mother was lovely when I met her. We got along swimmingly. She was very impressed with my body of work."

The way he said it made it sound as if he'd handed the woman a resume. "But only her mother was nice? Not her father?"

"Well, Cairny's dad wasn't in the picture," said Quinto. "She doesn't talk about him much. I'm not sure if there's some love lost or it's more of a cultural fairy thing. I'm hoping not, for my own sake. I met her sister though. She was pleasant."

Our rickshaw slowed and our driver skidded to a halt. He called out to us between gulps of air. "Here we are... Norman Family...Charters."

I looked up to see a wooden structure, painted a bright blue with pristine white trim and about twice as wide as it was tall, sitting along the elevated portion of the shore and with a brilliant backdrop of deep blue stretching behind it. A signpost planted in the soil near the road confirmed the business's identity. Behind the structure, a wooden pier led to a pair of ships moored there, wide, slow-looking vessels that were in much better condition than the fishing dinghies we'd chanced across all morning. A pair of workers in navy slacks and white, collared shirts toiled on each one, swabbing hatches or belaying the mainstays or doing whatever it is sailors did.

I hopped off and dug some coins out of my pocket to pay the driver. "Look, Quinto, help me out. You overheard enough to get the gist of what went down between me, Shay, and her folks last night. Shay and I are at opposite ends of the spectrum on this one, and to be honest, I don't have a lot of successful personal experience to draw from when it comes to resolving family conflicts. I haven't talked to my little brother in years, and my relationship with my dad isn't much better. Honestly the person I get along with best is my ex-wife, and as the title suggests, we're divorced."

Quinto shrugged as we headed along the gravel path toward the charter shop's door. "What do you want me to tell you, Daggers? I don't have many experiences to draw from either. You know I didn't date much before I hit it off with Cairny."

Much was an exaggeration. I pulled on the front door, which responded with a cheerful shopkeeper's bell as I did so. "Well, what about experiences with your own folks. Surely you've had fights with them?"

Quinto shot me a sideways glance as we entered the shop. "*My* family?"

"Yeah. You've got one, right?"

The interior of the shop resembled the exterior, with the same blue paint tinting the walls and white covering everything else, from the wainscoting to the counters to the displays. The latter were the only thing occupying the shop floor, two person-wide displays filled with glossy brochures hawking weekend fishing excursions for businessmen, summer pleasure cruises, and trips to New Welwic's famed Isla de Pajarose, which I'm pretty sure was just an enormous granite outcropping covered in bird crap.

"Well, yeah, sure, I have a family," said Quinto. "But if you're hoping I can give you advice on how to solve interpersonal problems based on my experiences in that realm, you're barking up the wrong tree."

"How so?" We walked toward the sales counter.

"Well...how much have I told you about my folks?"

"In all the years we've been together? Honestly, I'm not sure you're mentioned your family once. That's why I asked."

"Well, don't you think there might've been a reason for that?"

"Look, Quinto, if it's about your heritage, it doesn't matter to me what you are. You're my friend. One of the best detectives in the precinct. And beyond that, you're thoughtful, intelligent, and observant."

Quinto pshawed. "Come off it. Look, I'm a half-troll. I admit it. I don't talk about it because there's no reason to. But that's not why I kept my family history to myself."

"So why then?"

A latch clacked. A door in the back opened, and a middle-aged gentleman with a thick moustache wearing dark blue pants and a crisp white shirt emerged. He gave us a friendly wave. "Hullo there! Welcome to Norman Family Charters. Looking to hire a crew for a private jaunt, or schedule something for a business get-together, maybe?"

I held up a finger in Quinto's direction. "Hold onto that thought. Norman, I presume?"

"In the flesh," said the owner, approaching. "How can I help you?"

"I'll make this quick. I'm Daggers, this is Quinto. We're detectives with the NWPD. I don't suppose you've had an employee go missing, probably within the last week or two?"

"Uh...no," said the man. "Can't say I have. Everyone's been coming to work, same as always."

"Thanks," I said. "That's all we needed to know."

I clapped Quinto on the shoulder and headed for the door, leaving the dumbfounded Norman in our wake.

"So, where were we?" The front door chimed as I let myself and Quinto out. "You were about to tell me about your folks?"

Quinto glanced at the door. "Well, ah...here's the truth, Daggers. You know I had a rough upbringing. That I spent time on goon squads of questionable legality before ending up on the right side of the law. What I don't think I ever told you was *why*."

"Well. I'm here now."

"Daggers...I ran away from home when I was fourteen. I haven't seen my mom or brother in almost two decades."

I felt my jaw plummet. "Seriously?"

Quinto nodded. "Yeah. I had my reasons. Mostly it was typical teenage angst. But I was big enough to get by on my own. It wasn't until much later, when I'd started working for the boys in blue, that I fully regretted my decision. I went back, looking for them, but they were long gone. Cleared out of the slum. I talked with folks in those parts who might remember them, but I found nothing but shadows and vapor. Someone thought they'd gotten fed up with the slum life and skipped town, but I never heard anything concrete."

"Did you check with Public Records?" I asked.

"Of course I did," said Quinto. "But you've got to understand, Daggers, I was never listed in Public Records myself until I started working for the government. Most of the folks in the slums aren't. The public assessors are too scared to go in there. Taxation and Revenue is another story, but that was another dead end. Mom always was talented when it came to avoiding the tax man."

"So that's it? You really haven't had any interaction with your family for twenty years?"

"Almost, yeah."

"Wow. I envy you."

"Don't say that, Daggers. You don't know what you're missing until you've lost it. Sure, you might have some beefs with your brother and old man, but you've still got time to fix those relationships. I'll never have that option."

I swallowed back my snarkiness. "You're right. That was inconsiderate of me. I'm sorry, Quinto."

"Don't be. It's not your fault." He shot a thumb in the direction of the charter shop as we walked along the path toward the street. "Hey, don't you think we should've grilled that guy more about his business? It's not like you to take someone at their word so freely."

I shook my head. "He's wearing the same outfit as the guys on his boats in back. It doesn't match Fishy's attire. He's telling the truth."

Quinto shrugged. "If you say so."

"I do. Come on. Let's head back to the precinct—after we pick up lunch on the way, of course. I'm starving."

8

Quinto and I accepted the station's loving embrace, stepping through her front doors and returning to our desks. Shay sat at hers, leaning back in her chair and reading the contents of a file. She must've heard us as we approached, as she suddenly pulled her head back.

She sniffed the air. "Something smells good."

Apparently, I picked the wrong sense to give us away.

I deposited a paper bag at the edge of her desk. "Butter chicken, which as far as I can tell is a misnomer. My palate isn't as polished as yours, but I tasted cream, yogurt, and a host of spices, among them pepper, cloves, cinnamon, nutmeg, cumin, coriander, and turmeric. Oh, and there's chicken in the dish, too."

Shay raised an eyebrow. "No way you picked out all of those spices on your own."

"He asked the vendor what was in it before buying," said Quinto. "But he didn't write any of them down, so he deserves *some* credit."

"I'm guessing you ate without me." Shay shot me a wounded look, but a facetious one. I think...

"I was hungry," I said. "Sorry. But it's still warm. Have at it."

Shay grabbed the bag. "Did you snag naan to go with it?"

"Never you worry. They're in there."

Steele opened the bag and breathed deeply, a smile spreading across her face. "This'll do nicely. You forgot chili, though."

"What, like, as a side?" I said. "Come to think of it, the vendor had been hawking roasted peppers, but you've never gone for those before."

"Not chilies. *Chili,*" said Shay. "I can smell it in the butter chicken. You left it out of your list of spices."

I snorted and took a seat. "Now you're just showing off."

Shay carefully lifted the meal out of the bag, the flatbreads stacked atop the bowl to keep them warm. She fished a spoon out of her desk and went to work, but not before sharing her smile with me. "Thanks."

"Don't mention it."

Quinto grabbed a chair from his desk, pulled it over, and deposited his bulk in it, eliciting a groan of displeasure from the wooden throne—none of which made him seem like any less of a third wheel, but at least he acknowledged that standing over my partner while she ate was unnecessarily creepy.

He waited until she'd slowed before giving her a nod. "So. Care to share what the Captain drew you aside for?"

To the casual observer, it might've seemed as if I'd pressured Quinto into asking the question for me, but I swear upon the might of the gods, I had nothing to do with it. We hadn't even discussed the matter on the ride back from the ethnic food cart. Still, that didn't stop me from leaning forward in my chair and perking my ears at the mention of it.

Shay looked up from her bowl. "If that's a round-about way of asking whether what she had to tell me pertained to the case, then no, it didn't. And if you're simply being nosy and prying into my personal conversations, then maybe I'll bring *that* up the next time the captain pulls me aside."

Quinto's cheeks colored. It wasn't a particularly good look for him—not so much because of his otherwise manly appearance, but because the rouge mixed terribly with his skin tone.

Shay shot me another glance, almost daring me to ask a follow up, but I didn't. She'd already let the butter chicken out of the bag, so to speak.

Obviously, the captain had talked to her about me, though about which aspect, I couldn't be certain. Probably something related to our morning spat, though I couldn't envision Captain Knox delivering life advice. Then again, I'd only known her for a few months, and the entirety of my interactions with her had been in the work environment as opposed to the old Captain with whom I'd occasionally drank and socialized with, against any number of regulations, probably.

Regardless, I'm not sure the particulars of the advice mattered that much. Hopefully whatever it was had helped set Shay's mind at ease, but from my point of view, she could've delivered a platitude along the lines of 'boys will be boys' or shared a heartfelt experience about a quarrel from her own life and it wouldn't have made any difference in my attempts at reconciliation. I'd already developed the initial inklings of a plan. Based on the look of pleasure on Shay's face and the speed with which she devoured her sauce-lathered chicken and bread, step one had gone over quite well.

Step two might prove to be more difficult. Though I'd long since abandoned my irrational, masculine fear of asking for forgiveness, I found my inherent sense of right and wrong made it harder for me to make the same plea when I knew I was in the right. Then again, maybe it didn't matter. Maybe some things were worth the moral sacrifice. White lies and all that.

Yet despite my newly concocted plan and a willingness to come to the negotiating table, a lingering fear sat in the pit of my stomach, poking me, niggling me, flashing me its sharp teeth and honing its claws. It was a fear that had surfaced in the company of Shay's family, a fear I thought I'd banished long ago but had apparently only been in hibernation. I wanted no part of it, but there it was, making itself a nice home despite my best efforts to shoo it back into oblivion.

"So did you guys discover anything at the charters place?" asked Shay between a mouthful of food.

"Only that they're not involved," said Quinto. "Their owner and ship crews wore the same outfits, ones decidedly different from Fishy's."

Shay made a face like she'd smelled the guy in question. "You're sticking with that nickname, too?"

"You know better than to fight it," said Quinto. "You might as well take on a Taxation and Revenue auditor."

I smiled. "Thanks. I think…"

Shay swallowed the last of her chicken and started to mop up the sauce with the remaining naan. "Well, that's not particularly surprising. Knox suspected it wouldn't prove to be a fruitful trip."

"So you *did* talk shop," said Quinto.

"Some."

I looked through the captain's windows into her office. She sat at her desk, sifting through a pile of paperwork. "Hold on. If she didn't think heading to Norman's Charters would prove useful, why did she send us?"

Shay's smile revealed the real answer before she could dispute it with a fake one. "You know we have to check every lead. Besides, she didn't become convinced it wouldn't be fruitless until I related the fisherman's comment about the ocean currents."

"That they travel west to east," I said. "Which means, what? That she wants us to travel to Aragosto to check out the next likely business?"

"You hit the nail on the head." Shay popped the last bit of bread in her mouth.

"Knox really wants us to head all the way there?" said Quinto. "That's a two hour rickshaw ride away, easy. My driver might die, never mind the cost."

"Would you have made a different call?" said Steele. "We don't have a lot of other leads to go on right now. Aragosto is to the west and within the range from which we might expect a body to wash up. And if you're surprised Captain Knox is willing to shuttle us out there and back, you'll be *really* shocked to hear she's already authorized us to spend the night in the event our investigation requires it."

"No way," I said.

"Way," said Shay. "Between this and the raises, I think it's time we accept she's better at securing funds for our department than Captain Armstrong was."

"Well, I think it's rather optimistic of her to think anything will come of that lead," I said. "But given what time it is and how long it'll take us to get there, I guess I can see where she's coming from. Thinking ahead. Apparently, it's qualities like that which get you promoted to Captain."

"Don't even start," said Shay. "We've been down that road before, and it wasn't worth it."

"Fair enough. You ready to go?"

"Let me grab some tea for the road, then sure."

That wasn't a bad idea. Quinto and I followed Shay to the break room to stock up for the trip.

9

I should've brought a book. The ride to Aragosto really did take two hours, and not because we picked a sickly rickshaw driver with gray hair and a concerning cough. Rather, we secured the services of agile young guys, one for Shay and myself and another for Quinto, both of whom after hearing where we intended to go demanded payment in advance.

Still, despite the length of the journey, it wasn't an unpleasant one. Other than my luxury poker cruise with Shay a few months back, years had passed since I'd left our metropolis. Though the first half of our excursion carried us through congested neighborhoods and loud, garishly-decorated markets, they were sites I was only vaguely familiar with, which made them ideal for sightseeing and people watching. Half-breeds and full breeds of every shape, size, and color filled the streets, conversing in a dozen different accents and insulting each other in twice as many foreign tongues. It seemed to me any other city would have a hard time matching the cultural and racial diversity of New Welwic, but I was an uncultured slob who rarely traveled, so what did I know?

Eventually, the multi-story apartment buildings and crops of groceries and eateries gave way to a strip of urban sprawl that surrounded New Welwic, a slapdash collection of wooden shacks and lean-tos constructed by folks eager to gain entry to the city but without the means to live there full time. The military occasionally swept through the areas, culling the worst parts and torching the structures that posed an imminent threat to human life, but like an infestation of black mold, the hastily constructed tenements always grew back.

On the bright side, compared to the bulk of New Welwic, the sprawl was a mere scab on its surface. Soon enough we were through that, too, and into the countryside, enjoying the floral, sweet scent of the blossoming irises and bleeding hearts, feeling the cool ocean breeze on our faces, and gawking at the preponderance of trees, ones with bark and leaves and everything. Shay and I exchanged pleasantries about the greenery and glimpses of wildlife, each of us picking at the wall of ice we'd built overnight but unwilling to address the mammoth in the rickshaw.

Eventually, new structures appeared. A farmhouse here, a general supply shop there, then a collection of homes. Before we knew it, our driver had careened around a bend and was hauling us into a quaint seaside town. Two-story cottages with steeply-pitched roofs, jutting chimneys, and two-toned façades lined the gravel road, conceding their plots to three-story inns and bed and breakfasts as we neared the shore. Neatly-manicured crepe myrtles with pink blossoms sprouted from brick rings built into the sidewalk at regular intervals. Planters hung from lantern posts, spilling tendrils of pinks and purples toward the street. In the direction of the gusting ocean breeze stretched a sprawling boardwalk, filled with shops and eateries, carnival games and sideshows.

Our driver skidded to a halt, the crunching of rickshaw wheels over gravel reduced to a lingering crackle. "Here we are. Downtown Aragosto."

I hopped out and held a hand for Steele to help her down. As she reached solid ground, I instinctively reached for my pocket before remembering I'd already paid the driver.

"Not much of a *downtown,* really," I said.

The driver shrugged his thin shoulders, still gripping the handlebar in front of him with his wiry arms. "It's what passes for one around here."

Despite demanding payment upfront, the driver hadn't asked an exorbitant price, at least not for the amount of work involved. I almost felt like I was short-changing him, and I was notoriously stingy when it came to tipping. Maybe my empathy resulted from the man's physique. The poor guy looked like he could use a good meal or twelve. Then again, he wasn't even breathing hard. Perhaps adherence to a strict diet was his secret to success.

"You, ah...sure I covered the charge?" I asked.

The driver nodded. "I should be able to secure a return passenger. Lots of tourists from the city around here this time of year."

That explained it. I'd assumed I was covering his time out and back, meaning I'd overpaid by at least fifty percent. My miserly tipping instincts kicked back in. "Well, if you don't find any takers soon, circle the wagon back around. I doubt we'll be here long."

Gravel crunched behind us. Quinto's rickshaw arrived, through his driver didn't seem to be the pinnacle of physical fitness ours was. The poor sap gasped and wheezed and nodded as Quinto thanked him.

"Nice town," said the big guy as he joined us.

"You ever been here?" asked Steele.

Quinto shook his head. "Can't say I have, though now that I see it, I think maybe I should've. Perhaps I'll bring Cairny out at some point. You?"

Steele shook her head. "I think I passed it by a long time ago on a trip to see relatives, but that doesn't count."

"If we're lucky, we'll have time to see some of the sights before we head back for the evening," I said. "First things first, though, let's find the local station."

"Heading straight for the police?" said Steele. "From what you told our driver, you made it seem as if we weren't going to find anything here."

"It doesn't matter what I think," I said. "This isn't our jurisdiction. If we start poking around without permission, the local fuzz might get persnickety. Besides, in a town this size, they'll probably know if one of their own went missing a week or two back."

Shay and Quinto nodded, and we set out in search of a local to point us in the right direction. It wasn't hard. The first gentleman we chanced across, a septuagenarian by the name of Howard William Wadlow, provided a simple roadmap for us to follow, as well as gave us a completely unprompted and unwanted account of Aragosto's history as a fishing port. Upon finally ripping ourselves free from his company, we ventured into the heart of the suburban sprawl, fighting past four or five blocks of curio shops and homes that would've had to have been made out of cardboard and shoe polish to have been affordable in New Welwic.

Not wanting to feel left out, the police station was as quaint and compact as the surrounding structures: only a single story tall, taking up a quarter of the footprint of the 5th Street Precinct and painted in a thoroughly non-threatening baby blue. If not for the sign above the front door, I might've mistaken it for a day care.

I yanked on the front door and let myself in, Shay and Quinto following behind me. To my right, I spotted a pair of offices with open doors. In front of us was an open area, much like our pit but without the ancient stink of coffee and desperation and with only four desks instead of a few dozen.

A pair of uniformed officers stood in the middle, chatting as we arrived, one a husky dark-skinned woman with short, side-swept hair and the other a balding dwarf with close cropped auburn hair up top and a ruddy brown bush of beard below. They both peered our way as we entered.

The woman approached us, hooking her thumbs into her belt loops as she shot us a smile both genuine and guarded. "Hi there. Sergeant Samantha Mines, Aragosto Police. Can I help you?"

Her smile might've been cautious, but her stance wasn't. She stood tall and proud, even with big old Quinto looming behind me.

"Nice to meet you, Mines," I said. "I'm Detective Jake Daggers. This is my partner, Detective Shay Steele, and our associate, Detective Folton Quinto. We're from New Welwic's 5th Street Precinct."

"New Welwic," said Mines, nodding. "I figured you were law. You had that air about you as you walked in, like you owned the place."

"Force of habit," said Quinto.

"Don't worry. I get it," said Mines. "What brings you to our neck of the woods?"

"Probably nothing," I said. "A case we're looking into. I don't suppose someone's gone missing from your town recently? Lost at sea, perhaps? From a Nicchi Fishing and Crabbing?"

"As a matter of fact, someone has." The dwarf had approached, taking a stand next to the Sergeant. He didn't shoot us a smile, and his stance indicated he could do without us entirely.

Mines shot a thumb at the height-challenged cop. "This is Officer Bronmuth Silverbrook. And yeah, someone did go missing. Johnny Nicchi, owner and operator of Nicchi Fishing and Crabbing. About a week and a half ago. Did he pop up in New Welwic? The whole town's been worried sick."

I gestured toward the quartet of desks in the center of the station. "Perhaps we should have a seat. I have some bad news."

10

Rather than settle in the makeshift pit, we ended up in one of the offices, which turned out to be a conference room. I cradled a mug of coffee in my hands, having long extinguished the cup I'd grabbed from the precinct before leaving. Mines and Silverbrook had secured their own cups, though Steele and Quinto went thirsty. Apparently, the Aragosto PD didn't have a line in their budget for tea. Either that or none of the officers in the city's employ drank any.

Mines leaned back in her chair, having absorbed our story of Fishy's discovery, retold in painstaking, gory detail.

She took a sip of her coffee and stared at us with wide eyes. "Wow. You're sure it was murder then?"

"We'd let you talk to our coroner if she'd come along," said Steele. "But unless the man tripped and fell on a trident while at sea, then in his death throes got his feet tangled in a rope attached to an anchor, the lot of which followed him to the bottom of the ocean as he fell overboard, then yeah, he was murdered."

Mines set her coffee down, shaking her head. "Sorry. This is coming as a shock. I'd talked to him a few weeks ago. Didn't know him *that* well, but I knew him. In a town this size, you get to know almost everyone, at least their faces. When he went missing, some people thought the worst. Not that he'd been murdered, of course. Just that he'd met his makers another way. But plenty of us held out hope he'd run off, disappeared into the night. Set sail for bluer seas or something."

I gestured with my mug. "So Johnny was...what? A fisherman?"

"More of a crabber, really," said Mines. "But guys in the industry do both around here. Depends on the season, and the weather to a degree. Lots of blue crabs in the shallows this time of year. Snow crabs in the winter. More fishing in the summer and fall."

"Obviously, you knew he'd gone missing," said Shay. "You said it happened at night?"

"As far as we know," said Mines. "At least that's when he went missing. I think it was...ten days ago, was it?"

She looked to Silverbrook. The dwarf nodded as he took a gulp of his joe.

"Ten days, then," said Mines. "He wasn't reported missing until a couple days after that. Let's call it a week ago. Silverbrook did the legwork on his case, but he didn't pull up much of anything. His wife, Bianca, said Johnny never mentioned what he was up to when he went out that night. Didn't even tell her he was leaving. Said she figured he'd gone out to work, but...I guess not, right?"

"Apparently," I said. "Johnny have any kids?"

Mines shook her head. "Just the wife."

"And how old was he?"

Mines looked to Silverbrook for help. The dwarf looked like he'd rather be wrestling a grizzly bear than stuck rehashing an old case with us and his boss. "Uh...I'm not sure. Twenty-six. Twenty-seven, maybe. Why does it matter?"

"Curiosity," I said. "The body wasn't in the sort of condition where we could make an educated guess."

Steele soldiered onward. "What time did Nicchi leave his home the night he went missing?"

Bronmuth waffled. "Well...I'd have to check the files, but I want to say around eight. At least according to Bianca."

"And in accordance with the wife's testimony, you worked off the assumption Johnny went to work. Presumably he took his own ship, or one of his?"

"Just the one," said Mines. "His was a small operation. He worked it alone, for the time being anyway."

Steele nodded. "Alright. So is that normal behavior? Going out to fish in the middle of the night, either for him or for fishermen in general?"

Mines shrugged. "For him, I can't say. But lots of crabbers around here work through the night. Pull thirty to thirty-five hour shifts sometimes. It's a tough living. Some men die, to be honest, but for the guys who are good at it, know where to lay their traps, it can be lucrative. The Abano brothers have built quite an empire at it. Others pay their bills with plenty left on the side."

"Were there storms the night he went missing?" I asked.

"None," said Mines. "Which is why it was odd he went missing. If there'd been high winds or lightning, I think we all would've assumed he'd found his way to the bottom of the ocean."

"So he took his boat out that night?" asked Quinto.

"That's what we'd assumed," said Mines. "His ship was missing the following morning. Silverbrook talked to the folks on the docks, the ones who'd also been working that night."

Mines looked to Bronmuth for help again. The dwarf's sunny disposition hadn't changed.

"Yeah," he said, shifting in his chair. "Uh...I forget the exact testimonies, but one of the guys mentioned the ship was still docked around ten. Someone else mentioned it was out of its slip when he got back around...I want to say four?"

"And no pieces of his ship washed ashore?" asked Quinto.

"Not in town," said Mines. "Though I can't vouch for anything outside our beaten path. None of the other fishermen have reported seeing any, that's for sure."

"Which implies his boat was stolen," I said.

"Or scuttled," said Quinto.

I shrugged. "Depends on the motive for murder. If our killer was driven by coin, then you can be sure the boat is still in one piece. If Nicchi was murdered for another reason, then maybe you're right and the killer valued the destruction of evidence over the boat itself. Still, based on the quality of knots tied to Nicchi's ankles, I'm guessing we weren't dealing with professionals. Thieves seems like a more likely bet."

"In that vein," said Steele. "Was Johnny in debt, perhaps over the boat?"

Mines blinked. "Well...I'm not sure. We haven't put much effort into investigating his disappearance. Like I said, we had no reason to think he hadn't simply sailed away. To be honest, I'm still trying to wrap my head around the fact that he was murdered, and with a trident of all things. You're sure about that?"

"It's an educated guess," I said. "Speaking of which, you've mentioned your town's fishermen and crabbers. Any spear fishermen among the bunch?"

"None that I know of," said Mines. "They wouldn't be able to make a living that way. Everything here is net, line, or cage caught."

"Is there anyone who even sells tridents?" I asked.

Mines looked to Silverbrook. He grunted.

Mines shrugged. "I don't think so."

We all sat at the table, nursing our drinks and our thoughts alike.

Bronmuth finally took the opportunity to assert himself. He placed his coffee on the table, stood, and took a step forward. "Well, officers, we certainly appreciate you coming all the way out to Aragosto to let us know about Johnny. It's a tough thing to hear, but we'll do right by him. We won't rest until we've tracked down his killer. Unless there's something else you need before you go...?" He gestured toward the door.

Mines shot her associate a confused glance. "Bronmuth, what are you doing?"

The dwarf frowned. "Uh...thanking the detectives for their help?"

"Really? Because it sounds like you're trying to shoo them off."

"They've told us what they know. We need to get to work, don't we?"

"*We* do. All of us," said Mines.

Bronmuth's frown deepened. "Sam, this is our town. We know the folks here. We've got this."

Mines shifted her weight in her chair, cocking her head. "Have you forgotten Gentry retired three years ago?"

"No, I thought he was still working the beat in his free time," said Bronmuth, his face darkening. "Come on. We don't need Gentry, or anyone else for that matter."

"Is...everything alright?" asked Steele.

Mines pulled her gaze free of Silverbrook's. "We're a small town, detectives. We survive off fishing, crabbing, and tourism. I don't know if you noticed our boardwalk on the way in? Tons of folks from New Welwic drop by to visit, to play the carnival games, watch Doc Fowler's ridiculous horse show, and stay in our inns. Thankfully, our problems usually don't grow much bigger than our size. We get bar fights and disagreements among the fishermen, sometimes they come to blows, sometimes a tourist even gets involved, but by and large, Aragosto is a safe place to live. There hasn't been a murder here in six years, and even that was a run of the mill mugging gone south. The detective who investigated that case, Gentry, retired a few years ago. When it comes to homicide experience, we have none."

"That's not true," said Bronmuth. "I was here when Gentry cracked that case. So were you, Sarge. You act like neither one of us paid any attention while he was here, or that we haven't studied countless cases over the years. We can handle this on our own."

"Well, I'm sure you can," I said, leaning forward and setting my mug on the table. "But unfortunately, it's not that simple, for either of us."

"What's that supposed to mean?" asked Silverbrook.

I spread my hands in appeal. "Aragosto is your town. Nicchi lived and worked here, no question about that, but he washed ashore in New Welwic. That's our jurisdiction. As of now, we have no idea where he was murdered, but our best guess is it happened at sea. Add those things together and you're looking at a situation in which none of us has the upper hand. The fact that Steele, Quinto, and I are homicide investigators is immaterial. We're all involved in this, like it or not."

Mines adopted a self-satisfied smile and turned it on Silverbrook, who looked as if he'd swallowed a lemon. He cleared his throat and jutted his chin toward me.

"Fine. And I guess since I'm the one who took statements after Johnny's disappearance, that means you're with me."

Shay smiled. "Glad to be aboard, Officer Silverbrook."

I nodded in agreement, thinking to myself how much better of a liar Shay was than me.

"So," said Bronmuth. "You're the homicide cops. Where do you propose we start?"

"With the worst part of the job," I said, standing. "Breaking Nicchi's wife the bad news."

11

B ianca Nicchi's home made me jealous, but not because of its great opulence or incredible size. The
house was a mere two stories, and probably in the
range of fifteen hundred square feet. The exterior
looked lively, with a coat of cornflower blue paint popping against white trim in the porch railing and posts,
all surrounded with a rickety picket fence and a mob of
green bushes that were taking full advantage of spring.
Trees shaded the property, too, a pair in front and a half
dozen in the back, rustling delightfully in the mid-
afternoon breeze, but it wasn't a hatred of shrubbery or
a deep-seated aversion to foliage that fueled my ire.
Rather it was the home's cost. Not that Officer Silverbrook had shared with me insider knowledge of Aragosto's real estate market, but the fact that a fisherman
could afford a home such as this gave me some idea as
to the town's housing costs. In New Welwic, the best I
could ever hope to achieve would be to upgrade from
renting a small apartment to owning a similarly small
condo. As for owning land, I'd have to settle for what I

managed to drag with me in terra cotta pots up the stairs.

We followed Silverbrook through the gate, down the path to the front, and up the porch stairs. The dwarf knocked on the frame of the exterior door, a hinged cover made of cheesecloth and wire. We waited.

After a moment, the interior door creaked and opened. A young woman stood behind it, clad in a yellow, sleeveless sundress with a deep slit that plunged into her bosom. Dark hair fell to her shoulders, kept out of her face by bangs in the front. Thick, shapely eyebrows curved over light brown eyes like pouting lips, the latter of which the young woman also possessed.

"Bronmuth?" she said through the screen door. "What are you doing here? And who are these jamooks?"

"Nice to see you, too, Bianca," said Silverbrook. "And these jamooks are cops, so maybe lighten up on the attitude? I know it's hard for you, but give it a try sometime."

Bianca cast a judgmental eye over us. "They're no cops I've ever seen. You and Sam been hiring at the station?"

"They're from New Welwic," said Bronmuth. "Detectives Daggers, Quinto, and Steele."

"Detectives?" The exterior door squeaked as Bianca pushed it open. "This about Johnny? They find my sorry excuse for a husband drunk in a puddle of his own piss?"

I lifted an eyebrow and shared it with Steele.

"Look, Bianca, you mind if we come inside?" said Bronmuth. "We need to talk."

The young woman snorted. "Fine. Whatever. Come on in. Not like I've got anything going on."

Silverbrook nodded to us and led us inside, following Bianca through a corridor into a small living room fitted with a mismatched couch and loveseat, one of them upholstered in brown corduroy and the other with a teal and gray paisley design. What sunlight made it through the trees in the backyard filtered through the room's windows, dying in the layer of dust that caked the coffee table and upon the threadbare tapestry hanging from the wall.

Bianca settled on the couch in the far corner, crossing her arms and legs alike and turning a good fifteen degrees away from the center of the room. Silverbrook took the opposite corner of the couch. Anyone stupid enough to risk the center spot risked having their head bitten off by Bianca.

"Well?" said the young woman. "What is it? You going to make me sit all day before you tell me?"

"Look, Bianca," said Bronmuth. "There's no easy way to say this, so I'm just going to come out with it. Johnny's dead. I'm sorry."

Bianca blinked, furrowing her brow. "What? Seriously?" She eyed Quinto, Steele, and me, none of who'd helped ourselves to the loveseat. It looked as if there might be a colony of mice living inside it. "So that's what the three of you are here for? You're emissaries from the city, here to tell me my husband's dead?"

"We found him this morning," said Steele. "The embroidery on his jacket led us to Aragosto."

Bianca shook her head, her brow still furrowed and her lips pressed together tightly. She worked her mouth for a few seconds until words came out. "Well...I can't say I'm surprised. He would've shown up by now if he wasn't. And it's not like he'd be alive for long if he did show his face, not after I got my hands on his sorry ass."

"You might want to cool it with the threats," I said. "Johnny isn't just dead. He was murdered."

Bianca recoiled as if she'd been wafted with smelling salts. "Murdered? What are you talking about?"

"You noticed the part where Officer Silverbrook mentioned we were detectives, right? We're with New Welwic's homicide department."

Bianca blinked, staring as much into a fourth dimension as at anyone in particular. "But...why? Who would kill him?"

Steele settled onto the edge of the loveseat, shelving whatever misgivings she might have and adopting her best look of concern. "That's what we're in town to find out, Bianca. Do you mind if we ask you some questions about your husband, Johnny?"

Bianca started to close back up again, her folded arms tightening. "Well...sure, I guess. What do you need to know?"

"Maybe you could tell us about the night he went missing."

"What about it? I already talked to Bronmuth after the fact. He took my statement."

"I think they want to hear it from you," said Silverbrook. "Start at the beginning. You said Johnny left around eight, right?"

I clenched my teeth. Shay's jaw tightened as well. Bronmuth might claim he didn't need our help, yet in our very first interview, he bungled an opportunity to allow a key witness to contradict herself.

"That's right," said Bianca. "There was nothing special about the night, really. Johnny'd gotten back from a fishing trip the day before, then spent most of the day in and out of the house, buying supplies for his ship or hitting the bars or gods knows what else. Anyway, he left for good about eight. Didn't say where he was going, or even give me so much as a goodbye. Just left, like I didn't even exist. I figured I'd be able to tell where he went when he came back by the smell, either of the bottle or the sea, but he never showed. And here we are, with you all saying he got murdered."

"You didn't pay much attention to his business, I take it?" I said.

Bianca shot me a dirty look. "Huh?"

"You said he could've been up to gods know what during the day. Clearly he didn't talk to you much about his affairs."

"We didn't talk about much at all, if we're being straight," said Bianca. "Haven't for a while. I'd pretty much given up on him."

"What do you mean by that?" asked Steele.

"Just that I couldn't tell you much about Johnny," said Bianca. "Not anymore. When we started dating, and the first couple years of marriage, things were great. Johnny doted on me, cared for me, spent time with me.

But that all went away. Got too caught up in his work, or got bored with me. I can't tell you what I don't know, and I already told you he didn't talk to me anymore."

"Do you mind if I ask you when these...*marital troubles* began?" asked Shay.

Bianca shrugged. "A year ago? Maybe two. I don't know."

"And do you have any idea what might've caused the changes in your husband?"

"It's just the way men are, according to my girlfriends. Who knows. Maybe he was stressed about money, or over problems with his brother. Maybe both."

"His brother?" I asked.

"Joey," said Bianca. "They worked together. That's why it was called Nicchi Fishing and Crabbing, not Johnny's Fishing and Crabbing, capiche? Joey left a year ago. Started doing his own thing."

"Speaking of money," said Bronmuth, "how are you holding up with Johnny gone, Bianca? You doing okay?"

The young woman gave Silverbrook a dismissive nod. "Thanks, but I'm fine. The whole community's pulling together. Sent the collection plate around, same as they always do, you know? Besides, I'm sure something'll come through sooner or later. I'll be alright."

The young lady still hadn't uncoiled. The wall she'd built around herself loomed over us all, capable of fending off attacks from catapults and ballistae alike. Though her tone of voice had softened in response to Silverbrook's inquiry, it struck me as odd how she hadn't shed a single tear for her husband. If what she said was true, her relationship with the man wasn't much to write home about, and she'd already convinced herself he'd exited the picture, but she surely hadn't expected the man to have been *murdered*. And still no tears. Not even the threat of any. Could she really be that cold? Who drove away who, exactly?

"I hate to harp on financial matters," said Steele, "but since we're on the topic, do you know if your husband suffered from any money problems? Was he heavily indebted to anyone?"

"I don't know," said Bianca. "I already told you he didn't include me in his business dealings—not that I wanted to be. Maybe money had been a little tight lately. Didn't I say it might've been? But Johnny wasn't in a bad way with worse people, if that's what you're asking. Not to my knowledge. Why?"

"Well, his boat went missing the night he did," said Steele. "We presume it was stolen. Maybe it was an act of chance that thieves targeted your husband, but given what we've learned about Aragosto, that seems...*unlikely*."

Bianca shrugged and rolled her eyes. "Well, I don't know what you want me to tell you. If Johnny was up to anything, I didn't know about it. And I doubt he was. We might've grown apart, but he was a good man. An honest man. Now, Bronmuth, if you and these government mooks are done firing the grill, maybe I can get some privacy? It's not like I just learned my husband was *murdered* or anything."

The anger and annoyance radiated off her quite convincingly, but still no tears.

"You bet, Bianca. You need anything, just call." Silverbrook stood and gave us a nod.

A half-dozen steps brought us out the door, which clattered shut behind us.

"Well, that sucked," said Bronmuth, passing a hand over his close-cropped hair. "You deliver news like this all the time?"

"Not every day, but close," said Quinto. "You get used to it."

Silverbrook shook his head. "I'd rather not."

"How well do you know Bianca?" I asked as we descended the steps.

"About as well as I know anyone," said Bronmuth.

It wasn't a useful answer. "She a good woman?"

"Of course she is," said the dwarf. "Rough around the edges, but yeah. What are you getting at?"

"Nothing," I said. "Let's keep moving."

"And where exactly are you in such a rush to go?"

"The scene of the crime," I said. "Or at least as close as we can get without getting wet."

12

A sense of déjà vu accosted me as I waltzed down the
rickety wooden dock, the slats clacking underfoot
with each of my steps, but the sensation faded as I
failed to encounter an impertinent fisherman at the
end of it all, sassing me as I asked him about a man in a
monogrammed maroon jacket. Instead, there wasn't anything at the end of the dock. No fisherman, no boat, no
crates of cargo that reeked like Quinto's breath after he
binged on fish cakes of questionable freshness. All I
spotted was a collection of coiled rope, a few bollards,
and a wide expanse of sapphire blue ocean beyond.

"Here we are," said Silverbrook, spreading his arms.
"Pier seventeen. Johnny's slip. Not sure what you expect to find."

"Evidence of something untoward, of course."

Spindly piers stretched into the shallows on either
side of me, some with boats moored and some without.
All manner of crafts were represented, some with low
hulls and wide bodies, others narrow with peaked bows,
some adorned with figureheads of ocean gods or dol-

phins or half-naked women. Service buildings lined the wharf behind us. Off to the left, past the seventeen piers and the piled stones of the breakwater, I spotted the colorful flapping banners of the tourist-friendly boardwalk.

"What kind of evidence, exactly?" asked Bronmuth. "Blood? Guts?"

"Steele, you want to take this?"

My partner nodded as she searched, crouching to get a better look at one of the fastening posts. "I understand where you're coming from, Officer. Homicide investigation is its own beast, as are arson and burglary and the other felony subdivisions. Most of the investigative techniques carry over, but you look for slightly different things depending on the type of perpetrator you're after. Obviously we'd love to find physical evidence tying a scene to Johnny's death. Blood is the most likely, but there could be other markers. Signs of struggle or of a quick exit. Unintentionally misplaced non-sanguineous bodily evidence."

"Non-whatinous?" said Bronmuth.

"Anything other than blood," said Quinto.

"The usual then," said Bronmuth. "And?"

"And what?" asked Steele.

"Have you found anything *non-san-guin-aeous?*"

Shay rose and sighed. "No. Nothing sanguineous either. It's an old dock, rickety and in need of care, but if there was ever any evidence of an assault or kidnapping here, it's long since washed away. Has it rained in the past ten days?"

Bronmuth nodded. "Middle of last week."

Shay lifted both her brows. "Wonderful."

"Hey. Bronmuth!"

The voice, salty and rough like a gust of ocean spray, arrived simultaneously to the footsteps. A wiry graybeard with a red tartan shirt and tan carpenter pants approached, his mop of faded, straw-like hair mostly concealed under a plain knit cap, a garment I was starting to think was mandatory for anyone who worked on or near a boat.

"Hey, Keonig," said Bronmuth, tipping his head toward the newcomer. "How you been?"

"Every day a little older and a little creakier," said Keonig. "But I'm still kicking. Who're your friends?"

At least Bronmuth was polite enough not to correct the man on his assumption. "Detectives from New Welwic. Daggers. Steele. Quinto." He pointed us out in turn, and we each nodded or waved.

"Detectives, eh?" said the graybeard. "You still looking into Johnny's disappearance?"

"Murder, apparently," said Bronmuth. "These folks found him washed ashore in the city."

I ground my teeth again. I wanted to punch the stupid dwarf. "Silverbrook? How about you ixnay the assual-cay omicide-hay talk, mmkay?"

His eyebrows scrunched. "*What?*"

"Your tongue's lolling," I said. "Maybe you should keep it in your mouth."

Bronmuth added a cocked head to his eyebrow contortions. "Are you mad I told Keonig about the murder?"

I tapped the side of my nose and gave him a bug-eyed, toothless grin.

Silverbrook snorted. "Give me a break. We told Bianca. You think word's not going to get out?"

"I've no doubt it will," I said. "But it doesn't have to be the first thing out of your mouth. You want to learn how to investigate a homicide? Consider revealing as little as possible to witnesses rule number two, right after don't trust the guy with the bloody knife in his hand."

"*Witnesses?*" said Keonig. "I don't know anything!"

Bronmuth growled, the edge of his lips curling. "I know what I'm doing. I didn't graduate from the academy yesterday."

Quinto clapped me on the shoulder, gently pulling me back. "Don't mind Daggers, Silverbrook. He's been having an off day."

"Off day and a half, more like," muttered Steele from the end of the pier.

"The point is, we all want the same thing," continued Quinto. "To figure out what happened to Nicchi. Keonig, was it? You work here?"

Keonig looked like he'd rather be anywhere but between me, Quinto, and Bronmuth, but he nodded anyway. "Yeah. I'm the docks' super. I make sure everyone's got their paperwork on file, everyone's following proper safety procedures, and I handle disagreements. If someone ties up on somebody else's pier or tangles their mooring lines. That sort of thing. Boring stuff, mostly, but I saw Bronmuth and I figured I should check in to make sure I hadn't missed something."

"Were you here the night Johnny Nicchi went missing?" asked Quinto.

"Well, no, not at night," said Keonig. "Earlier that day, sure. I go to bed early."

"So you didn't see Nicchi arrive, or leave in his ship, for that matter?"

Keonig shook his head. "Sorry."

"You have a logbook?" I asked. "To keep track of what ships come and go and when?"

Keonig laughed. "What do you think this is? The New Welwic Transport Authority?" His face suddenly lost it's mirth, probably as he remembered where we were from. "Oh. You were serious. No, we don't. Guys barely interact with me unless they're in trouble. They pay their slip fees, usually on a monthly basis. Other than that? I'm telling you, I'm a mediator more than anything else."

Silverbrook grunted. "Please. You sit and nap at your desk six hours out of eight."

"Hey, you don't see me denigrating what you do," said Keonig. "You're not much more than a mediator, yourself."

"Maybe not, but I'm a hell of a lot better at it than you are, you old fart."

Shay joined us, having given up on her search. "Do you know if anyone else around here might've had a view of what happened to Nicchi's ship that night?"

"Sure," said Keonig. "Any of the guys on the neighboring piers. I think Bronmuth already talked to them, though, didn't you?"

The dwarf nodded. "I did, and I told them that."

"Still, might be worth talking to them again," said Steele. "Not that we don't trust your testimony, Silverbrook, but sometimes you can get more juice out of a lemon on the second press, if you get what I mean."

It was kind of a kinky turn of phrase. It was also one that suggested Shay's plan of action included something I most certainly did *not* want to do any more of today.

"You, ah...know if anyone *else* might've noticed what ships came in or out that night?" I asked Keonig. "Some nosy Nancy with a bad case of insomnia who lives on the shore, perhaps?"

Keonig's squinty eyes suggested he didn't get my sense of humor. "There's Old Man Connors. He mans the lighthouse at the tip of the cove. He's a night owl, and if memory serves me right, it was a clear night that night. If anyone saw anything in the bay other than the fishermen and crabbers, it would've been him."

Silverbrook groaned. "Oh, come on, Keonig. *Crackpot Connors?* There's a reason he never leaves that lighthouse."

"Hey, I'm just answering the man's question."

Silverbrook shot me a look. "You don't want to meet him. He's a total kook."

"Are you kidding?" I said. "Kooks are some of the best sources, provided you know how to handle them."

"I'm with Silverbrook," said Steele. "Let's canvass the docks, see what the witnesses who don't jump at shadows and mumble to themselves have to say."

"We can do both, you know," I said. "I count four of us."

"Seriously?"

"Seriously."

Steele sighed and rolled her eyes. "Fine. Not like I've had any luck changing your mind on anything else today. Quinto. You're with me. Meet you back here in an hour or two, okay, Daggers?"

She didn't give me time to respond, heading down the dock with purposeful steps. Quinto gave me a reluctant shrug before following.

Shay's vacuum left me both relieved and hollow. On the bright side, I'd avoided banging my head into another brick wall of fishermen and crabbers. On the other, I'd apparently volunteered to be the solitary companion of one Bronmuth Silverbrook during my hiatus, and he looked none too enthused about having been surrendered to my guardianship.

Still, I could deal with his mean-mugging. It was the butter-thick tension between me and Shay that concerned me.

13

Trees shaded the path to the lighthouse. Birds twittered in the leaves above, bees buzzed in the underbrush, and gravel crunched underfoot. A persistent sea breeze whisked up the path, enough to flutter my hair and cool my cheeks but not enough to make me reach for my pockets, not with the warm bursts of sunlight that punctured through the canopy like an intermittent rain of arrows.

It was an idyllic setting—except for the dour dwarf who marched beside me.

Silverbrook hadn't talked since leaving the pier. To be fair, I hadn't made an effort to break the ice, either, but if the small town cop was fishing for an apology, he was casting in the wrong spot. He needed to learn to hold his tongue if he hoped to investigate homicides successfully on his own, and even if he didn't, a measure of restraint would help the rest of us solve the current case for him. Perhaps I'd have been more forgiving if his tongue had only slipped with Keonig, but he'd gushed over Bianca as if he were a school girl trying to ingratiate herself with the cool crowd. I understood the desire to serve and protect, but that had to be tempered when a murder investigation was afoot.

Still, I probably owed the guy an apology, and getting my feet wet with him could be a good warm-up for what I needed to do later with Shay.

I cleared my throat. "Look, Silverbrook. I'm, uh...sorry about my behavior back there. Keonig seems like a good guy. And you're right. News of Johnny's death is sure to travel regardless of what we do. It's an investigative habit, I guess. Give away as little as you can. Let other people insert feet into their mouths, free of influence."

"It's fine," said Bronmuth. "I get it. You're probably right."

His tone said he didn't want to talk about it. Fair enough.

"You like Aragosto?"

He shot me a suspicious look, like he thought I might be trying to sell him a sickly goat in a horse disguise. "Sure. Why?"

"Well, it's just, ah..." How could I say it without seeming insensitive? "It's not terribly diverse. Mostly humans in these parts, as far as I've seen."

"What are you talking about? There's me, Thoringill, Tall Mike, Big Norma and her kid, the Flutterbright clan."

"A half dozen individuals isn't exactly a lot, even in a town this size."

"So what are you trying to say? That folks here aren't welcoming? That they don't want me around? Or elves or pixies or ogres, for that matter? I thought living in the big city would make you *more* open to other cultures, not less."

"I'm not saying that at all. I'm just wondering what brought you here."

Silverbrook shrugged. "It's a nice place to live. Rent's cheap. It's safe. What else is there?"

I could think of a dozen other things off the top of my head, but fate decided I shouldn't have to respond. The trees thinned in front of us, revealing a lighthouse that watched over the bay, five stories of bricks and mortar capped with an oversized, upturned lowball glass. A long crack ran from the whitewashed bricks at the bottom through the painted red bricks at the top, giving me serious reservations about the building's structural stability, but it didn't sway in the stiff, salty breeze that whipped over the exposed sea cliff some twenty paces before it, nor did it wobble when Bronmuth pounded on the front door, a warped hunk of peeling wood that might've been salvaged from a shipwreck a few decades ago.

"Connors? You in?" he called, before looking back at me and muttering, "As if he'd be anywhere else..."

A squeak sounded from inside, then a cluster of rapid footfalls followed by a loud clunk and the squeal of two dozen mice being tortured with a hot poker—which turned out to be the sound of front door opening.

A frantic man popped into the gap, hunched over as much by age as by an obvious sense of suspicion. He stuck his head out the door, whipping it back and forth and sending the long tendrils of pale hair that hung from the sides of his head flying. One of them grazed me, but I doubt the man noticed. He seemed more pre-occupied with seeing what lurked in the trees than taking note of us. When his head finally stilled, his eyes refused to follow suit, darting around and only briefly pausing on Silverbrook.

"Bronmuth," he said. "You weren't followed were you? And who's your friend? Are you here for the delivery?"

"*Delivery?*" I said.

"Why would anyone follow me, Connors?" said Bronmuth. "Everyone knows where you live."

"Not true. This guy doesn't." Connors waggled a long, skeletal finger at me. "Well, he does now. See what you've done? Now every deliveryman within a hundred miles will know where to find me."

"I'm not a deliveryman," I said. "And wouldn't you want them to know where to find you? How would you get your deliveries, otherwise?"

"*Delivery.* Singular," said Connors, bringing his finger dangerously close to my face. "I only have the one, which is why I don't need your kind banging down my door. Or not your kind, if you're who you say you're not. Sure you don't have my spyglass tucked away inside your pants?"

"Nope. That's all me. One hundred percent natural Jake Daggers."

I didn't expect him to get the joke. He didn't disappoint.

"Well, then? What is it? Can't be you came here for nothing, Bronmuth. Spill it. I don't have all day."

"You don't?"

Connors started to scold me but was forced to stop in mid waggle.

"This is Detective Daggers," said Silverbrook. "From the city? He was, ah...*convinced* it would be helpful to talk to you about a case of ours."

"*Case?* What case?" Connors gave us the shifty eye, which seemed to be his default.

"You'd heard Johnny Nicchi went missing, right?"

"Nicchi!" cried Connors. "Why didn't you say so? Get in here!"

The man grabbed me by the jacket and yanked, pulling me into his abode. I blinked, as much in response to the man's speed as the darkness that swallowed me. Or dimness, more like. A pair of narrow slits cut through the brick walls to the afternoon sun outside, and a bit more light filtered down past the metal spiral staircase in the middle of the lighthouse. A cot had been pushed against a wooden desk covered in junk, the pair of them making a hundred and twenty degree angle against the curved wall. A single worn chair sat in front of the latter, an unlit lantern occupying the space a posterior normally might, but the makeshift home's opulence ended there.

At least Connors didn't invite us to take a seat. After releasing me, he waved at Silverbrook. "Go on. Get in here and close the door. Keep out prying ears."

Bronmuth grudgingly obliged, plunging the room further into the grip of shadows. "For the second time, Connors, no one followed us. No one's here to spy on you."

"Says you," said the old man, "and yet you're the ones here asking about Nicchi, who so *mysteriously* disappeared into the night."

"So you've heard, then." I'd started to think the trip might be a waste.

"Course I've heard," said Connors. "What do you take me for? Some crazed reclusive hermit?"

I glanced at Bronmuth, mostly because I didn't think I could keep the mirth off my face. Either way, I was grateful for the dim lighting. "Right. Well, that's why we're here. To talk to you about that night."

Connors narrowed an eye in my direction. "What night?"

"Uh...the night Nicchi went missing?"

"Is that a question?"

"It started out as a clarification and turned into a question as I went along."

Connors crossed his arms. "For real, Bronmuth, who is this guy? Can we trust him?"

"I already told you, his name is Daggers. He's a detective, of the public kind. As far as whether we can trust him? Probably. *You* certainly can."

"Why *me, certainly?*" said Connors. "What's that supposed to mean?"

"Just tell him what he wants to know so we can leave, will you?"

Connors didn't relax. He scowled, then waved me in. "Alright. Here."

"Here, where?" I asked.

"*Here,* here. Close in. I already told you about the prying ears."

My patience was wearing thin, but I did as he asked. He'd piqued my interest.

"I remember the night as if it were yesterday," said Connors in a low voice. "I was on the catwalk outside the lantern room, feeling the breeze whipping through my hair and filling my lungs with the smell of the sea. I was gazing onto the bay, probably around midnight—I don't sleep as well as I used to—and then, I spotted it. Out past where the breakers start, a fog started forming. Slow at first, then thick as a bowl of clam chowder. And out of it—*a ghost ship!* Tendrils of fog creeping along the sides, tatters in the sails, barnacles eating every inch of the sides—"

"Whoa, whoa," said Bronmuth. "Connors, what the *hell* are you talking about?"

"The ship, man," said Connors. "Night of Nicchi's disappearance. What? Don't give me that look. Okay, maybe it wasn't a ghost ship. But that fog sure was creepy, and with the wind flapping the sails, you'll forgive me for thinking they were in tatters. Hard to tell by the light of the moon. But I'm pretty sure some of them had seen better days."

Bronmuth held a couple fingers to his temple. "I don't even know where to start. Nicchi's ship wasn't big. It was a diminutive sloop, barely bigger than a catboat, and last I saw it wasn't covered in barnacles or flying tattered sails. Also, if Nicchi disappeared and his ship along with him, don't you think it would've been *leaving* the harbor, not entering it? So I don't know what ship you saw, but it sure as hell wasn't Nicchi's, because it also *wasn't foggy the night of his disappearance.*"

Connors blinked and scratched his head. "It wasn't? How long has it been since he went missing?"

"Ten days ago tonight," said Bronmuth.

Connors mumbled to himself, ticking fingers in the air as he stared into nothingness. "Oh. Right then. I was off by a night. Never mind."

Bronmuth gave a labored sigh. "Come on, Daggers. Let's go."

"Wait," said Connors. "Just because I was off by a night doesn't mean I don't remember. Ten nights ago, right. I didn't see his boat leave. Wasn't outside much. Was sawing logs, actually. One of the few nights in recent memory I managed a few hours of uninterrupted sleep."

"So you didn't see his boat. Got it. Daggers?" Bronmuth shot his thumb toward the door.

"Hold on," said Connors. "I didn't see it. That doesn't mean I didn't *hear* anything. That's what woke me, see. After a few hours of rest. The sound. The cries."

"Cries?" I asked.

"That's right. The pained cries—of the merfolk!"

"Oh, for the love of..." Bronmuth shot a symbol of piety toward the skies. "Daggers, I'm leaving. You coming or not?"

"Just a sec," I said. "You said you heard *mermaids?* What do they even sound like?"

"Like people, normally, lest you hurt them, then they're more like dolphins. High-pitched, squeaky, haunting. And I didn't say mermaids. *Merfolk.* Males and females, savvy?"

"Right. Of course."

"Oh, come on. You can't honestly believe this crap, can you?" said Bronmuth. "Nobody's seen merfolk in a hundred years, and even then they were probably nothing more than a horny sailor's sunstroke-induced fantasy."

"Not true," said Connors. "I've seen 'em with my own eyes. Not ten nights ago, mind you, but recently. A few years past."

"Right," said Bronmuth. "And I'd bet your army of made up ghost pirates would back you up on that, if we asked them?"

Connors shook his head, suddenly embarrassed. "Martinsvale would if he were around. He's the one who took me to 'em one night, rest his soul."

"So all we need to corroborate your story is the testimony of a dead man," said Bronmuth. "Perfect. We'll get on that as soon as we find a medium. Not that it matters, because we're not looking for mermaids, we're looking for a fisherman who was murdered at sea."

"Merfolk." Connors crossed his arms and shrunk into a corner. "And I saw them. Heard them, I mean. I did..."

Silverbrook yanked open the door and glared at me. "You coming?"

I nodded, even though I thought continuing to interview Connors might prove fruitful. Based on Bronmuth's look of frustration, he hadn't made the connection. We *had* mentioned that Nicchi had been murdered by trident, right?

14

Daggers of color stabbed across the twilit sky as Silverbrook and I returned to the docks, tendrils of carnation pink and coral, orange peel, lavender, and ultramarine, as vibrant as a painting against a backdrop of steel gray.

The metaphor wasn't lost on me, but if the gods intended to send me a message via sunlight and clouds, they'd have to be more blunt. Form the clouds into letters, perhaps, or focus the sun's rays onto a target to catch my eye.

I spotted Shay and Quinto on a quay in the distance. I waved, expecting to be ignored, but despite his thinning hair, Quinto's eyes remained sharp. The big guy waved back, nudged Shay, and the pair started toward us.

We met by a set of pilings covered in fragrant white droppings, at least a portion of which belonged to the gray and white gull who currently perched there. He cawed repeatedly as we approached. I thought he might fly off as we closed to swatting range, but the sucker paid us as much attention as he might a stiff breeze. He just kept on cawing and decorating the post with his excrement. He must've been a local.

Shay gave the bird a sidelong glance as she and Quinto arrived. "Well. That didn't take quite as long as I expected, though I suppose your timing is right."

"Why?" I asked. "Did you just unearth an exciting clue?"

Shay pointed to the sky. "I simply meant we're running out of daylight. What did you learn from this Connors fellow?"

"That's he's battier than I remembered," said Bronmuth. "The rest doesn't even merit repeating. I can't believe you convinced me going out there was a good idea."

"Come on, Silverbrook," I said. "I thought we bonded on the walk. To say it was a waste of time hurts me deeply. Besides, we did learn the coastal waters of Aragosto are haunted by ghost pirates and mermaids, among other things."

"*Ghost pirates* and *mermaids?*" said Steele.

"Well, one of them makes sense."

The gull cut loose with another undulating set of caws, cutting off whatever question Shay might've prepared for me, but I could see the wheels turning behind her corneas.

"So what about you two," asked Bronmuth when the gull finally shut up. "Learn anything new?"

"Not precisely," said Quinto. "Talked to a number of the local fishermen, some of whom didn't trust us, but your friend Keonig vouched for us and soon enough word got around. Loosened some lips. Ultimately we found a trio of witnesses who remembered the night in question. Said Nicchi's boat was there early in the night but went missing later on. No one remembers seeing Nicchi on his dock the night of the disappearance, though."

Bronmuth frowned. "Which is exactly what I told you in the first place."

"True," said Shay, "but we may have narrowed the timeline. According to our witness statements, Nicchi's ship went missing between eleven and two. It's not much more to go on than what you provided, but every bit helps."

"And his wife said he left the house about eight." Technically, it was Bronmuth who'd said it, but Bianca had confirmed it and I didn't have any reason to question the information—yet.

Shay nodded. "Which gives us at least a three hour window during which Johnny Nicchi is unaccounted for. Silverbrook. How thoroughly did you look into Nicchi's disappearance, outside of talking to folks around the docks?"

"I mean, I looked into it, if that's what you're asking. Just because I didn't think he'd been murdered doesn't mean I ignored the case, you know."

"I wasn't implying you had," said Shay. "Just wondering if you'd had any leads on him after he left his house that night."

Bronmuth shrugged. "As of now, no. I'll hop on that in the morning. For now, it's getting late. I'm sure you all want to head home before the last of the light disappears."

"Actually, our captain authorized us to spend the night should we find a lead on Nicchi," I said.

"Really?" Bronmuth lifted an eyebrow. Apparently his superior was as stingy with the funds as ours was, or at least as much as our old captain had been.

Shay shrugged. "She was thinking ahead. Got any hotel recommendations?"

"Well...sure, I guess," said Bronmuth. "Most of the seaside inns are overpriced. Targeted towards New Welwic schmucks who can't tell a bed and breakfast from a bungalow—which I'm sure excludes all of you fine folks. But I know the manager at the *Osprey*. He's a good guy. Can probably give your department a discount rate if I introduce you."

"And it's close by?"

"Sure. On 2nd Street, right behind the more expensive oceanside properties. Hopefully they still have rooms available. You never know this time of year. With the weather warming up, we'll be inundated with visitors soon."

"Sounds like we shouldn't dawdle," said Quinto.

Bronmuth nodded and showed us the way. Luckily, he'd been honest about the distance. Within ten minutes we'd arrived, and though we hadn't crossed the entire town by any stretch of the imagination, it still boggled my mind that we could reach so much of Aragosto in such short order. Come to think of it, I hadn't seen any rickshaws patrolling the streets until I spotted a number waiting outside the inns on 1st street. I guess they weren't needed.

The *Osprey,* which to me sounded more like the name of a ship than a hotel, was a narrow three-story building painted a shade of yellow that was probably brighter than it appeared to be in the fading light of day. White-trimmed four pane windows flanked a door with the hotel's sign hanging over it, with a smaller sign reading 'Vacancy' hanging from hooks underneath the first.

Bronmuth led us into the lobby, similarly painted yellow and populated with rustic, upholstered furniture that had been restored enough to make it presentable but not so much as to lose its charm. A man with thinning gray hair and a beard that matched Silverbrook's in size if not color waved at the dwarf from the confines of the front desk.

"Bronmuth," he said with a smile. "What's it been? A month? Don't tell me you've brought goons with you to force me into making good on my bet?"

"Goons?" said Steele.

"Bet?" I said.

Bronmuth rolled his eyes. "Don't mind Weston. It was a friendly wager made over beers, one that doesn't hold the weight of my department, as he well knows."

Weston shrugged, his smile firmly in place. "Don't I, though. Who are your friends?"

"Steele. Quinto. Daggers." He pointed. "They're from New Welwic, with the PD there. Could use rooms for the night. Got any—at a fair rate, I might add?"

"I do as a matter of fact," said Weston. "Though it's a good thing you got here when you did. Ten minutes later, and who knows if I'da had anything left."

"Don't go trying to fabricate demand out of thin air," said Bronmuth. "You said a fair price. We all heard you."

Weston held up his hands in mock offense. "Hey, I wouldn't dream of such a thing. I'm just telling the gods' honest truth, I am. So, what'll it be? Three rooms?"

Quinto looked to me. I looked to Steele. She didn't look at either of us, nodding to the clerk in agreement. "Three, yes. Thanks."

"Not a problem," said Weston. "I can give you two oh three, three oh two, and three oh three. Stairs are behind you to the right. Breakfast starts at six thirty, in the dining room at the base of the stairs. It's not included in the price of the room, mind you. Just noting for your convenience."

"Remember, a fair price," said Bronmuth, shooting a finger at Weston. "Otherwise I'll hear about it. And if I have to collect on that, I *will* bring goons, trust me. Guys? I'm headed out. If you need a place to eat, try the cafés and bars on Main. Or hit the boardwalk, as long as you're not looking for health food. You need anything else, laundry, courier service, you name it. Ask Weston, he'll point you in the right direction. I'll see you tomorrow, I'm guessing. At the station?"

I nodded, and Bronmuth showed himself the door. Under other circumstances I might've ruminated on how the dwarf's temperament had improved in only a few hours under our watch, but I had other things on my mind of greater importance.

The number of rooms we'd secured, notably.

15

I sat on the bed in my room, my back against the headboard, staring vaguely in the direction of the lone window overlooking 3rd Street and the collection of homes and leafy green trees beyond it. The sky had darkened to a deep purple, a sea of eggplant with the streaky color variations included. Soon the purple would darken to a midnight black, lighting the fires of a thousands stars should the clouds choose to play along. They'd been noncommittal during the day.

I tried to shift my mind to the case, but try as I might, every time I conjured thoughts of Fishy's dead corpse or his speared sweater or Old Man Connor's unhinged testimony, I found myself staring at the wall or back out the window with no idea where I'd been going or what I'd intended to accomplish. I couldn't seem to wrap my brain around much of anything. At least, anything other than the fact that I was in breezy seaside Aragosto, in spring, in a quaint bed and breakfast, yet in a room all by myself.

I sighed. Seemingly in response, a knock sounded at my door.

I rose, undid the latch, and opened it. Shay stood in the hallway outside.

"Hey," she said.

"Hey."

Silence stretched for several seconds, or so I assumed. They felt like minutes. I could've peeled a five pound sack of potatoes while I stood there.

Steele looked me in the eyes, but she didn't crack a smile as she so often did. "Any chance you're getting hungry? I thought it might be nice to go out, grab some dinner, maybe go for a walk afterwards."

"Yeah. Sure. That would be nice," I said. "But what about Quinto?"

"He's a big boy. He can fend for himself for a night."

I nodded.

"Need anything from your room?"

"I'm good to go if you are."

"Great. Any thoughts about dinner, in that case?"

I closed the door behind me and locked it, to be on the safe side. Not like I'd left anything there. "I'm amenable to just about anything. But I'll be honest, Bronmuth made the Boardwalk fare sound pretty appetizing."

Shay lifted a brow. "Unless you discussed it on your trip to the lighthouse, all he said was it was the furthest thing imaginable from health food."

"That's enough, isn't it?"

"I thought I'd trained you out of that obsession."

"There are a lot of things I thought you'd trained me out of."

Shay looked at me, but she didn't say anything. She led the way down the stairs, out the front and onto the streets of Aragosto, past the lantern-lit facades of the inns on 1st Street and toward the sea. A long boarded path, the boardwalk proper, snaked over the sandy dune at the foot of the ocean, eventually opening up onto a broad dock, more of an esplanade, really, but my niggling over terminology wouldn't make it less of a boardwalk to Bronmuth or any of the locals and tourists who milled about its planks.

A boxy building stood to my right, a sign featuring a mishmash of large and small, bold and subdued fonts proclaiming it to be 'Max William's Marvelous, Miraculous, Mystical and Magical Wax Museum of Wily Warriors, Masculine Madmen, and Mesmeric Maidens,' not to mention any number of other boasts that populated the sign in distinct bubbles. Another structure further down the esplanade promoted itself as a house of mirrors, and beyond that, a labyrinth, though based on the building's footprint, I didn't think it could be much of one. Mummers put on a puppet show to my left, one in which the puppets in question seemed to do little other than bash each other in the head with clubs. Beyond that I heard more than saw the efforts of a fiddler playing for coins.

"I see a sausage cart down that away," said Shay, pointing. "Maybe someone selling meat pies, as well, and a dessert cart if I had to guess based on the smell. Fried dough, of course. Your favorite."

"One of them, anyway."

"Or we could keep looking," said Shay. "Looks like the boardwalk extends for about a third of a mile. We might even find a place with patio seating."

"You had me at sausages."

"Yeah, I figured that mistake out as soon as I said it. Not that you wouldn't have noticed them. Or smelled them, given your pork-attuned olfactory system."

As suggested, I followed my nose to the cart, buying a foot-long pork kielbasa slathered in spicy mustard for myself. Shay opted for a more modestly sized turkey sausage covered in a corn relish. We ate as we walked, passing a few couples here and there but not as many as I'd expected given the season and Bronmuth's prognostications of incoming tides of tourists.

"How's your dog?" I asked.

Shay waggled her head. "I've had better. I probably shouldn't have sprung for the relish."

"You tempted fate by choosing a topping supposedly made of fresh ingredients. You knew the risks."

"Indeed."

We kept walking, passing a haunted house and a fortune teller's tent on the boardwalk's landward side before arriving at a much larger structure facing the ocean, with rows upon rows of benches overlooking a number of contraptions on a jetty. It was hard to tell what, exactly, given the darkness and the benches obscuring the view, but I thought I spotted a stage, a crane, and an elevated platform. A haggard sign above the entrance glimmered in the light of a few nearby lanterns, proclaiming the attraction as 'Doc Fowler's Fantastic Flying Foals and Fillies, An Extravaganza of Natural Wonders and Delights.' I think Sergeant Mines had mentioned it in passing, but that familiarity didn't help me under-stand how in the world Doc Fowler made the poor foals and fillies fly.

I gestured at the sign, its peeling paint and faded let-tering having seen better days. "You have any idea what kind of show this is?"

"I wouldn't even be able to speculate, but for Doc Fowler's sake, I hope business is better in the day than at night." Shay glanced at what remained of her turkey dog with a look of uncertainty, as if determining whether a full belly was worth the effort.

"Yeah, I'd hope so, too. Not a lot of action here at night. I figured there'd be more after what Mines and Silverbrook made it out to be."

"Daggers, can we talk?"

I crumpled my kielbasa wrapper into a tight ball. "Aren't we talking now?"

"You know what I mean."

Lacking a nearby wastebasket, I stuffed the greasy ball of paper into my pocket. "Of course."

Shay rewrapped what remained of her own dog. "Jake, what are we doing?"

"Having dinner. Going for a walk."

"Stop being so literal. I mean, what are we doing to each other? Why are we fighting? Neither of us wants this."

I shook my head. "Obviously not."

"So why are we?" asked Steele.

I sighed and gave a tiny shrug, more with my lips than my shoulders. "It's...hard to admit you're at fault sometimes. Especially to someone you care about, over a matter that doesn't have an easy fix."

"Well, it shouldn't be," said Steele. "I mean, honestly. I can start. I admit I overreacted. Maybe not to the events of last night, per se. Between you kicking Barnabus and spilling an entire bottle of wine over the table and my mother, I can't imagine things could've gone any worse. But even with all that, I did overreact. I treated you as if you'd planned it all, when inside, I know it was an accident, or at least a series of unfortunate events that were unavoidable given your pathological aversion to cats. And more than that...I trust you. I believe you that, even though they meant well, you interpreted my family's overprotectiveness as something less welcoming. As a sign of dislike."

"And I'm sorry, too," I said. "Obviously I could've handled things better. Not just while pouring the wine. While talking to your father and brothers. Even while your mother prodded me at the dinner table. I should've expected I'd get questions about my personal life, about Nicole, about Tommy, about my past, about how and where I fit into your life. I think maybe I expected the worst coming into it, and I let it get to me. Either way, I know I owe you an apology, and I certainly owe one to your family, more than the one I already gave in the immediate aftermath."

"So we both admit we made mistakes."

I nodded. "Absolutely."

"Great. That's precisely what I was hoping to hear."

"Me, too."

"Are you sure? Because you still look miserable."

I lifted my head, realizing I'd been staring at the ground. "I do?"

"Your cheeks are tight, your brow is furrowed, and you're sure as hell not smiling."

She was right. It took a conscious effort to unclench my jaw. "Sorry."

"You don't have to apologize for that," said Shay. "But if there's anything you're still upset about, now's the time to tell me."

"I..." I swallowed hard, not sure how to voice what was bothering me.

"Just tell me, Jake."

Shay's bright blue eyes glimmered in the glow of the boardwalk lanterns. I couldn't keep it from her. She deserved to know.

I took a deep breath. "What if... What if they're right?"

"What if who's right?"

"Your family," I said. "You dad, your brothers, your mom. What if they're correct, that I'm not right for you. That I don't...*deserve* you."

"What?" Shay's face softened. "Why would you think that? You know how much I care about you."

"On the surface, sure, I know," I said. "But at the same time you're young and beautiful and brilliant. You're sophisticated and clever, you're hardworking, you come from a great family, you have people who love you. You may not be a psychic, but you have every other possible thing going for you, and I'm just...*me*."

"And who else would I be with?"

"Someone younger. More attractive. Smarter. Someone more like you."

Shay's eyebrows furrowed and her face fell. "Jake, this crisis of confidence isn't like you. Not anymore. I thought you'd progressed past this. I thought *we* had."

"I thought so, too."

Shay's lips parted, and I could tell she wanted to say something, but nothing came out. After a moment, she took a breath and released it. Her head shook almost imperceptibly.

"Jake, I could stand here all day and tell you the things I like about you, the qualities that make me care about you, but it wouldn't help, would it? I've already told you those things. You know them. Up here." She tapped her head. "But that's not where the problem lies. The problem is a little lower. And I can't offer a solution for that. I can't make you feel worthy of me, of anyone. That's an issue you'll have to tackle yourself."

"I know."

Shay gestured down the rest of the boardwalk. "You want to keep walking? Maybe visit an attraction?"

I shook my head. "Not tonight. Not right now."

Shay nodded, understanding. "I'm going to head back to my hotel room, then. Don't hesitate to reach out. And don't wander off, okay?"

She knew me too well. "I won't."

Shay gave me a shy smile and squeezed my arm before turning and heading toward the boardwalk entrance. I watched her go, keeping my eyes on her until she disappeared behind the dune. With her words fresh in my mind, I plunged my hands into my pockets and walked off toward what remained of the attractions.

16

The sun greeted me as I cracked my eyes, streaming in through the lone window in my room. I blinked, once, twice, yawned, and pushed the blanket off of me. Rubbing my eyes, I stumbled to the quarters' rudimentary washroom, where I splashed my face with water from the basin. The chill shocked me as intended, widening my eyes despite my anticipation. Staring into the mirror, I took a deep breath.

I felt okay. Not fantastic or even above average. My legs and feet ached from yesterday's walking, and I could feel the accumulated grime from a day's toil rubbing between my fingers and greasing my brow, but deep down in the middle where it mattered, I felt acceptable. After the bout of self-misery I'd fought through during my solitary journey across the boardwalk, I'd take it.

I stripped my shirt off, doused my face again, and went to work on my grubbiest parts with a towel. Luckily I'd had the foresight to borrow a razor from Weston before heading to bed the night prior, though I wished

I'd also had the foresight to stop by my apartment to grab a change of clothes before leaving New Welwic. At least I could console myself with the knowledge that Steele and Quinto had made the same mistake.

With my face cleaned and shaved as well as I could get it, I threw on the rest of my clothes, stepped into the third floor hallway—and almost ran into Quinto.

"Whoa there." I put my hands up to avoid barreling into him. "What are you doing here, big guy?" He'd taken the second floor room, while Shay and I had taken the third story offerings.

Quinto swayed, trying to regain his balance after almost trampling me. "Sorry. Looking for you, actually. Time to get going."

"And what time is that?" I asked, glancing at the nearest window.

"Eight thirty, give or take," said Quinto. "Apparently your stint as an early riser was short lived."

"I don't think I ever could've been considered that, even during these past few months. An on-time riser, on my best days. Still, don't give up on me yet. I might surprise you. Steele up?"

"Would I be looking for you if she weren't?"

"Fair enough. Is she downstairs?"

Quinto nodded. "But not waiting on you. We tried the breakfast portion of our B&B."

I thought I'd smelled black pepper and sage on Quinto's breath, but I couldn't be sure. Lacking the comforts of home, I hadn't brushed my teeth after my kielbasa last night. I'd hoped it hadn't been me.

"And?" I asked. "How it is?"

"You should ask Steele. I don't have the most delicate of palates."

"Is it all you can eat?"

Quinto nodded.

"So it was worth it."

Quinto didn't argue the point. We headed downstairs, weaved through the adjoining hallway into the dining hall, and found Steele seated at a round table covered with a white cloth. Her plate held a few egg remnants and scraps of toast, whereas the plate that must've belonged to Quinto had been picked clean, tainted only by a few sticky specks of syrup or honey. A third plate had been set at the side of the table, containing a biscuit, cut in half, piled with scrambled eggs and a pair of sausage links.

I pointed at it. "This for me?"

"I figured you'd appreciate it," said Steele, giving Quinto a small nod. "And it's something we can take with us on the road."

"We're leaving already? What's the rush?"

"You mean other than someone having been murdered and there being a killer on the loose?" asked Shay. "That should be enough, but beyond that, I'd rather spend tonight in my own bed. Room three oh three's was on the lumpy side."

I picked up the sandwich and took a bite, speaking between a mouthful of buttery goodness. "You realize we have literally no leads right now."

"All the more reason to get started as soon as possible. But we've made quick work of trickier cases before. I have faith." Shay stood, tossed her napkin on the table, and gestured toward the door. "Come on. Might as well bring that with you."

Another garbled sentence spoken between bits of egg and flaky crust. "Think Weston'll mind you snagged this for me?"

"Oh, I have no doubt he'll charge us for it whether we eat or not," said Shay. "I don't think he's quite as scrupulous as Bronmuth made him out to be."

I followed Steele and Quinto out the front of the hotel and down the streets of Aragosto, eating my sandwich as the other two conversed.

"So where were you thinking we should begin?" asked Quinto.

"Well, we didn't get much done yesterday, so we have a lot of options."

Quinto snorted. *"Didn't get much done?* We covered more ground by four in the afternoon than we do over the entirety of most cases."

"True," said Shay, "but it wasn't functional work. The majority of that was spent trying to figure out who Nicchi was and where he was from. And don't act so righteous. Most of that *covered ground* was spent in a rickshaw."

Quinto shrugged, but I saw him smile.

"The point is, all we really accomplished before checking in for the night was to look into Nicchi's last known location, the dock where his ship went missing."

"And technically, we don't even know if he was there at all," said Quinto. "Remember, nobody saw him. They saw his boat, or lack thereof."

I swallowed a mouthful of eggs, sausage, and biscuit, another bite or two left in my hand. "You're forgetting my meeting with Old Man Connors."

Shay shot a sly smile back at me. "You're right. How *dare* I discount that? But lacking any more crazy coots to gather conspiracy theories from, I think our next course of action is clear. We need to dig into Nicchi's life. Talking to his wife was a start. They may not have had kids, but surely he has parents. Bianca mentioned a brother. And I'll bet he had friends. Chances are one of them will be able to help us identify Johnny's murderer."

I finished my sandwich in the time it took us to reach the precinct. Quinto held the door for us as I wiped my hands on my pants and forced the last mouthful down my gullet. The biscuit had proven less fresh with each of my bites, and now my throat screamed for some coffee. At least I'd arrived at the right place to solve that problem.

Once again, the station was mostly empty. Only Sergeant Mines sat at one of the desks, scribbling away at some forms.

She waved when she saw us. "Hey. I didn't realize you were spending the night, but it sounds like Silverbrook helped you get settled. Come in. Make yourselves comfy."

I wasn't sure how that was possible given the limited furniture options, but I tried not to take her literally. I headed to the coffee pot while Shay and Quinto made a beeline for Samantha.

"Morning, Mines," I heard Shay say over the gurgle of coffee cascading into a mug. "Sounds like Silverbrook got you caught up. Is he in?"

"No," said Mines. "Well, he was. But that's not when he caught me up. He left a note last night, after hours. I found it this morning."

Quinto's face scrunched, like a brick spontaneously crinkling. "He already left?"

"Duty called," said Mines. "He's back at Nicchi's house, talking to his wife, Bianca."

That perked my ears. The dwarf had been a little too friendly with the woman yesterday. I walked over, holding my coffee carefully to avoid spilling. "He's back there? He said he'd meet us here before continuing the investigation."

"And he would've," said Mines. "If Bianca hadn't reported a break-in at her place overnight, that is. He left fifteen minutes ago."

I glanced at Steele and Quinto. They each returned piqued looks.

"Well, I'm good to go," I said, lifting my mug. "Assuming you don't mind me borrowing this, Mines."

The Sergeant gave me the a-okay, and back out the door we went.

17

We let ourselves in through the white picket gate at the front of Bianca's home and headed up the porch steps. We would've knocked, but the interior door stood open. Sounds of heated discourse filtered through the exterior screen. I tested the latter, finding it unlatched, so I pulled it open and went in.

We found Bianca and Silverbrook in the same small, haphazardly decorated living room as before, Bianca's cheeks pink as she gesticulated wildly with her arms.

"Well, you tell me, Bronmuth," she said. "You're the one who was showing concern over me yesterday, and yet here we are. One day I find my husband's been murdered, and the next I find my home's been vandalized. What if they'd been after *me,* Bronmuth? Did you consider that? I could've been brutalized, or worse. Where were you and the rest of the police for that, huh?"

Silverbrook pressed fingers against his forehead, and the response he hacked out was slow and measured. "Look, Bianca, you know your safety, *everyone's* safety, is of our utmost concern. We're here to serve and protect, I *promise* you. But obviously you're okay. No one came after you, regardless of whether you were here or not at the time—which you still haven't given me an answer on, mind you. Now could you *please* calm down and try to answer my questions?"

"*Your* questions? Yes, it's all about *you,* isn't it? No concern for me at all. For the widow's mental state." Bianca glanced toward us. "Oh, wonderful. Company. Just what I wanted."

Silverbrook took note of us, too. He gave us a resigned nod. "Hey."

"Hey," said Steele. "Mines told us we'd find you here. Said you had a break-in last night, Mrs. Nicchi?"

"You figured that out, did you?" said Bianca. "What do you think? I could've been murdered, same as Johnny. I bet whoever came into my home was the same man who killed him. I thought this town was *safe,* Bronmuth."

"It *is* safe, Bianca. You're over—" He caught himself in mid-sentence, glancing to the heavens for guidance.

Eying us, he started over. "Bianca's home was broken into at some point last night. She says she—"

I held up a hand. "No offense, Silverbrook, but I'd rather hear it from Mrs. Nicchi, if that's okay with her."

I think the young woman took my rebuke of Bronmuth as a sign of confidence. She beamed, triumphant, as she launched into her story. "Someone who's willing to listen, finally!"

Silverbrook groaned and rubbed his temples again.

"As I was trying to explain to Bronmuth," continued Bianca, "*someone* violated my privacy last night. I didn't notice it until the morning, but when I woke and happened to wander through Johnny's old office, I found the place a total mess. Someone rifled through his things, trashed his personal belongings, desecrated his memory. It's a disgrace, and extremely upsetting, to boot! To think some man barged in here with who knows what on his mind and got away scot-free? It's terrifying. Do you realize what he could've done to me?"

I was well aware what the intruder *could've* done, but Bronmuth had already tried to convey to her without any success that said intruder *hadn't,* so I didn't see why I should venture down the same losing path. "Did you hear anything that tipped you off to the intruder's presence? Banging or clatters or latches being tripped?"

"No. Not at all," said Bianca. "Which is what makes the intrusion so upsetting!"

"Is your bedroom upstairs?"

Bianca blinked, confused. "Uh...yes."

"And Johnny's office? Downstairs?"

Bianca nodded. "Yeah, why?"

"Curiosity, that's all. Your intruder would have to be quite the mouse for you not to hear them on the same level if what you say about the state of Johnny's office is accurate. With a floor between you? Maybe..."

"I assume you were home all night," said Steele.

"Well...no, actually," said Bianca.

Quinto lifted an eyebrow. "You went out?"

"Don't give me that look," said Bianca. "You think I'm in a state to be alone right now? I went out with friends, had a drink or two to dull the pain."

While that seemed an eminently logical response to losing a loved one, Bianca hadn't seemed particularly bent out of shape when she'd learned of Johnny's death. She still didn't. Instead, she was simply angry at us for being in her house, or not having caught her intruder red-handed. One of the two. Maybe both.

"Where did you go, if you don't mind my asking?" said Steele.

Bianca crossed her arms. "Does it matter?"

"It's part of the police process, gathering information," said Steele. "If the intruder who broke into your house did so while you weren't here, it's possible they might've seen you out earlier. Knowing where you went could help us find them."

Bianca sneered. "Fine. I was at the Muddled Mermaid, over on Second and Main. Shared a few drinks and a good cry with some friends, as I said."

"And what time were you gone from your house?"

"I don't know," said Bianca.

"It could help us crack the case," said Steele with a hint of a smile. "You don't even have a guess?"

Man, she was getting to be masterful.

Bianca shrugged. "I left at...I don't know. Nineish? I don't remember when I got back. A few hours later, I guess."

"And you didn't notice the mess in your husband's office at the time?"

"Well, of course not. I didn't pass through there. Why would I? I went straight up the stairs to bed. It was late, and I was tired. A little tipsy, too, if I'm being honest."

"So the disturbance is only visible in the office?" I asked.

"That's what I've said, isn't it?"

"Do you mind if we take a look?"

"Sure," said Bianca. "Not like it can get any messier *now*. First room past the stairs on the left."

I left to seek it out, Steele and Quinto wisely following me and leaving Bronmuth to deal with Bianca's ire. I skirted the stairs and paused at the foot of the office.

I lifted an eyebrow as I looked in. "Hmm."

"Hmm is right," said Steele.

In keeping with the home, it was a small office, perhaps six feet by eight with a single window peering over the grassy path between it and the neighboring house, and while perhaps the room was a bit messy, *trashed* it was not. Sure, I could tell someone had come through recently—either that or Johnny hadn't bothered to tidy up in a while—but by and large things appeared to be in place. A pile of ledgers, haphazardly stacked but in a stack nonetheless, occupied the left half of the room's small desk. The right hand drawer of said desk hung open, laying bare the contents—purchase and sale agreements and a collection of nautical charts, by the looks of it. A few random sheets had made their way to the floor, and the room as a whole desperately needed a thorough dusting, but beyond that, it wasn't in bad shape.

"Not exactly what I'd call trashed," said Steele.

"You took the words right out of my mouth," I said.

Shay headed in, putting her eagle eyes to use, scanning them over the room from floor to ceiling to see if she could glean anything. Quinto shouldered his way past me and sat down at the desk chair, cracking open the topmost ledger. I made my way back to the living room.

"Excuse me," I said as I arrived, once more interrupting one of Bianca's tirades against Bronmuth. "Do you know if anything was taken from your husband's office?"

She shot me a dirty look, whatever good will she'd afforded me having vanished in the past two minutes. "Like what?"

"I don't know. That's why I'm asking."

"Well, I don't know, either," said Bianca. "I already told you I didn't pay a lot of attention to Johnny's business deals, didn't I?"

She had. "Do you keep your home locked when you're not away?"

The dirty look got grungier. "Aragosto might be safe, but I'm not dumb."

I lifted a finger. "I'll be right back."

I returned to the front of the house and took a look at the interior door, kneeling in front of the deadbolt. A dull coating of oxide covered it, and though there were a few small nicks by the keyhole, there weren't any major scratches. No sections where the oxide had been scraped away.

I wandered past the stairs, past Johnny's office, and into the kitchen. There, to the left of the sink and a bank of cabinets, I found a door leading to the back patio. I opened that and took a look at the deadbolt on it as well.

Same deal. Oxidation, wear, no fresh scratches.

I rubbed my chin.

Quinto remained in the office, reading, as I passed the room by, but Steele had left. I found her in the living room. She must've just returned.

"I already told your partner," said Bianca. "I don't know if anything's missing. There he is. Ask him. I have no idea."

"Find anything?" Steele asked.

I shrugged, but I tried to convey with my eyes that maybe I had. "Bianca, we appreciate your help, and you can be sure we're going to try our best to find out who broke into your place. For the time being, it makes sense for us to assume the intrusion into your home and your husband's murder are related. With that said, can you think of anyone who might've shared a close relationship with Johnny, someone he might've confided in? Friends, family. Or if he had any enemies?"

"Johnny? Enemies?" Bianca shook her head. "I doubt it. He was too aloof to have any. And friends? Well, he had a few. Émile. Rigger. Maybe Skillethands, I don't know. And there's his brother, of course. Joey."

I looked to Silverbrook. "Rigger? *Skillethands?*"

Bronmuth nodded. "I know who she's talking about. Émile Rodan? And Danny Peabody? He goes by Rigger because he's good at rigging ships. Brilliant, I know. And everybody knows Skillethands. He's big Norma's boy."

"Well, if everyone knows him..." My sarcasm was wasted based on everyone's lack of responses.

"You said Johnny's brother used to work with him, for the family fishing business?" asked Steele.

Bianca nodded. "Yeah. Left about a year ago."

Steele gave me a look. "I think that should be our first stop."

"Agreed," I said. "Silverbrook? Mind showing us where he lives?"

"I would, but I have to finish some procedural work with Bianca," he said. "You should be able to find his place, though. He works giving hunting tours. Sea Ridge Preserve. Follow the road out of town, first right, and follow the signs. Can't miss it."

"You're okay with us continuing the investigation without you?"

He gave a resigned shrug. "It is what it is. It's a small town. I'll find you."

He was probably right about that, and with Bianca shooting icicles at anyone who bothered to get within eyeshot, I figured there wasn't any point in me questioning him on it further. I gave Steele a nod and we left to gather Quinto.

18

"So, you learn anything from those ledgers, big guy?"

Bianca's home shrunk into the background as we hoofed it toward Aragosto's main thoroughfare. A menagerie of small birds chirped from the trees lining the avenue, looking for love while spring was still in the air.

Quinto shook his head. "Not much. Not that I know a ton about the market price for live crabs and fresh caught cod, mind you, and I didn't have the ledgers in my hands long enough to start crunching any numbers, but on first glance, they seemed clean."

"You know," I said, "for as many killers as we've caught who happened to drop their murder weapon in a wastebasket at the scene of the crime, you'd think we'd come across some brain dead money launderers sooner or later, but that breed always seems to possess at least a modicum of smarts."

Quinto smiled. "They don't like to make it easy on us, that's for sure. But as I said, a quick glance didn't suggest that Johnny was trying to hide anything about his earnings or finances. And more importantly, all his ledgers seemed to be there, at least going back a few years."

Steele's voice floated over my shoulder. "Which begs the question, what was the intruder after?"

I glanced at my partner, who followed Quinto and me closely. "No idea. Bianca certainly didn't seem to know, or didn't want us to. Whether it was knowledge or something tangible could make a big difference. My first thought was that the murderer came by to remove a piece of incriminating evidence from Nicchi's belongings, but why would they wait until now to do so? Why not take care of that right after they murdered him?"

Shay shrugged. "I can't answer that. But since we're on the subject, you gave me a look when you came back to the living room. You found something else in the house?"

"Rather I *didn't* find anything," I said. "No signs of forced entry, specifically, at either the front or back doors. Either Bianca didn't lock the place up as tightly as she claimed, or whoever broke in was exceptionally talented with a pick."

"Or they had a key," said Quinto.

"Or that."

We followed the path our rickshaw had taken us through on our way into town, back to the main road. There, we saw the first of the signs for the Sea Ridge Preserve, following it onto a dirt path that meandered through the trees. As we walked, I pondered the similarities between a reserve and a preserve, ultimately coming to the conclusion that they were in fact the same thing, making the additional 'p' superfluous. So why did preserve get a free pass when other words with similarly useless additional letters, like irregardless, didn't? Someone at the Department of Language should've been fired over that one.

Eventually, the path opened onto a field of aromatic yellow wild flowers, full of bees and butterflies and swaying with the motion of hares that bounded between them, nibbling at their petals. Behind them all was the headquarters of the hunting tours business.

And what a dump it was.

Rotted beams barely held up the aging home's sagging roof, one covered with a mossy green growth and pocked with holes. Vines grew over half of the front siding, and what little peeked through was so faded it would've taken the skills of a forensic painter to determine what color the home originally was.

"Joey went from the family fishing business to working *here?*" I said. "I think we just discovered a motive for murder."

"Uh...Daggers?" Shay pointed up the road.

I followed her finger. Another of the Sea Ridge Hunting Tours signs had been pounded into the earth at a bend, and beyond that I spotted a hint of a much newer, much less mossy farmhouse roof in the distance.

"Oh. My bad."

Past the bend we found the real Sea Ridge Hunting Tours, a perfectly respectable ranch home painted in a rustic but pleasing red and white, surrounded by a field of grass and wildflowers that were overgrown but not to the point where a machete would be needed. A stone path led from the sign to the front of the house, behind which loomed a barn painted in the same traditional red.

We followed the path to the front door, knocked, and waited, but no one answered.

I tried again. "Joey Nicchi? Anyone there?"

Still no response.

Quinto shrugged. "Maybe we should try the barn."

It was worth a shot. We ventured off the path into the flowers, agitating the bumblebees who worked among them, skirting the house and heading toward the barn. One side of it stood open, the space in front of it tramped down and covered with hay.

I poked my head into the cavernous space. Rays of light sliced through the boards at the barn's side, lighting dust motes that hung in the air like dirty snowflakes. Old farm equipment lay discarded throughout: rusted plows and haggard carts, harnesses with cracked leather and splintered yokes for animals, not to mention some metal contraption with dozens of rusted spikes that would make for a wicked weapon of war should anyone be able to lift it. Racks on the walls held hand tools, hoes and pitchforks and pickaxes, most of them rusted, but I spotted a number of well-oiled knives as well, not to mention a pair of glossy hunting bows.

Quinto and Steele pressed into the open door beside me, looking in.

"Hello?" I called. "Anyone home?"

"Hey, there!"

We all turned, but the voice wasn't close enough to make us jump. A man approached from around the side of the barn, a big guy, probably my height or even an inch taller, with wavy, light brown hair that reached to his collar bone and a bushy beard of the same color. He wore a heavy shirt with a tartan pattern, the sleeves of which he'd rolled to his elbows, and though the shirt certainly hadn't been designed to be form-fitting, it played the role on him well enough. The man's biceps pulled the sleeves tight, and there wasn't much room for his chest, either. As for his face, it bore a faint resemblance to a certain crab mangled one I'd recently seen.

"Joey Nicchi," he said, putting his hand out. "Welcome to Sea Ridge Hunting Tours. Are you all...looking to schedule an expedition?"

He cocked a flint-gray eye at us as he asked the question, clearly expecting a certain answer but knowing he had to ask anyway.

I shook his hand, taking note of the strength in his grip. "Jake Daggers. This is Shay Steele, and that's Folton Quinto. And no, we're not here to schedule a hunting trip, although I'm sure that would be fun."

He didn't bother shaking anyone else's hand when he finished with mine. "You're cops."

"What gave it away?" said Shay.

"Not much," he said. "Just the way you stand, talk, look, and smell."

I thought about cracking a joke about my hotel room's limited amenities, but Joey didn't look the type to appreciate that. "Do you know why we're here, Joey?"

"Something to do with Johnny, obviously. You don't look like run of the mill flatfoots, so...it can't be anything good. Where are you from?"

For all my admonishment of Bronmuth, apparently the rumors from town hadn't reached all the way here yet. "We're detectives, from New Welwic. You want to head inside, maybe?"

The man's jaw bulged, his eyes glinting. "I'm a big boy. Just tell me."

"We found your brother," said Steele. "Dead, I'm afraid. Washed ashore in New Welwic. But it's worse than that, I'm afraid. He was murdered."

Joey spun, turning his back on us, and took a few steps away. His head hung as he ran his hand through his beard, and I heard him sigh.

We gave him his time.

When he turned back, it was with wet eyes. He nodded. "Alright, then. Okay."

The grief I understood, but I'd expected a different reaction. "You're not surprised?"

He turned his eyes on me, which despite the nascent tears were still hard as rocks. "Johnny was my family. My blood. We may not have been as close as we'd once been, but I grew up with him. Laughed with him. Cried with him. I know how he thought, and I know what he was capable of. He wouldn't have left his wife. He wouldn't have disappeared without telling a soul. He wouldn't have given up on all of us, on his life, for no apparent reason. So am I surprised to find out he's dead? No. Not at all. That he was murdered? Yeah, maybe. But I knew, in here—" He pounded his chest. "—that he was dead. But that doesn't make it any easier to hear it."

"I understand."

We gave him another moment of silence before Shay tried again. "We're sorry for your loss, Mr. Nicchi.

You said you weren't as close to your brother as you once were. Do you mind if we ask you about that?"

"It's Joey. Just Joey. You're homicide detectives?"

We nodded.

He sighed. "Sure. Though I'm not sure how much there is to tell. We were close...once. Like any other siblings, I guess. Better, really. We had the kind of relationship most brothers dream of. We did everything growing up. Hunting. Fishing. Fighting. Screwing around, almost killing ourselves doing stupid stuff. Going after the same girls and failing at the same time. It's only natural we went into business together when we got older. Nicchi Fishing and Crabbing. Johnny owned it. He signed the loans for the ship and the equipment. Told me we'd be like partners, but he didn't want me liable for it all if things went south. I guess it was a fair trade. He got the house, after all."

"What house?" asked Shay.

"The family house, where he lived with Bianca," said Joey. "That was our parent's place before our old man died. With him gone, it was too big for mom, and she was starting to suffer from mental issues anyway. She let Johnny have it, what with him marrying Bianca, and she moved out to live with our sis. She's in New Welwic. Better medical care there than here."

"Bianca suggested the fishing business wasn't doing too well," I said. "Is that why Johnny pushed you out?"

Joey shrugged, gazing into the distance. "Maybe. I don't know. He tried to keep the financial stuff to himself, keep me protected from it if it soured, just like with the loans. But if I had to guess? Yeah, sure. We weren't pulling in the hauls everyone else was. We might've grown up here, grown up around ships, but we don't come from a line of crabbers. Just seemed like all we could really do, you know? It was either that or work on the boardwalk, and I've never much cared for juggling or breathing fire."

"So Johnny fired you?" I asked.

"Pretty much," said Joey. "Pulled me aside one day and told me he couldn't afford to keep paying me. Told me I'd have to find something else. I told him that was crazy. He couldn't do everything aboard his ship by himself, and I'd stay by his side even if I had to work for free. I didn't care about money. We were family, bonded by blood! But he told me I couldn't. That he couldn't ask that of me, couldn't do that to me. Swore he'd keep me protected, just like he'd said he would. It got heated. It...wasn't a good encounter. And actually..." Joey turned his head away. "It was the last real conversation I had with him."

"And that was a year ago?" asked Shay.

"More or less."

"But Johnny kept operating his business throughout the year, right?"

"As far as I know."

"So he couldn't have defaulted on his loans for the ship and equipment," said Shay. "It would have been repossessed, wouldn't it?"

"That would make sense, but I really couldn't tell you. As I said, we'd...grown apart."

"You have any idea who gave him the initial loan to start the business?" asked Shay.

Joey shook his head. "Some bank in New Welwic. As you might've noticed, there's not a thriving financial services industry here in Aragosto. You'd have to check Johnny's records to find out who. He never told me."

I nodded toward the ranch house. "So after you left the fishing biz, you went into hunting?"

"The job was available, and I'd always been sharper with knives and bows than Johnny."

"Business okay?"

"Not really," said Joey, "but I'm not too bent out of shape about it. I just work here. The Abano brothers own the place, and they make enough money from their fishing and crabbing enterprise that I don't think they're too concerned about this venture. They pay me whether people come by for tours or not. Not well, mind you, but they let me catch as much deer and water fowl as I can eat, and I get to live at the house, which is a huge bonus."

"Not surprising," I said, looking around. "This place doesn't look too touristy."

"What's that supposed to mean?" said Joey. "I do what I can to keep the place welcoming and tidy. I'm the only guy who works here, you know."

"I didn't mean any offense," I said. "I simply meant it's off the beaten path. And that dilapidated farm house can't be doing you any favors. My advice, I'd move one of the signs for this place a little further up the road so people see it before they notice that rotted old husk."

"Oh. That place," said Joey. "It belonged to an old guy. The head of a naturalist group. He passed away some five or six years ago. He was a real pain in the ass to hunters and fishermen around these parts, but I guess I shouldn't badmouth the dead. Never did anything to me, anyway, but his old place sure is an eyesore. I'm surprised the Abanos haven't bought it and torn it down, but again, I don't think they're too invested in this business."

Joey's eyes had finally dried. Though I could still notice the tension in his shoulders, he'd uncrossed his arms and his jaw had loosened.

Shay took his state as an invitation. "Joey, I'm sorry to have to ask you this, but other than his possible financial problems, can you think of anything else your brother might've been involved in. Anything *unsavory?*"

Joey gritted his jaw again. "Not that I know of. Like I said, I hadn't talked to him in a long time. Too long..."

His stare got distant again.

"Please, Joey. Anything could be helpful. Surely you—"

"I told you, *I don't know,*" he barked, his eyes suddenly fierce. "Ask Bianca. Maybe she'll know."

"We already did," I said.

"Then I guess you're out of luck. All of us. You. Me. And *especially* Johnny."

Joey turned and stormed into the barn, in the general direction of the hand tools. Quinto gave me a look, but I shook my head. I didn't think he'd hurt himself, but the man clearly needed to be alone.

19

The bees, butterflies, and rabbits ignored us as we skirted the edge of the dilapidated estate and headed back into the woods. I thought at least the latter might be more skittish given the whole 'Hunting Tours' thing, but apparently their size kept them from getting targets put on their backs. Strapping young Joey probably would've needed to catch a whole family just to make himself a decent breakfast.

"Well, that wasn't as helpful as I'd thought it would be," said Steele.

"Really?" I said. "You don't find it interesting that Johnny kicked his brother out of their family business due to money problems and yet showed no outward signs of financial distress for the next year?"

My partner glared at me. "Of course I do, but I'd already considered the possibility that Johnny's death was related to his money woes, and there's a few issues with that line of thought. For one thing, it's extremely difficult to collect on a debt when the person who owes you money is dead. You also realize the law is already on the side of the party owed money. If Johnny was behind on payments, the bank could've repossessed his boat. Why would a bank from New Welwic send a hitman after him instead?"

"Perhaps Joey's wrong," I said. "What if Johnny didn't use a reputable New Welwic bank like he thought? What if Johnny secured his loan a different way?"

"That still doesn't explain why his creditor would want him dead."

"Either way," said Quinto. "It's probably worth going through Johnny's ledgers in more detail. Hopefully he has them going back to incorporation. Not that I'd expect him to write down the source of his loan if it was from a suspicious source, but still. There'd be clues as to what happened, I have to think."

I lifted an eyebrow. "And you want to be the one to sweet talk your way back into Bianca's good graces?"

Quinto shrugged. "She might be willing to part with them freely. We may not have a warrant, and Mines would have to be the ones to procure one if we needed it, but I don't see why Bianca wouldn't be amenable to that. Other than her being an unpleasant individual overall, that is."

"That's more of what I was getting at."

"Speaking of Bianca," said Steele. "What's everyone's read on her? Beyond her personality, I mean."

"She's colder than an ice wine snow cone."

Quinto snorted.

"I said *besides* her personality, Daggers."

"I know," I said. "But in all seriousness, I'm not sure we can separate her personality from the case. Bianca readily admitted her relationship with Johnny was on the rocks. There's no way her grating persona didn't affect Johnny's mental state."

"I get that," said Steele, "but again, it's not what I was asking about. Her story about last night is of more immediate concern."

"Well, as angry as she was, I didn't get the feeling she was hung over," said Quinto. "Which isn't to say I doubt her story about going out for drinks. She'd have to be dumber than a sack of rocks to think she could get away with a lie like that, but...well, it doesn't seem as if she's telling the whole truth, does it?"

I scoffed. "That's an understatement. I wonder if anyone broke into her home at all."

"You think that's a lie, too?" asked Steele.

"Could be. Remember, I didn't see any signs of forced entry. She might've mussed up the office on her own, maybe even disposed of a crucial piece of evidence before anyone arrived."

"But then why would she report it?" asked Quinto.

"To cast suspicion on someone else," I said. "I don't know who. Anyone other than her, maybe."

"So you think she played a role in her husband's murder?" asked Shay.

"Perhaps, but I'm not sure. Despite her abrasive personality, she doesn't strike me as the type who would kill, at least not to perform premeditated murder. I *definitely* don't buy her as the kind of person who would spear her husband with a trident, tie his ankles down with weights, dump his body at sea, and scuttle his boat, all without anyone noticing."

Shay nodded. "Probably not."

The wind rustled through the leaves overhead, bringing with it the scents of a cluster of blossoming cherry trees off to the side of the path.

"You know," I said. "Something else that surprised me about Bianca was her *lack* of surprise. She wasn't shocked at hearing of her husband's murder. But neither was Joey. He was more shaken up by the news, but he wasn't surprised."

"They must've suspected he was dead," said Quinto. "They both said as much."

"Right. Dead, but not murdered. There's a difference."

"So you think they're both in on Johnny's murder?" asked Steele.

I shook my head. "Not likely. Besides, in a town this size, news of Johnny's death must be on every tongue by now. Bianca was the first to know, but Joey could've heard the rumors elsewhere. Still, if he'd heard them, he didn't let on about it to us."

"It's possible neither of them are involved in his death but still know more than they're letting on," said Quinto. "What if each of them knew Johnny was involved in some illicit activity, something they knew would catch up to him sooner or later, might even kill him. They wouldn't want to admit that for fear of being charged as accessories. It might also explain Johnny pushing Joey out. Could be that he managed to solve his money problems only by going underneath the law, and *that's* what he wanted to protect his brother from."

Shay nodded. "That actually would make a lot of sense. But how would that fit in with Bianca's potentially faked break-in...?"

None of us had any answers, so we walked in silence—or as close to silence as we could get between the rustling leaves, buzzing insects, chirping birds, and gurgling streams of the forest. And here I thought the city was noisy.

"Anyway," said Steele after a moment. "Something to think about. So what should we do next? Track down those friends Bianca mentioned?"

"She gave you names?" said Quinto.

I'd forgotten the big guy had been sequestered in Johnny's office at the time.

Shay nodded. "But we don't know where any of them live or work. We'll have to track down Silverbrook first."

While voicing our concerns, I wondered if I should mention my misgivings about the dwarf, too. I voted against it for the time being. "You know, we could kill two birds with one stone."

"How's that?" asked Quinto.

"Head to that bar, the Muddled Mermaid," I said. "We can check on Bianca's story. If there's anyone who knows everyone in a small town, it'll be a bartender. He can probably tell us where to find Rigger and Skillethands and that other guy."

"Skillethands?"

"I know, right?" I said as we reached the main road. "He kind of sounds like *you*. Come on. Let's get a move on."

20

The Muddled Merman's front door creaked as we pushed our way into the bar. I wasn't expecting much. The exterior sign of a muscled merman holding a trident in one hand and a mug of ale in the other had swayed in the breeze, faded, cracked, and grimy, much like the joint's exterior facing windows, so I wasn't shocked when the interior of the bar was of a similar ilk. Round, rib-height pub tables, worn smooth by countless encounters with mugs, elbows, and dishcloths, dotted the floor, while lower, square tables of a similar wear level lined the edges. A long bar ran along the edge of the L-shaped room, hiding a kitchen behind it, most likely.

I was, however, surprised at the place's popularity. Despite it being the middle of the morning, there were a good half-dozen groups at tables, sipping on their beers. An old guy at the bar noticed us lingering at the door. He nodded to a youngster who sat near the back entrance who scuttled off toward the kitchens in response. Telling the cooks to throw another roast beef in the oven, perhaps?

"What were the name of those friends Bianca told you about?" asked Quinto.

"Émile, Rigger, and Skillethands," I said. "Why?"

"I figured I'd pester the clientele for information while you and Steele take on the bartender. Divide and conquer, right?"

"You sure that's a good idea?" I said. "If anyone's likely to sweet talk bar flies into giving us juicy tidbits, I think it would be Steele, not you."

Quinto grinned. "Hey, we coerce people in different ways. My method is effective."

Shay gave him a nod. "Go ahead. Try not to crack any skulls."

"You wound me, my lady."

Quinto headed toward the nearest group of townies, while Shay and I sauntered over to the bar. The bartender gave us a nervous smile as he wiped off a spot in front of him.

"Howdy folks," he said. "Haven't seen you around. In town for anything special?"

"We're not part of the goon squad," I said. "Or with the liquor commission, for that matter."

"Huh?"

"Sorry. I saw the kid, heading to the kitchen... Never mind. My name's Jake Daggers. This is Shay Steele. We're detectives with the New Welwic PD."

Our barkeep added a few more wrinkles to his collection, but his nervous smile didn't disappear. "New Welwic, you say? What brings you down here, then?"

"You've heard about Johnny Nicchi, I assume?" said Steele.

Keep's face fell. "Oh, yeah. Damn shame, that. Him disappearing, and then last night I hear a rumor he got murdered. And...*oh*. That's why you're here. Right."

Keep wasn't the quickest on the draw. "Exactly. We're trying to track down who might've done him in. Looking into his life, his friends, his family. Speaking of which, we heard his wife, Bianca, came by last night. Were you working the evening shift?"

The old guy snorted. "*Shift?* Do I look like the kind of guy who hires out?"

"So you were working," said Shay. "You saw Bianca?"

"You're darn tootin' I was working. And yeah, I remember her coming in. She met some friends, had some drinks. The usual."

"Do you remember what time she arrived?" Steele asked.

"Hard to say."

"Any guesses?"

Keep snagged a mug that lingered nearby and wiped it down with his dish towel, the same one he'd used to clean off the counter. "I mean, I don't know. Nine? Nine thirty?"

"And she left...?"

The old man shrugged. "Eleven?"

That jived with what Bianca had told us. "You seem like the kind of guy who remembers a face. Probably know most of the locals."

Keep gave me a narrowed eye sort of look. "My mind's as sharp as a steel trap. 'Course I am."

"Do you recall who Bianca met for drinks?"

"Sure, sure. Let's see. It was, ah..."

His long pause didn't engender confidence in the validity of his boast.

"Oh. Right. There was Mallory and her husband, what's his name... Alessandro. Also little Rialta and her cousin, Carmine. All friends of Bianca's. I've seen them hang out before."

I felt in my jacket for my notepad. Luckily I'd remembered it.

I pulled it out. "You said Mallory, Alessandro, Rialta, and who?"

"Carmine."

I wrote down Bianca's name, and next to it I jotted those of her friends. While it was on my mind, I also jotted down the names of Johnny's friends Bianca had mentioned earlier, Émile, Rigger, and Skillethands. "And the mood at the table. Did you happen to get a read on it?"

"*Mood?*" said Keep.

"Yeah. Were Bianca and her friends somber? Festive? Upbeat?"

"Sorry to disappoint, champ," said the old man, "but I'm not that in tune with the inner feelings of the folks drinking my beer. Besides, I had too many patrons to attend to last night to pay them much mind."

"Still do," said Steele.

"Pardon?"

"Patrons," said Steele. "Is it always this busy in the middle of the morning?"

Keep gave us that same nervous smile. "Hey, what can I say? Folks like to drink around here. And the locals don't bother distracting themselves at the board-walk."

Shay shot me a look. "That explains the turkey dog."

I gave Keep a nod. "Tell me about the Muddled Merman."

I caught him off guard. He blinked. "You want to learn about the bar?"

"Yeah."

"What do you want to know about her?"

"*Her?*"

"Hey, she might be a Merman, but she's still a she."

"Just tell me about her origins. The name. Is there a long history of merpeople in and around Aragosto?"

"Well, sure," said Keep. "Legends and old wives tales, mostly, but still. People love their merfolk around here. You'll see then on signs, in names. Boats named after them. Lots of mermaid figureheads on the ships in the bay, too."

Steele gave me a sidelong look. "Daggers, where are you going with this?"

"Just curious," I said. "I've heard rumors there haven't been any merfolk in these parts in over a century. Other people claim to have seen them within the last decade."

"Really, Daggers," said Steele. "You can't honestly think a semi-mythical sea creature could be involved in this."

Keep sported a genuine look of confusion. "Well, I'm not sure where you're going with all this either, but for what it's worth, I think the legends are just that. Can't say I've heard of any credible mermaid sightings, or seen any myself for that matter. Though I sure wouldn't mind." He shot us another smile, this one much more creepy than nervous.

"Uh. Right. Thanks."

I heard heavy footsteps. When I turned, I found Quinto approaching, his eyelids narrowed and his gaze elsewhere.

"You okay?" I said. "You look like you might've been interviewing ghosts."

Quinto blinked. "Huh?"

Steele weighed in. "Were the locals less than friendly?"

"Oh. No. Nothing like that. They were willing to talk. Gave me a few leads on Johnny's friends. Said to talk to Norma at the bait shop to find this Skillethands guy. But..."

"But what?" I asked.

"I don't know." Quinto shook his head. "There was something about the way most of them looked at me. Gave me a strange feeling."

"No offense, big guy," I said. "But this isn't the most diverse place in the world, and you stick out like a sore thumb. It's not surprising."

Quinto stared back at a group in the corner. "I guess..."

"You get directions to that bait shop?"

Quinto nodded.

"Great." I gestured toward the door.

Quinto led the way, but he didn't look terribly focused as he did so.

21

"So, Daggers," said Steele. "You want to explain to me why you continue to obsess over every utterance of merfolk rumors and lore we come across?"

The sun shone down from the heavens, lending a toasty warmth to my jacket's embrace, all while the breeze that accelerated off the ocean filled my lungs with a cool freshness. A gull flew overhead, cawing as it flapped its wings. Seeing as I lacked an umbrella, I hoped it wasn't my hard to shoo, loose-stooled friend from yesterday.

"Come on," I said to Shay as we walked toward the docks, Quinto leading the way. "It's not a surprise. Johnny was murdered with a trident. That's the stereotypical weapon of choice for mermen and mermaids. To our knowledge, no one around here spear fishes. So where did that trident used to murder Johnny come from, hmm?"

"Yeah, that part came across fine," said Steele. "My questions is, why in the world would you suspect

Johnny Nicchi was murdered by an angry merman when literally *everything* other than the murder weapon is pointing in a different direction?"

"*Everything?*" I said. "Not even close. I think you haven't considered the evidence fully."

"Let's see. Man murdered. Dumped at sea with weights around his ankles. In a troubled relationship with his wife. Estranged brother. In debt. Possibly involved in illegal activities to cover his debts." Steele ticked off the points on her fingers as she went. She shook her head. "Yeah. Nothing there about mermaids. Or mermen, if we're being sticklers for proper gender identification."

I frowned. "Alright, fine. I admit on the surface it appears other less legendary factors are at play in Nicchi's death, but until we find a local spear fishermen's guild or a blacksmith who specializes in tridents, it's not a terrible assumption to make that Nicchi was murdered by a mermaid or merman. You weren't there with Silverbrook and me at Old Man Connor's, but he brought up mermaids *unprompted.* He said he heard their cries the night Nicchi went missing. You can confirm with Bronmuth if you don't believe me. And while his testimony is suspect, it's a weird coincidence he would mention the creatures considering Nicchi's manner of death. Besides, there are scenarios in which this case could be about merfolk and still fit into the more predictable mold you already outlined."

Shay lifted a brow. "I feel like I'm about to get served a dose of wild, unfounded speculation."

I smiled. "It's my specialty. And you're absolutely right, but hear me out. Let's assume Johnny was having serious money problems which caused him to alienate his wife and brother, and let's assume Johnny also wanted to protect his brother from something when he pushed him out of the family business. Something seedy. Or maybe he didn't want to share the profits with his brother, or he thought Joey wouldn't approve. One or more of the three. Doesn't matter which."

"And this something seedy would be...?"

"Human trafficking."

"What?"

"Or not *human* trafficking, per se. More like mermaid trafficking."

Quinto hadn't turned around at my bold statement, apparently lost in his thoughts. Shay blinked and shook her head. "Again, *what?*"

"It's not that crazy," I said. "Are you familiar with mermaid history and lore?"

"Not as familiar as you, apparently."

"You know me. I have a soft spot for the weird, wacky, inexplicable elements of our world. Now, I don't remember everything I've read on the subject, but if memory serves me right, mermaid populations started to disappear about a century ago, right around the time populations of the other sentient races started exploding. I don't recall any wars, but they went into hiding out of fear regardless. Communications problems, supposedly, maybe due to their underwater nature. I couldn't speculate as I've never met one. But that doesn't change humankind's obsession with them. It's on display all over town. Just look at the Muddled Merman. Sailors in particular have been infatuated with mermaids for as long as mankind has been sailing the seas.

I have to imagine there'd be a market for them, if one knew where to look."

Shay put a hand to my arm. "Daggers, I don't know how to tell you this, but humans and mermaids? They're not...compatible. The parts are different, if you catch my drift."

"Hardy-har," I said. "While most human trafficking does contain a sexual component, it doesn't have to. Mermaids would make for a great show to the right audience, like that stupid flying horse show but with actual patrons. Or they'd make a great conversation piece—for someone who wasn't planning on making their purchase public."

"Or," said Shay, "and this is just one suggestion of any number of possibilities, Johnny was covering his debts not by abducting mermaids but rather by smuggling crank through the harbor at night. He stepped on some toes or was found out by someone who had a competing interest, and they axed him."

I shrugged. "Another good theory. Show me an angry dope dealer with a bloody trident in his posession, and I'm on board."

Shay snorted and shook her head. "You're incorrigible."

"But predictable!"

Quinto, who continued to lead us in silence, wove us through a few supply buildings as we neared the docks, clearly following directions he'd received from a patron. When we stopped, it was in front of a squattish block of treated lumber and shingles with a battered door set square in the middle of it. A sign above the latter read 'Aragosto Bait and Supply.'

A shopkeeper's bell sounded as Quinto pushed through. Steele and I followed him inside. Rows of metal shelves stretched across the store interior, filled with fishing lures, hooks, spools of wire, coils of rope, and utility knives. Wooden stands dotted with fishing poles stood at their ends like oversized porcupines, and other racks held a selection of hats, jackets, and overalls. An earthy odor emanated from a section near the front counter filled with buckets and paper sacks—likely the live bait. Whoever had situated that next to the jar of beef jerky on the counter hadn't thought things through.

"So, remind me, Quinto," I said. "Who are we looking for?"

"Norma, the shopkeeper," he said, that distracted look still on his face. "Supposedly she knows some of Nicchi's friends and can point us in the right direction."

"Skillethands?"

"That's right."

"What kind of name is that, anyway?" Somewhere in the back, a hinge squeaked as I spoke, and heavy thuds sounded. "Honestly, if I didn't know any better, I'd say—"

A figure squeezed through the door at the side of the front counter—literally, *squeezed*. Seven feet tall at least, maybe four or five hundred pounds, with long, black hair, blunted fangs poking through thick lips, dusty skin like a rhinoceros, and hands like serving platters. A full-blooded troll. Here, in Aragosto of all places.

"Holy crap," I said.

The troll blinked, its brow creases deepening. Its mouth made an 'o' the size of a grapefruit. "Folton?"

Quinto turned. His consternation faded, replaced instead with a look like he'd been slapped with a mackerel. "*Mom...?*"

22

"Folton!" The troll surged forward, enveloping Quinto in a hug that lifted him off his feet and might've broken lesser mortals. When she released him, both she and Quinto started yammering, talking over each other while trying to adapt to each other's responses on the fly.

"Mom. What the... How did you...?"

"Folton, by the gods, I can't believe it!"

"So you're here? In Aragosto? When?"

"Yes! What are you doing here?"

"This is unbelievable! It's been—"

"Ages, Folton! Ages! I thought I'd lost you!"

After another round of hugging and incoherent half sentences, both of them seemed to remember they weren't alone.

Quinto extracted himself from his mother's grip and turned to us, his face slack from shock. "Oh. Uh. Guys. I can't believe I'm saying this, but...this is my mother. In case you hadn't figured that out already."

Shay waved, a warm smile on her face. "Pleased to meet you, Mrs. Quinto. I'm Shay. This is Jake. We're good friends of Quinto's. I mean, Folton's."

I gave a friendly wave, too, but I wasn't able to hide my shock as well as Shay had. Quinto's mother ran a bait shop in Aragosto? And more importantly, Quinto got his troll heritage from his *mother's* side? I'd always assumed his father had been the troll, mostly because I couldn't imagine being attracted enough to a troll to make my body participate in the reproductive deed. Then again, I'd always argued that no matter how kinky the matchup, there was someone, somewhere in New Welwic willing to play along. This only cemented the idea.

Quinto's mother waved one of her huge mitts through the air, almost bowling me over with the resulting whoosh of air. "Please. Quinto was Folton's father's name. Call me Norma. But forget all that. Folton? I can't believe my eyes. What in the world are you doing here?"

"I'm working a case," he said. "What are you doing here?"

"I run the bait shop," she said. "What do you mean, *working a case?*"

"Well...I'm a detective, mom. With the New Welwic PD. Homicide division. These are two of my fellow detectives."

Norma glanced at us, then back at her boy. "*Detective?* You're kidding."

"No," said Quinto. "Ranger's honor. Been working for the boys in blue for a decade."

Norma smiled as she shook her head. "My boy, a detective. I can't believe it. I always knew you had ˙righteous streak in you, but I mean...wow. After yǒ ˙an off with those Twelve Points thugs—"

"Mom..."

Norma threw up her hands. "You're right. What am I doing? This calls for a celebration! I think I have a bottle of something or other in back. Either way, come with me. The shop'll practically run itself. We can sit. Talk. We have *so much* to talk about..."

Beckoning with her hand, Norma turned, ducked, and squeezed through the doorway at the side of the counter, shaking the building with each of her steps. We followed her into a miniscule break room, or so it appeared with both her and Quinto in it simultaneously. A quartet of chairs sat before a round table, two of them heavily reinforced with crossbeams and metal brackets. While the rest of us seated ourselves, Norma hunched over, digging through a cabinet.

"I know I had something in here at some point. A fifth of gin, or at least a pint of whiskey. If Felix took either of those without telling me..."

"So it's true then," said Quinto. "Felix is here. Skillethands."

I could've slapped myself. I'd thought Norma, with her saucer-like mitts, must've owned the nickname, but Bronmuth had referred to her separately. That's why everyone had looked at Quinto with confusion while he asked about Johnny's friend. Because he looked just like him. Because Skillethands was Quinto's brother.

Norma turned from the cabinet, her hands free of liquor and a correspondingly sober look on her face.

"That's right, Quinto. He's here. And if he took my gin without letting me know—"

"Mom, forget the liquor," said Quinto. "I don't care about that. None of us do. Just have a seat. Tell me...about Felix."

Norma settled into her chair, the support system groaning despite the reinforcements. "Well, Folton, he's doing well. Real well. He's safe. He works hard. Hasn't found himself a girl, but there's time for that. But...it all worked out. When we came here? That was a tough time, Folton. Without your father. Without you..."

Quinto shook his head, his shoulders slumping. "Mom, I'm so sorry. I was an idiot back then. I should never have left."

"It's okay. You were fourteen." She reached a hand out and set it upon Quinto's shoulder, her voice softer than I thought anyone her size would be capable of. "We were all in a bad place. You, running around getting into trouble with those gangs. Me, with my drinking. I still haven't totally kicked the habit, as you can tell. And without your dad there to provide a decent example? That's why I left, Folton. I had to get Felix out of there. I really... I thought I'd lost you. For good. I couldn't lose him, too."

I'd never seen a troll cry until then. Contrary to popular belief, Norma's tears weren't droplets of blood or unpolished diamonds. Just wet streams of emotion, same as anyone else's.

Quinto looked like he might be on the verge of tears, too. I thought Shay and I might be better served anywhere else, but we'd been invited in. We couldn't sneak out now without it being awkward.

Quinto held it together. "I looked for you, you know. After I got my life back on track. After I joined the force. I couldn't find you."

Norma wiped her face on her sleeve, her sobbing muted but punctuated by roaring snorts as she tried to suck it all back in. "I don't doubt it. I left everything I could behind, Folton. I wanted no part of it."

"So how did you get here?"

"Luck? Coincidence? A miracle? It's hard to describe. When I saw Felix trending toward the same path you'd taken, I pulled up the stakes, grabbed your brother by the ear, and started walking. We barely had more than the clothes on our backs, and even those I wasn't sure if we'd finished paying for. I didn't know where to go or what I'd do, but I figured I didn't have anything to lose, just Felix, and I'd lose him anyway if I stayed, so why not try something different. We walked as far as we could that day—I don't even remember how long ago it was. Seventeen, eighteen years? It was a winter's day, I remember that. Cold. Blustery, and us without so much as a jacket between us. We walked until the sun started to set, with our bellies rumbling and the wind chilling us. I knew for sure I'd made a mistake then, traded a life of misery for a slow, cold death in the woods if we didn't turn back, but that's when the miracle found us. *Our* miracle. Annabell."

"Annabell?" asked Quinto.

Norma nodded. "Our savior. She spotted us from the porch of her farmhouse, just off the main road into town. In those days, it was about the only thing there. I would've figured an old country-bred lady like herself would've run off screaming, trying to rouse the villagers to drive us away with pitchforks and torches, but I couldn't have been more wrong. She came over with a lantern and a blanket, told us we could sleep in her barn. The next morning she offered us bread and honey, and when she heard our story and saw what dire straights we were in, she told us we could stay in the barn as long as we needed. To this day, I've never met such kindness anywhere else."

"So you stayed?" asked Quinto.

Norma rubbed her hands together, as if she was trying to start a fire between them—or remembering a certain fire on a cold winter's night. "Annabell's kindness didn't end after a few days. Her husband had passed away, see. She needed help around her home, on the property. Felix provided that in exchange for meals and a roof. But Annabell needed more help than that. She owned the bait shop, this shop, or had with her husband. She tried to keep it running, but couldn't, not at her age. So she offered me the job. At first I was mortified. I was sure the folks here would be scared to death of me, but she introduced me, showed me around. Folks took a while, but they warmed up. Soon enough, I was running the place on my own. Doing well by Mrs. Annabell. And then..."

She sighed, and it looked like she might start crying again.

"Then what?" asked Quinto.

Norma sighed, a sound like a fog horn. "She passed away, Folton. Quietly, in her sleep, like she should've. But she left me the shop, and the farmhouse. In her will. She'd never had any kids, you see... I told you she was our miracle."

I didn't have any words for that, and I didn't bother trying to find any. Norma dabbed at her eyes with her sleeve and took a deep, labored breath.

Shay smiled at the enormous troll woman. "That's amazing, Norma. A miracle is right."

I wasn't sure Shay believed in that sort of thing, but she'd always been far better than me at empathizing with others.

"Mom, I'm so sorry," said Quinto.

Norma shook her head. "No. Not now, Folton. There'll be time for apologies, time aplenty. But right now? I want to savor the moment. Savor you, here. I still can't believe it. Honestly what *are* you doing here?"

"Investigating a case, just as I said. A homicide. Johnny Nicchi. Did you know him?"

"Ah. Johnny. Yeah." Norma nodded. "I'd heard the rumors. I didn't know him well, not as well as Felix does. But he'd come in every now and then. Wasn't the friendliest individual, if I'm being honest. But that wasn't what I meant. Fates be praised that they brought us together, but I wanted to know how you got *here,* to this point, in life. Are you happy? Are you married? Your friends seem nice. Tell me about them."

"They're my coworkers," said Quinto.

I snorted. "Hey, now. *Just* coworkers?"

"Friends, too," said Quinto. "And no, Mother, I'm not married, though there is someone. Someone special. Another coworker."

"Well, tell me all about it, Folton. Trust me, I have nowhere else I'd rather be, and if anyone comes in through the front, I'll shout at them to leave money on the counter. Nobody around here would dare steal from me, tell you what."

"Mom, I would, and I will, I promise," said Quinto. "I'll tell you every bit I can remember. What happened when I left home, how I ended up on the force and in homicide. I'll tell you about the Captain and my girl-friend, Cairny, and everyone else, but first...where's Felix?"

"On the docks, I suspect," said Norma. "I think he was helping the Morrisons, the Formentis, and the Abanos today. Unloading cargo, probably. He still picks up odd jobs. Doesn't like working the shop with his ma, which I get."

Quinto pushed back from his chair and stood. "Thanks. I've got to find him, Mom. I've got to talk to him. I owe him that. Guys? Feel free to chat with my mother. Catch her up, if you have the time. I'll be back. Promise, Mom. I won't run away again."

Before his mother had a chance to object, he turned and headed into the bait shop proper. Big Norma looked at Steele and me expectantly, smiling.

"So...you're Quinto's friends? Tell me all about him."

Suddenly I felt hot under the collar. Not that I was under any pressure to give Norma a positive first im-pression, but in general I wasn't the best with mothers. "Well—"

The shopkeeper's bell sounded, I assumed from Quinto's exit—until I heard Silverbrook's voice. "Whoa, Quinto. Where are you—"

"Can't talk," came Quinto's echoing rumble. "Steele and Daggers are in the back. Check with them."

A moment later Bronmuth appeared in the doorway. "Hey. There you guys are. Morning, Norma. Everything alright?"

"More than alright," said Norma. "I'm whole again."

Bronmuth squinted. "Huh?"

"Quinto," said Shay. "He's Norma's son. Felix's brother."

Bronmuth stared at Norma, then us. His eyes widened. "Well. Now that you mention it, I see the resemblance. With Skillethands, I mean."

And Bronmuth thought he had the deductive instincts to solve a homicide case on his own...

"So," I said. "You finished with Bianca?"

He nodded. "Got her squared away as well as I could. What are you up to?"

"Trying to locate Nicchi's friends," I said. "Quinto's on his way to take care of his brother. Mind helping us track down Émile and Rigger?"

"Sure," said Silverbrook. "We can try Émile first. He works on the boardwalk. You ready?"

Shay shot Quinto's mother a regretful smile. "Sorry, Norma. Duty calls, you understand? But don't worry about Folton. He won't skip out on you again. I've never been more certain of anything in my life."

"It's probably for the best," said the massive troll woman. "I could use some time to...*process* everything. My doors are always open—at least from seven to five. Best of luck in your investigation."

Silverbrook nodded toward the door. Norma looked sad as we headed out, but I consoled myself with the knowledge that it wasn't my fault. It wasn't me she was sad to see go.

23

The problem with heading back to the boardwalk around lunchtime was that my stomach was unwilling to accept how mediocre the sausages we'd secured the night before had been, certainly not while receiving an onslaught of scents, those of fried dough and charred meats and roasted peppers. My stomach grumbled, and I might've echoed its concerns with a grumble of my own. Steele, of course, reminded me of the nature of the sausages, which I had no logical argument against, but luckily, Bronmuth proved his worth for once.

After expounding on our unsuccessful venture into Aragosto street cuisine, Bronmuth told us we simply had to know which stands to target and which ones to avoid. The real gems, he confided, were from the carts that offered the strangest cuisine. To prove his point, he led us to a dinky stand that sold what to my ears sounded like 'Catch a Purry,' which turned out to be a cheese-filled pastry brushed with hot butter and topped with a fried egg.

I could barely understand the guy working the cart, but apparently Bronmuth had worked out a system to interact with him, and good thing, too. The 'Catch a Purry' was as mouthwateringly delicious as something made entirely out of bread, eggs, butter, and cheese had every right to be. Steele and I devoured ours while Bronmuth took a more measured approach to his, all as he led us to our next destination—none other than Doc Fowler's Fantastic Flying Foals and Fillies show.

If anything, the place looked even dingier in the full light of day. The faded sign over the entrance had only three real colors left, a light gray, a lighter blue, and a 'so light it might've just been dirty white' yellow. Sun glinted off the bleachers that surrounded the place, highlighting the frequent rust spots that corroded the battered metal. Past those, I still couldn't make out more than the crane, platform, and rigging I'd spotted before, all set against a gleaming ocean backdrop that glimmered like the bleachers, an endless sea of gray liquid steel.

Of audiences, however, the show had none. Not a single butt pressed into the seats around the main stage, and no line stretched from the kiosk that stood underneath the faded sign. A young man stood behind the counter, however, his unwashed shoulder length hair and ratty beard in perfect harmony with his thin, equally ratty t-shirt.

He noticed Silverbrook and held out a hand. "Yo, Bronmuth. How's it hanging, my man?"

Bronmuth clasped hands with the guy, an awkward cross between a high five and a handshake. "Good, Émile. You?"

"Same as always, man. Still living the dream."

Émile said the last part with such conviction that I couldn't tell if he was joking. I hoped he was.

"So what brings you to my neck of the woods?" said Émile, resting his elbows on the counter in front of him. "You got, like, some hot leads on missing circus freaks or something? Or you just showing your new friends around?"

"More of the latter," said Bronmuth. "These are Steele and Daggers. They're detectives."

"Whoa," said Émile with raised eyebrows. "Cool names. Wish I had one like that. I'm just Émile. Though I prefer to be called The 'Milester.'"

"You actually prefer that?" I lifted a brow. This guy couldn't be for real, could he? Of course, he was working the front kiosk at a barren flying horse show. Maybe he was.

"Just a joke," he said. "But not really. Either way is fine."

"Émile," said Bronmuth. "We need to talk to you about Johnny Nicchi. You've heard, I'm guessing."

"Dude, that he went missing? Course I've heard. That was like a week or two ago. Unless you mean did I hear about him dying, in which case, yeah, I heard that too. Murdered, someone said. Damn shame, man. So I guess I've heard everything."

"Silverbrook tells us you two were friends," said Steele.

"Well, sorta," said Émile. "We grew up together. I hung out with him and his brother. Can't say we were that close anymore. We'd go drinking every now and then. That's about it."

The answer assuaged my fears a little. I'd started to fear Johnny had been a complete ignoramus like Émile, which didn't bother me in the slightest as far as his murder investigation was concerned, but it would've been a bad sign for the mental aptitude of Quinto's brother.

"You'd go drinking with Johnny and his brother, or just Johnny?" I asked.

"Both," said Émile. "More recently, just Johnny."

"And when was the last time you did that?"

Émile shrugged. "Not sure. A month, month and a half ago?"

"That's the last time you saw him?"

"Might've seen him on the docks, from a distance. I've got good eyes, man."

"A month and a half," I said. "And you were one of Johnny's *best* friends?"

"Was I?" Émile eyed Silverbrook. "That's news to me."

"Bianca named you as one, for what it's worth," said Bronmuth.

Émile shrugged. "Well, straight from the horse's mouth, I guess. Not that I'm saying Bianca's got a horse face or anything. She's actually pretty hot. But yeah, me and Johnny didn't talk much anymore. If I was one of his best friends, I'd hate to see his worst, know what I mean?"

None of us laughed.

"So you wouldn't know much about Johnny's recent activities, I suppose?" said Steele. "If he was involved in anything underhanded?"

"Underhanded?" said Émile. "You mean like, *illegal?*"

"Yes."

Émile's eyes widened, and he shook his head. "Nah. Not that I know of. I keep my head out of that stuff. My body, too."

Again, none of us laughed. I don't think Émile was getting the hint.

I looked at Steele. "Anything else you want to ask?"

She replied with a taut shake of her head. It wasn't much to go on, but it was enough. I felt the same way.

"Silverbrook?" I said. "Maybe we should move on."

"I was thinking the same," he said. "Émile? Until next time. Be sure to keep the horse show spectators in line."

"Don't I always, dude." He held his hand out over the kiosk again. "Come on. Don't leave me hanging."

Bronmuth gave the young guy another of those awkward high five handshake things, and back up the boardwalk we went.

I nodded my head toward the attraction as we left. "Was that some sort of inside joke?"

"What?" said Bronmuth. "You mean about the horse show?"

"It doesn't seem to be very popular. At all."

Silverbrook snorted. "I'm giving him a hard time. It's an Aragosto landmark. It'll pick up when tourist season hits. It always does. So, what's next? You want to try and find Rigger?"

"You actually want our input?"

"Why wouldn't I? You have more experience in these matters than I do. Only makes sense for you two to take the lead."

I blinked. I wished I could get a better read on the dwarf. Yesterday, he'd come across as a huge jerk, one that was more than simply ornery. For a time, I'd been sure he'd been leading us astray, sabotaging our case by feeding us misinformation. Then today he'd cheered up, even gone out of his way to be helpful. Maybe he'd just been hungry?

Of course, despite his newfound cheerful personality, it still bothered me that he knew all our witnesses and suspects so well. First Bianca, now Émile. I would've chalked it up to a small town congeniality, but I couldn't help but feel there was something else going on.

"Rigger, then. Yeah," I said. "Any idea where we can find him?"

Silverbrook nodded. "We'll swing by the pier. If his boat's in its slip, he'll either be there or at home."

We reached the end of the boardwalk and crossed the breakwater that separated it from the docks. When we reached the twenty-first pier, Bronmuth took it and stopped at the side of a medium-sized ship by the name of *The Blue Albatross*. He called out for Rigger, but no one answered, so we headed back the way we came, continued past the end of the dock, reached the road Bronmuth and I had taken to see Old Man Connors and instead took it in the opposite direction, skirting the edge of town as we headed into a residential district. The homes in the area were slightly nicer than the ones in Bianca's neighborhood. A little larger, a little cleaner, but still nothing fancy, nothing that would look out of place in a town of Aragosto's size and standing. Not like the handful of houses that poked through the trees on the hill overlooking the neighborhood. I only spotted a few of them, but they looked spectacular, with dark slate roofs and facades of gleaming hardwood or stone, looking like a group of patricians in suits and matching fedoras.

"Don't tell me Rigger lives up there," I said as we walked.

Bronmuth glanced at me. "What's that?"

I pointed. Given Émile's oafish nature, having one of Johnny's other friends turn out to be a wealthy upper cruster would've stretched my belief to the breaking point.

Silverbrook shook his head. "On Millionaire's Row? Please. Only the cream of Aragosto's crop live up there. Some of the inn owners, Orlando and Carmine Abano, and Doc Fowler. Rigger does well for himself, far as I know, but he's here in town with the rest of us plebs."

"Wait, Doc Fowler?" said Shay. "Seriously? The horse show guy?"

Silverbrook snorted. "I'm telling you, that Fantastic Flying Horse show is more popular than it looks. That and he owns a number of bars around town."

"Like the Muddled Merman?" I asked.

"I don't know. Maybe," said Bronmuth. "Does it matter?"

I gave Steele a look. I'm not sure if she was thinking the same thing I was, but the curiosity was written plainly across her face.

Silverbrook pointed at a two-story house down the street, one painted a pale green with an enormous oak tree in the front yard. "There's Rigger's place. Let's see if he's in."

24

A woman opened the door in response to our knocking, strands of her blonde hair falling out of the bun in which she'd pinned it. She wore a yellow floral print apron, a frown, and a baby over her hip. The baby looked at us and promptly vomited.

"Oh, dear gods," said the woman. "Are you kidding me? Sorry. What is it? I really don't have time for this."

"Sorry to bother you, ma'am," said Silverbrook. "It's Catherine, right? I'm Bronmuth, from the police department."

The woman tried to wipe vomit off her child's face with her apron, not really paying attention. In the back, I could hear children screaming and a dog barking. A big dog, by the sound of it.

"Yeah, right. Sorry," said Catherine. "Bronmuth. I remember."

"Is Rigger in?"

Catherine pulled the edge of her apron away just as an aftershock hit the baby. A second wave of vomit spilled out. Luckily we were out of the splash range.

"Oh, gods damn it! His name is Danny, not Rigger. Danny? *Danny!* Oh, just go in. I think he's in the living room."

Catherine retreated from the door, leaving it open, so we stepped on through. Immediately, we were accosted by a herd of children, at least four of them, though they moved so fast it was hard to keep track. They bounced around, grabbing Shay's and my legs, waving, shouting over each other, and smacking each other in the face. One of them was showing me a stick, telling me it was actually a sword and that he'd slain seven pirates with it including one with a wooden leg and another with a bum eye and he'd poked a third in the eye with it and the eye had popped out and that made him the pirate king now and wouldn't I tell his brother that he was the pirate king, because boy was he being a pain about it, and hey, LET GO OF MY STICK! And then more smacking commenced, right as the dog came bounding in, a hulking brute that probably could've swallowed the smallest of the children whole. He barreled into my legs, almost taking me out at the knees, and deposited a huge rope of saliva over Bronmuth's shoulder.

"Alright, that's enough!" A tall man with a thick black beard and equally thick black hair came in through an adjoining hallway, waving his arms. "Out, all of you! In the backyard. And stop screaming, for the love of the gods. Take the dog! Take him!"

The kids' eyes widened, and they ran off, the dog stampeding after them and creating an unholy ruckus. Despite the command, they all kept on shouting. A door slammed shut, and the sound of yells and pounding feet faded, though I could still pick up a muted argument about pirates and why someone refused to share a stick.

The man in front of us sighed, his voice tired. "Sorry about that. Hey, Bronmuth. What brings you out here?"

"Some business. You doing okay? You look like you got run over by a scow."

"I got home less than half an hour ago. Thirty-six hour shift. I'd be asleep already if it weren't for the kids. Either way, I'm ready to die. Whatever it is you need, make it quick." He finally noticed Shay and me. "Hey. Danny Peabody. You can call me Rigger if you like."

"Nice to meet you," I said. "And your family. They're, ah...*energetic*."

"You have no idea."

"You want to have a seat, Rigger?" said Bronmuth. "Your living room maybe?"

He shrugged, but I don't think he really cared. "Sure."

We followed him into the hallway from which he'd appeared and into the living room, taking seats on a pair of couches, one of which overlooked the backyard, now filled with whirling dervishes armed with sticks and covered in mud, their little legs a blur. I'd always thought my Tommy was hyperactive, but if Rigger's kids were any indication, I'd hit the jackpot.

Rigger sighed. "So what do you need, Bronmuth?"

"We've got to ask you about Johnny, Rigger. When was the last time you saw him?"

The man wiped a hand through his hair. "Beats me. A few days before he went missing, I guess. On the docks. He was working. So was I. Didn't say a word."

"You still hung out with him, though, right?"

"*Some*times. But not often. Tell me, Bronmuth. I heard a rumor as I tied the *Albatross* up. Is he really dead?"

Silverbrook nodded. "It's true. Sorry, Rigger. That's why these detectives are here. Daggers and Steele. They're trying to figure out what did him in."

Not *who* did him in, I noticed. Bronmuth was finally exercising some restraint.

Rigger turned his tired eyed to Steele and me. "You the ones who found him?"

"We were."

"Is the rumor true? Was he killed?"

Apparently Rigger already knew. Whispers travelled fast in Aragosto. "That's right."

Rigger sighed and hung his head. "Damn. I mean, I wasn't that surprised when he went missing, but dead? *Murdered?* Who would do a thing like that? And to Johnny, of all people. Yeah, he wasn't the most outgoing guy, not anymore, but that makes this all the weirder, don't you think? He didn't put himself out there. Why would anyone go after him?"

"Sorry," said Steele. "You weren't surprised when he went missing?"

"Not really, no," said Rigger. "Honestly, I thought he might've simply...packed it up. Given up and left."

"Why would he do that?" I asked. "Was he having money problems?"

"I think so, yeah," said Rigger. "Not that he ever mentioned them, specifically. He was pretty tight lipped about it. But we knew he'd kicked his brother out of his fishing business 'cause he couldn't pay him. That he was working long hours. I think that's why he didn't want to come drink with us anymore. The cost, you know. But he did anyway, to get away, I think."

"To get away from what?" asked Steele.

"You know. His wife."

I nodded. "I get it. I've only been in Bianca's presence twice, and I'm already certain I'd rather not go back for thirds."

"I think it was more than that..." said Rigger.

Bronmuth knuckled his brow. "Like what?"

"You hadn't heard?"

"Heard what?"

Rigger leaned in, as if he had a piece of juicy gossip to share. "I heard a rumor. I have no idea if it's true or not—for damned sure I never asked Johnny about it—but I heard tell Bianca was having an affair."

I shouldn't have been surprised, but I was anyway. "Wait, what?"

"With who?" asked Bronmuth.

"No idea," said Rigger. "Like I said, there's no way I was going to ask Johnny about it, and I don't spend any time with Bianca. I haven't seen her in a year or two."

"Who told you that?" said Bronmuth.

Rigger shrugged. "I don't remember. Honest. It was some night I was hanging out with Émile and Talbot and a couple other guys. Someone mentioned it. Maybe they made it up, I don't know. Seemed like it made sense, though, given the way Johnny'd been acting."

It *did* make sense. Not only did it explain why Bianca hadn't been particularly bent out of shape by her husband's disappearance and death, but it also explained why she wasn't more concerned about being a jobless widow. Because there was someone else she was relying on for help.

"Silverbrook," I said. "As much as I meant my statement about not wanting to endure another of her welcoming tongue lashings, I think we really need to have another chat with Bianca."

25

Bronmuth pounded on the front door of Bianca's house, the screen rattling under the force of his fist. "Bianca? You in there? We need to ask you some more questions."

"Honestly, Silverbrook," I said as I peered through one of the front porch windows, trying to see past the drapes. "How is it you weren't aware Bianca might've been having an affair?"

"Give me a break," snorted Bronmuth. "I don't know everything. You think I spend all my time lounging in bars talking to gossips?"

"I wasn't suggesting you should know *everything,*" I said. "But it sure seems you know everyone. Bianca, Émile, Rigger, Skillethands, Connors, that superintendent guy who runs the docks. You're on a first name basis with each of them. I have a hard time believing you wouldn't have come across Bianca's possible infidelities from *one* of them when you went around investigating Johnny disappearance the first time around."

Bronmuth turned from the door, a scowl stretching his face. "First of all, I didn't know he was dead at first, all right? He'd gone missing. That's it. So of course I didn't turn over every rock and look in every cranny in search of the guy. We all knew he wasn't in the best of shape, financially, mentally. So I thought like Rigger, alright? I assumed maybe he left. It's an honest mistake. And I sure as hell don't appreciate you suggesting I'm doing a crappy job, or *worse,* just because you don't agree with my conclusions. If you're going to come into *my* town with that attitude, you can turn your ass right around and take it back to New Welwic. Screw what Mines has to say about it. I'll kick your ass out myself!"

"Whoa there. Relax. Both of you." Steele stepped between us. "It doesn't matter whether or not anyone *should've* found something earlier. What matters is that we determine if there's any credibility to the rumor, and if there is, that we find out who she's seeing."

Bronmuth glared at us, having rediscovered the unpleasant nature he'd put on display yesterday. He banged on the door again. "Bianca? If you're there, open up."

"I don't think she's home," said Steele.

Silverbrook snorted. "Fine. I'm going to make some rounds. Hit my contacts. See if I can figure out who Bianca might've been dating. You two? I don't know. Do whatever you want. Just don't get into any trouble."

Bronmuth stormed off without so much as a second glance, heading down the steps, through the gate, and down the street in the direction of the inns.

Steele stared at me and shook her head. "What's wrong with you?"

"Don't tell me you don't sense it," I said. "There's something off about Silverbrook. Maybe he's just a jerk. Fine. But yesterday, I got the feeling he was intentionally leading Bianca and that super at the dock into certain answers. It could be inexperience. Or not."

"And you think pointing that out to him is going to help our cause? You realize we need him, whether he's telling us the whole truth or not, right?"

I took a deep breath, feeling my blood pressure drop. Without even realizing it, I'd physically prepared for a fight. "Sorry. You're right. I was hard on him yesterday for revealing crucial information without needing to, and here I am doing the same thing. But you see what I'm saying, right?"

"Of course. Either he's not very good at his job, or he's hiding something. Not necessarily something related to Nicchi's murder, but something."

"Any idea what?"

"Well, I don't think he knew Bianca was seeing anyone. His reaction was as surprised as ours. Other than that?" Shay shrugged. "You're usually the one with the conspiracy theories. You tell me."

I shook my head. "Trust me, I have a lot on my mind, but I don't have any answers."

Shay's gaze softened, as if she'd deciphered the true meaning of my statement from those few bare words. She looked like she might ask me about it, but I wasn't ready to rehash the events of last night. Not yet. Not without figuring out how I was willing to deal with my issues.

I nodded for her to follow me and descended the front steps, skirting the house en route to the back. I paused at the side window, the one that looked in on Johnny's office. The ledgers were still there, right where Quinto had left them. I kept walking, working my way to the back porch. There I peered into the available windows, into the living room and kitchen, but the house was barren.

The porch stairs creaked behind me in response to Shay's footfalls. "Still convinced she's here, in hiding?"

"Not really. Simply exhausting my options."

"She won't be able to hide for long. Assuming she's trying."

I nodded.

"Look, if you don't want to talk about us, that's fine, but at least let me in. Tell me what you're mulling about the case."

Damn, she was good. I pointed toward the door. "The break-in. You know, the one that wasn't really a break-in because either the door was unlocked or the intruder had a key? If Bianca had a man on the side, he would've had a way to get in."

"True," said Shay. "But why would he rob the house—assuming anything was actually taken. Wouldn't he snatch the object of his affection while he was here under invitation? And why would there be anything to take in the first place? If Bianca's squeeze murdered Johnny, he and Bianca would have to be monumentally stupid to leave something incriminating in her house, never mind to report the incident afterward."

I nodded. "True."

"Besides, this is all assuming Bianca wasn't with her beau last night."

"You mean after she went to the bar?"

"Maybe. Or during."

"Spending time with her paramour in public would be kind of a stupid thing to do, especially the night after she'd found out her husband had been murdered."

Steele lifted an eyebrow, as if to say, "I know."

I reached into my jacket and procured my notebook, flipping to where I'd written the names the barkeep had told us. Mallory, Alessandro, Rialta, and Carmine.

"So she was there with a married man, who happened to be there with his wife, and this Carmine guy."

"Aragosto is a small town, which isn't to say there aren't multiple people here who share the same given name, but Silverbrook mentioned a Carmine. The one who lives on the hill for the wealthy folks with his brother."

I blinked. "The Abano family. Right. If he's loaded, it would explain why Bianca wasn't worried about money after losing her husband."

"I mean, it could sort of explain Johnny's death."

I squinted. "What do you mean, *sort of*?"

"Well, there's still the matter of the trident."

"Right. How could I forget?"

I cast a glance at the back doorknob, wondering if Aragosto had a CSU team. They might be able to clear some things up if our story was shaking out how we thought it was.

I raised an eyebrow at Shay. "Moment of truth. Think we can trust the local PD?"

"Honestly? I'm not sure."

"Likewise. Come on. Let's track down Quinto."

26

We found the big guy sitting on a crate near one of the warehouses by the docks. At his side, sitting on another crate, lounged his doppelganger, or as close to it as I'd ever seen. Sure, he didn't look exactly the same as Quinto. He was younger and lankier, with more hair and bigger hands, but he had that same oval-shaped head as Quinto, the same light gray skin, and the same goofy grin with teeth in desperate need of work. He probably could've slung both of the crates over his shoulders if he'd wanted to. Still, I don't see how Bronmuth couldn't have immediately noticed the resemblance. He *must've...*

Quinto noticed our approach. He gave us a friendly wave as we reached conversational range. "Hey guys. Felix? These are my friends I was telling you about. Jake Daggers and Shay Steele. Guys? Meet my brother, Felix. Man, it feels strange to say that..."

"But, like, a good strange, right?" Felix's voice wasn't as deep as Quinto's but it still could've put most tough guys' best efforts to shame.

"Definitely a good strange." Quinto grinned, a reserved yet genuine smile I'd only seen him shine in Cairny's direction before.

"Anyway, nice to meet you," said Felix. "Folton told me a lot about you over the past couple hours."

"A pleasure," I said.

"Nice to meet you, too," said Steele. "I'd say the same about you, but...well, Quinto's always played his personal life close to the vest."

Shay must've struck a nerve. Quinto turned to his brother and sighed. "I just... I didn't know..."

"It's okay," said Felix. "I get it. We had no idea what had happened to you either. We thought that...you know. You were gone. For good."

"Felix. I'm sorry."

"Really, bro. It's okay. We made it. Mom. Me. You. *Somehow.*" He snorted. "Although you, man. A cop. I still can't believe it."

"Neither can the rest of us," I said. "I'm pretty sure he blackmailed his way onto the squad. Either that or he threatened to eat a bowl of chili and stay in the admissions office until someone gave him a definitive yes or no."

"Dude. Come on," said Quinto.

Felix's lip curled in mirth, but he gave me an odd look regardless.

"It's sarcasm," said Steele. "Mostly, anyway. It's a cop thing. You'll have to get used to it."

"It's cool," said Felix. "Sailors just curse a lot, but I'm down with a more subtle approach. Speaking of which, long lost family or no, I *really* need to get back to work. I get paid by the job, and those sacks of squid jerky aren't going to move themselves. I'd love to stay and catch up, but..."

"It's alright, Felix," said Quinto. "There'll be time. I promise."

"Sure. You bet."

The younger Quinto nodded, hopped off the crate, and started to head off. He paused before making it more than a few feet, looking back at Quinto with hesitation in his eyes. I thought he might toss caution to the wind and come back in for a bear hug, but he didn't. He simply shot his brother a wave and kept on his way.

Quinto watched him retreat. I clapped the big guy on the shoulder. "You doing alright, old pal?"

"Huh?" He blinked. "Yeah. You bet. Never better."

"You sure?" said Steele.

"Of course." Quinto hopped off the crate. "It's just...odd. I haven't seen him in forever. I barely recognized him. He's gotten so big."

"The ridiculously oversized apple doesn't fall far from the tree," I said.

"I'm actually surprised at how easy it was to talk to him," continued Quinto, ignoring me. "I thought, given how I'd left, and what I'd left behind? For sure he'd be angry at me. Furious, even. But he wasn't. He was legitimately happy to see me. He thought I was dead, or as good as. Still, our conversation, the relationship between us? It felt strained. It wasn't the same as it once was."

"You're brothers, Quinto," said Steele. "You'll always have room in your hearts for each other. But after all that's happened, if your relationship hadn't changed, I'd say that would be an even bigger problem. You'll figure it out, if you want to."

Quinto nodded. "I do. Absolutely, I do."

I checked the alley behind us, making sure Felix had disappeared. "I hate to break up the good feels, but did you ask him about Nicchi?"

Quinto sighed and shook his head. "You know, Daggers, I'm going to be honest. I didn't. I was too distracted. Didn't feel like the time was right."

I shot a look at Shay. "It's alright. I know the feeling."

Maybe I hadn't been as stealthy as I'd thought, or I'd put too much longing in my eyes, because Shay noticed. Quinto might've, too.

"Anyway," I said, trying to get the four piercing eyeballs off me. "It's not a big deal. We got what we were hoping to out of Johnny's friend Rigger, and Steele and I are hot on the trail of a new lead."

Quinto's eyebrows lifted. "Yeah?"

"Bianca might've been seeing another man," said Shay. "Possibly one of the Abano brothers we've heard about. We know where they live, give or take. I was thinking about heading up there. Seeing what they have to say."

"You think this guy might've had something to do with Johnny's death?"

"There's a chance."

"Might not be the safest thing to waltz up to his house and ask him about it, then," said Quinto. "Especially not without local backup. Speaking of which, where's Silverbrook?"

"Daggers charmed him, and he stormed off," said Steele. "You know. The usual."

"I don't think Steele was planning on pointing the finger at anyone yet," I said. "And it's entirely possible having Silverbrook with us wouldn't help. Everything we've heard so far is that these Abano brothers are made of money. If they were generous with their success, that might explain why we've had less than total cooperation out of Bronmuth."

Shay cocked an eye at me. "You think?"

"It came to me suddenly. Just a theory. Either way, we don't need Bronmuth when we have you, Quinto."

Quinto's face fell. "Guys. You know I'll always have your backs. Any other time, I'd be there in a hot minute, but I need to get back to New Welwic. I need to tell Cairny. I mean, I just found my long lost family, for crying out loud. Besides, someone needs to give Captain Knox an update, and if I'm being selfish, I wouldn't mind a shower, a change of clothes, and a night's sleep in my own bed."

Shay didn't quite sigh, but she emitted of wistful moan. "That does sound nice."

"I thought if I left now, I could make it back to the precinct before everyone packs up for the evening," said Quinto. "Assuming I can find a rickshaw that's ready and willing."

"Go for it," I said. "If she means as much to you as I think she does, you should tell Cairny. And keep the captain updated. Steele and I'll be fine. That's why we're partners and you're the third wheel."

Quinto snorted. "Thanks."

"You'll be back first thing in the morning, though?" asked Steele.

"Before the sun's up, if I can get a driver."

"Perfect," said Steele. "You mind stopping by my place, then? I could use a change of clothes. I can give you my key."

Quinto's face scrunched. "Uh...sure. No problem. It's just that, well, I don't know where everything is, and, ah..."

"You'll have to grab me fresh underwear, yes, I know," said Steele. "It's okay. You're a big boy. I don't expect it'll be weird unless you want it to be. Just don't look in the bottom drawer in my nightstand, right side of the bed."

"*Bottom drawer of the nightstand?*" I said. "What's in there?"

"Nothing you need to know about."

"Okay, *now* it's getting weird," said Quinto.

"Well, if you're going, grab me a change of clothes, too," I said. "I've got stuff at Steele's place. I tried to arrange it across the backs of furniture and on the floor to make it easily accessible, but she forced me to store it in a dresser, too."

"Two changes of clothes, fresh underwear, no bottom drawers," said Quinto. "Got it."

"Also, while you're at it," I said. "Do you mind popping by Taxation and Revenue? I know Johnny kept ledgers, most of which we think are at Bianca's place, but I'd like to see what the official record is on Nicchi Fishing and Crabbing. Might as well see what you can pull on the Abano brothers' businesses, too, specifically if they made any suspicious loans."

"You think Carmine lent Johnny the money to keep his business afloat?" said Steele.

"It's possible," I said. "I'm collecting possibilities at this point."

"Fair enough. Quinto, since you're going there, go ahead and pull anything you can on Doc Fowler, too."

"The horse show guy?" I said.

"We've been by twice now," said Steele. "Both times his Fantastic Fillies and Foals show hasn't had a single patron in the stands, and supposedly he's one of Aragosto's wealthiest individuals? Call me suspicious."

"Nicchi Fishing and Crabbing, the Abanos, and Doc Fowler," said Quinto, ticking them off on his fingers. "Alright. I'd better get moving then. No way Taxation and Revenue will be open when I leave in the morning. If I hustle, I should be able to arrive before they wrap it up for the day. I'm sure someone there will love seeing me walk in five minutes before closing."

"Get to it, then," I said. "And be sure to tip your driver."

"I always do." Quinto clapped me on the shoulder. "Real quick, though, before I leave. You mind if we have a word?"

I blinked. "Uh...sure."

Steele looked curious, but Quinto shot her a raised finger. She nodded.

Quinto escorted me down the alley, far enough to prevent Steele from listening in. He cast a glance in her direction just to be sure.

"What's going on?" I said. "Is something wrong?"

"No, not at all," he said. "It's just that, well... Finding my mom? Finding Felix? I never in my wildest dreams expected it."

"You want me to let your mom know you're not skipping out on her?"

"No. Well, sure, it you want. I already told Felix my plans. He should let her know. But what I was getting at is..." He took a deep breath and let it out slowly. "I thought I'd lost my family, long ago, so I tried to build my own. Rodgers. You guys. Cairny. You'll always be family. The family I *chose*. We can't always control the relationships with our blood, but we can with the family we surround ourselves with. And I don't know what's going on between you and Steele lately, but...make sure you make the right choice, okay?"

"I will. I may be an idiot, but I'm not dumb."

Quinto got my gist. He nodded, squeezed my shoulder again, and high-tailed it in the direction of the inns.

I returned to Shay. She cocked an inquisitive eye in my direction. "Everything alright?"

"Completely," I said. "You still want to try to find Carmine without consulting Silverbrook first?"

"He might not be happy about it, but I think it's our best bet. Better than searching aimlessly for Silverbrook, anyway."

"Fair enough." I held my hand out. "Lead the way."

27

I t took a bit of searching to locate the turnoff into Millionaire's Row, but once we did, I found the walk invigorating. As during our trek to Sea Ridge Hunting Tours, our senses were accosted by a barrage of nature. Buzzing dragonflies, chirping songbirds, and rustling leaves. Smells of damp earth, pine needles, and a thick, musky, tropical scent that tickled my nose when the wind blew, coming from a tree with milky white blossoms. Gardenias, Shay suspected. The proximity of it astounded me, how we could turn off a path lined with homes and suddenly find ourselves surrounded by trees and animals and flowers. In New Welwic I'd be lucky to find a single weed sprouting between cracked slabs of concrete before it was trampled by an unsuspecting ogre.

Of course, even here, we couldn't escape mankind's efforts. The trees thinned. On one side of the path, the forest disappeared entirely, falling off the edge of a steep cliff and providing a clear view into town. On the other side, in a cleared section, I spotted my first glimpse of the luxurious homes. From a stone's throw away, they seemed even more ostentatious than from afar, with sleek gray roofs and stone exteriors. Luckily for us, each of them possessed a plaque affixed to their front gates noting the owners of the estates beyond. Even more luckily, none of the homes featured any enormous guard dogs threatening to tear our faces off as we ventured through said gates.

Shay and I passed a few of the homes, each of them separated by a wedge of trees for privacy, before arriving at the Abanos' property. A delicate wrought iron fence surrounded the estate. A path of cut limestone led past a pair of cherub-laden fountains to the front door. Shay and I escorted each other to the front, and Shay knocked.

We waited for a moment, but no one answered. I tried again, with a more forceful set of knuckles than Shay had employed, but again, no one answered.

Shay tried the verbal approach. "Pardon me? Anyone home?"

More delicate wrought iron inlaid the home's front windows, acting as much as a decoration as a theft deterrent. I peered through them but saw only heavy drapes.

"So," said Shay. "Bianca isn't at her home, and it doesn't appear Carmine is either. Coincidence?"

"Maybe," I said. "Wouldn't they be at one or the other of their places if they were having an affair?"

"Not if they ran off."

"And leave both their homes and their stuff behind? Not likely."

Shay clicked her tongue. "Come with me. I have something else I'd like to check while we're here."

I thought my partner might have something less than legal on her mind, but instead of trying to break into the Abanos' home, she led me back up the front walkway and up the path. After crossing another stretch of woods, we came to the last house in line. The sign above this particular estate read, 'Doc Fowler's Fantastic, Fabulous Familial Farmhouse.' A farm it certainly wasn't. More of a mansion, but I could appreciate the alliteration.

"Really?" I said. "You want to talk to Doc Fowler?"

"Why not?" she said. "We're here. It can't hurt."

"And what do you plan to ask him? If his horse show is really a front for mermaid trafficking that he secretly killed Johnny Nicchi over?"

"You keep bringing up that human trafficking theory, but I'm not sure even *you* believe it. And no, I don't plan on asking him anything of the sort. But his name has come up numerous times. Obviously, he's wealthy. He's probably well connected. He might be willing to talk to us, and if so, something might slip. He just as soon might not be home, or he might tell us to get lost, but we'll never know unless we try."

I shrugged. "Alright. I'm going to follow your lead on this. Charm the pants off him. Or...*don't*. You know what I mean."

Shay snickered and shook her head. We walked to the front door and knocked. This time, something stirred within.

After a brief pause, the door opened. Behind it stood a middle-aged man in a fine gray suit. He eyed us with a measure of uncertainty. "Can I help you?"

"Doc Fowler?" said Shay.

"No. I'm Mr. Fowler's manservant, Mateo. You are?"

"Shay Steele and Jake Daggers. We're with the New Welwic police department."

Shay produced her badge. Mateo peered at it skeptically.

"We're not here to investigate Mr. Fowler in any way, I want to be clear about that. Rather, we're looking into Johnny Nicchi's disappearance. Had you heard of it?"

"*Yes...*" Mateo seemed to regret having to respond in the affirmative.

"We were hoping to talk to the Abano brothers about it, but they don't appear to be home," said Shay. "Since we were in the neighborhood, we thought it might be worth seeing if Mr. Fowler would mind spending a moment of his time with us. We hear he's quite knowledgeable of events in the city."

Mateo knew when he was having smoke blown up his hindquarters, but to his credit, he did his job anyway. "If you'll wait a moment please..."

He closed the door. Thirty seconds stretched into a minute.

"You still sure about this?" I asked.

"Worst case, he comes back with a broom," said Shay.

"Or something pointier."

The door opened again. Mateo waved us in. "If you'll come with me, please."

The manservant led us into the home, which opened dramatically as we walked into it. Before us stretched a spacious, circular living room the floor of which was almost completely covered in thick, white rugs. A wall of windows curved around the back of the room, looking upon a neat garden of white roses. A black grand piano with the lid propped open drew my attention, as did a freestanding bar whose lacquered wood had been stained a deep, deep brown. To the side, a quartet of pristine, white leather couches had been arranged into a square, separated in the middle by a steel and glass coffee table. Beyond that I spotted a massive roulette wheel and a felt topped table.

Mateo shot a hand out as we approached the rugs. He pointed to a set of cubbies built into the wall. "Shoes."

We removed the articles in question and stored them before continuing onto the carpeting. Mateo showed us to the couches, where we found an old man flanked by cushions sitting in the middle of one.

I hadn't even noticed him at first. Even if he'd been standing he couldn't have measured more than five feet, three inches, and I probably could've thrown him across the room if I'd been worked up. A shock of white hair stood upon his head, thin in spots but voluminous nonetheless, and his wrinkles could've swallowed un-suspecting houseflies.

"Welcome," he said as we approached, his voice aged but not weak. "You'll pardon me if I don't stand. My knees aren't what they used to be."

"*You* must be Doc Fowler," said Shay.

"Yannis Phalonopoulos, actually," said the old man. "But by all means, yes, call me Doc. I made the bed, and I've been lying in it my whole life. Please." He waved at the couches.

We sat. Mateo left and stood at the side of the room, by the bar.

"Can I get you anything to drink?" asked Yannis. "Well, not me personally, of course. But Mateo would be more than happy to."

He didn't look happy to do much of anything. I waved Yannis off. "No thank you, Mr. Fowler. We're fine."

The old man nodded. "Very well. I understand you're with the police, but not from our delightful town. New Welwic, then."

"That's right," said Shay. "We're investigating the disappearance of Johnny Nicchi, one of the local fishermen."

"Yes, Mateo told me that as well," said Yannis. "And of course I'm familiar with the situation. News travels fast. In fact, I was aware of your presence, too, which is why I had Mateo let you in. But I don't know what you expect to learn from me about Mr. Nicchi's disappearance. If I'd met the man, it was only in passing."

"I understand that, Mr. Fowler," said Shay. "But clearly you're a man with his finger on the pulse of the city. You knew we'd arrived. Perhaps you know something that can provide insight into Nicchi's disappearance. His frame of mind, his finances, anything."

Yannis smiled. "You flatter me, and even at my age, I can appreciate flattery from a lovely young lady such as yourself. If I could help you, I would, but I simply don't have any knowledge to share. Mateo mentioned you came to speak with Orlando or Carmine next door. I can leave a note, if you wish."

"I'm afraid that wouldn't help," said Shay. "What we require is a conversation, not delivery of a message. But thank you."

Yannis nodded in understanding.

"Are they good neighbors?" I asked. "Orlando and Carmine?"

"The best," said Yannis. "A more sophisticated, nuanced pair of young men, I've never met. Excellent business owners, and quite respectful of my property."

"Do you ever have them over?"

"On occasion. For parties and social gatherings, though I host fewer of those than I used to."

I glanced toward the roulette wheel, a thought building in the back of my mind. "Are you, by any chance, a gambling man?"

Yannis smiled. "Mateo said your name was Daggers, is that correct? You're...what? A detective?"

"That's right."

"Well, Detective, I'll have you know those are purely decorative. Conversation pieces. But if your question was about my personality, then yes. I enjoy taking risks. Making the occasional wager. I wouldn't have gotten where I am with a more passive attitude. Why do you ask?"

"No reason," I said. "You simply struck me as the sort of man who would be. In either case, thank you for taking the time to meet with us despite the circumstances. You'd be surprised how often we gain useful information from unlikely encounters."

"You stopped by my home," said Yannis. "I'd hardly say this encounter qualifies as *unlikely*."

"My mistake. Steele?"

"One moment," she said. "Mr. Fowler. Do you mind if I ask you one last question?"

"By all means," he said.

"How does a foal fly, exactly?"

Yannis laughed. "Magic and arm power, my dear. You'll have to come to the show some time, in a few weeks when we open it to the public. It's down at the moment, I'm afraid."

And yet Émile still worked there.

I motioned for Steele to rise. "We'll be sure to do that. In the meantime, best of luck with your other business ventures."

It might've been my imagination, but I think the old man's eyes glinted when I said that.

He nodded anyway. "Thank you. And best of luck to you in your investigation."

Mateo separated himself from the wall, and Shay and I went to get our shoes.

28

I sat on the bed in my hotel room, my feet up and once again freed of their shoes. After leaving Doc Fowler's mansion, Shay and I had returned to town, but at that point we'd butted heads on how to proceed. We'd both agreed we needed to find one or both of Bianca and Carmine Abano. I suggested we try Bianca's place again, but Shay contended that, like it or not, we needed Silverbrook's assistance, as well as that of the local PD as a whole. After all, Bronmuth had gone out in search of the same information we sought, though who knew if he'd keyed in on Carmine the way we had.

As was so often the case, Shay won the fight. We returned to the station, and though we found Mines— seriously, did she ever leave?—she didn't have any updates on Silverbrook's whereabouts. With frustration undoubtedly showing on our faces, we left a message with Mines telling Silverbrook to look for us at the hotel, grabbed a quick bite at a place on the way, and returned to our rooms.

As we reached the third floor of our hotel, I paused at the door to my room, my key in hand. I glanced at Shay, who pulled her own key and stared back at me. We both stood there, Shay's face hopeful.

The metaphor wasn't lost on me. Both of us, standing there, holding the keys to our problems and yet choosing not to use them. Or *me* choosing not to use mine, more like.

Shay only waited a moment. She unlocked her door and let herself in, leaving me in the hallway by myself. With a sigh, I'd let myself in, taken my shoes off, and flopped onto the bed, where I still found myself, and in a similar state of mind to when I'd entered.

I couldn't understand it. A beautiful, smart, compassionate, fascinating woman cared about me, had told me she cared about me, maybe even loved me, though neither of us had ever broached that particular thorny subject. I cared as much about her in return, desired her deeply, and thought she was perfect in just about every way. If I behaved logically, I would've moved heaven and earth to make sure I maintained that mutual level of affection and care, yet I couldn't stop sabotaging myself periodically. I might go a month or two without incident, but then, like clockwork, my foot would come flying in, knocking a handful of teeth out of my mouth with the force of its impact.

Why couldn't I believe I was worthy of her? Why wouldn't I let myself accept her love? Was it because I'd lost my mother, or let my relationships with my father and brother fall into disrepair? Perhaps it had more to do with my failed marriage, though I actually felt I'd been making progress on that front. My relationship with Nicole was better now than ever before, and I was making regular efforts to spend quality time with Tommy. His face lit up every time he saw me now instead of flattening out like it used to, with him knowing my presence was a mere speck in an otherwise desolate morass.

Maybe my issues of self-confidence were a result of all of the above, a consequence of roughly two-thirds of my life spent angry and upset and feeling unloved. If so, perhaps I was being too hard on myself. I wouldn't be able to reverse twenty years of bad habits in a few months with Shay, even with her support and affection as motivating factors. Debilitating injuries to muscles or ligaments could take years to repair, and the brain was a few hundred times more complicated than any of those fleshy parts. It only made sense.

Of course, it was also foolish on my part to assume whatever problems ailed me would simply go away. Sure, I'd been polishing my exterior with diet and exercise and regular shaving, but what about the interior rot that had taken hold of me during my baser moments? I thought I'd dug it out it, but perhaps I'd merely tiled over it, hidden it behind a fresh coat of paint. If so, I might have to really work to get myself on the right path, and like any good reconstruction project, major elements might come crashing down before my structure returned to its former glory.

I heard a noise in the hall, and I shook my head. Here I was, daydreaming about my problems again when I should've been focusing on the case, a case in which the pieces involved finally were falling into place. Johnny's financial troubles. His deteriorating relationship with his wife. Bianca's paramour, whoever he might be. They all painted a believable picture.

Except for the part where Johnny got murdered with a trident. I still couldn't make heads or tails of that. Sure, any object could be turned into a murder weapon in a moment of passion. Any port in a storm and all that. But that didn't answer the question of where it came from. Who would've had access to a weapon of that sort? I still liked my mermaid theory, but Shay was right. Even I had to admit the thought of illegal mermaid trafficking was ludicrous. The point of having a mermaid in captivity would be to showcase her, and no one would be able to do that and keep it secret for long. Even one held privately would cause rumors to swirl. And there's no way Nicchi could've financed himself off just one. He would've had to capture several, making the secrecy of the operation even less viable.

I heard more of a commotion in the hallway. Voices that sounded like Steele and Bronmuth, actually. I hopped off the bed and headed toward my shoes. Before I'd managed to slip on the second one, I heard a knock at my door. A forceful one.

"Daggers? You there?" called Silverbrook, his voice muffled by the wood. "We need to move."

I quickly finished the knot on my second shoe and tossed open the door. Shay stood there alongside Bronmuth, the latter looking haggard and flustered.

"Yeah?" I said. "What's going on? You find out who Bianca was seeing?"

"Not now," he said. "I just got reports of an incident near the dock warehouses. Carmine Abano got stabbed."

I shared a look with Steele. We hadn't shared our suspicions with Silverbrook. At least I hadn't.

He didn't give us time to sort it out. "There's no time to waste. He's at the local medical clinic, supposedly in critical condition. We've got to go."

I nodded. It sounded like things were about to come to a head. *Especially* if Carmine had been stabbed with a trident.

29

appreciated the fact that Silverbrook referred to our
destination as a clinic, because a hospital it certainly
wasn't. The place we arrived at was a collection of a
half-dozen doctor's offices, but in a town the size of
Aragosto, I supposed I couldn't expect much else. The
secretary in the lobby waved us through as soon as she
saw Silverbrook, pointing down the hallway to the left
of her desk. There wasn't as much of a commotion as I
might've expected, but I was used to New Welwic hospi-
tals, full of the hustle and bustle of doctors and nurses,
the clatter of moving carts, orderlies shouting com-
mands, adults screaming out in pain, loved ones screaming in grief, and small children screaming for no good
reason.

Aragosto's clinic had none of that. We passed a pair
of rooms empty of both patrons and staff before arriving
at a third. A window at the front provided a view inside,
but a white sheet had been drawn all the way across it.
As we approached, a doctor backed his way out of the
door leading in, his hands covered in blood.

"Excuse me," said Bronmuth as the door shut behind the man. "Is this Carmine Abano's room?"

The doctor looked at Silverbrook, his eyes more on the dwarf's uniform than his face. "You're police?"

Apparently, Bronmuth didn't know *everyone* in town. He nodded. "Officer Silverbrook. You are?"

"Doctor Pryor," he said, heading to a sink on the far wall. "And yes, that's Mr. Abano's room. Though I don't suggest you enter at the moment. He's in a bad way."

The white sheet might've obscured the view through the window, but a small porthole in the door remained unobstructed. Inside the room, I spotted a man lying prone on a hospital bed, his torso wrapped in thick bandages, many of which had soaked through to a dark red. His eyes lay closed, and his skin looked as pale as ivory against the midnight black of his hair. It didn't appear as if his chest rose or fell, but perhaps I couldn't see it from my vantage point.

In the corner of the room, another man sat in a chair, his head held between his hands. I couldn't see any of his face, but his glossy black hair was identical to that of the man on the hospital bed, and their builds appeared to be similar, as well. Stocky, but not fat. A faint wail drifted through the walls, choked sobs of grief coming from the corner chair.

I turned from the porthole. "Is that Carmine's brother?"

The doctor nodded as he began to wash his hands. "Yes. Arrived a few moments ago. He's in a...fragile position, I think."

"What happened to Carmine?" asked Silverbrook.

"Well, if you're asking me what occurred to land him in my clinic, I couldn't tell you," said the doctor. "He wasn't in any condition to speak when he arrived. But I can tell you everything I've seen since he was carried through the front doors, and I can tell you what I know about his injuries. Given what seems to have transpired, patient doctor confidentiality doesn't apply to you."

"Well," said Bronmuth. "Go on."

The doctor glanced at Silverbrook as he soaped his arms, the look on his face indicating he thought he should be addressed with a little more respect. "Mr. Abano arrived perhaps twenty-five minutes ago, carried here by a couple of citizens who said they found him among the warehouses by the docks. It's a good thing I was on call—I have the most surgical expertise of any of the members of our practice—and Mr. Abano was in dire need of immediate attention. I wasn't even sure he was alive when I first saw him."

"Is he now?" I asked.

The doctor glanced at me, his arms covered in suds to the elbows. "For the time being, yes. I had the citizens bring Mr. Abano in and lay him down. His shirt was soaked in blood, as were a good portion of the rest of his garments, so I cut them off and immediately got to work. I only found a single injury, but it was a bad one. A puncture wound over the right side of his chest cavity—not a cut mind you. The wound wasn't nearly clean enough, nor was whatever injured him particularly sharp. Based on the way it expanded and tore at the flesh, I'm guessing he was stabbed with a pointed object that grew thicker along the axis. Maybe a pickaxe or something similar.

"Either way, Mr. Abano was reasonably lucky. The weapon scraped across his ribcage and angled right, into his lung. Obviously that's bad, but if the attack had come from a different angle, it could've gone the other way, into his heart or any of the pulmonary arteries that surround it. If that were the case, he certainly wouldn't have made it here alive.

"Even so, he was on the brink of death when I started to operate. His right lung had suffered a minor pneumothorax—what you'd normally call a collapsed lung—and I had to aspirate a pint of blood from it as I worked. Given the severity, I think aspirating the fluid will be enough for his body to recover from it over time. If it doesn't, I might have to try something more drastic like an intercostal drain, but I hope it doesn't come to that."

"An inter-what?" said Bronmuth.

"A small rubber tube leading from his lung to an exterior water seal. It has a small chance of success, and risks infection, but it's a possibility."

"So you think he'll survive, then?" asked Steele.

The doctor rinsed the last of the soap off and reached for a towel. "Well, that's still very much in doubt, I'm afraid. Despite the ragged nature of the wound, I was able to stitch Mr. Abano up to my satisfaction, but the state of his lung is very concerning, as is the amount of blood he lost. His blood pressure is alarmingly low, and he's at risk for circulatory shock. And as I already mentioned, the entry wound was anything but clean. I'll be surprised if he doesn't come down with an infection, and if he does, all bets are off."

Bronmuth wiped a hand across his face. "And you said Orlando was in there with him?"

Doctor Pryor nodded. "Mr. Abano's brother, yes. One of my nurses tried to keep him out, but he wouldn't be denied, and I wasn't about to evict him either, given the circumstances."

"And the townsfolk who dropped him off?" asked Bronmuth. "Who was it?"

Pryor shrugged. "I'm not sure. I didn't ask. My secretary might've recognized them. She could give you descriptions, I'm sure. I was too busy trying to make sure Mr. Abano didn't die to pay any attention to them."

"Silverbrook?" said Shay. "Could we speak to you for a sec?"

"Give us a moment," said the dwarf to the doctor. We retreated up the hallway and out of earshot.

"Look, Silverbrook," said Shay, leaning in. "It's pure speculation at this point, but while you were investigating the identity of Bianca's lover, Daggers and I had an epiphany. Bianca was seen with Carmine at that bar last night. It might've been him."

Bronmuth grunted. "Yeah."

"You don't seem surprised," I said.

He frowned. "I didn't know, if that's what you're suggesting. But some of the rumors I heard this afternoon? Nobody could tell me anything specific, but I was cobbling pieces together. And with Carmine getting stabbed? It was a reasonable conclusion."

"In that case, we need to talk to Orlando," said Shay. "I mean, they live together, don't they? He would've had to have known what was going on."

"Oh, I'm sure he did," said Silverbrook. "But *we* aren't going to be talking to him. You don't know him like I do. He's not the most rational person on the best of days. Normally, he's loud and brash and a little on the combative side. Now? Who the hell knows." He shook his head. "I'll talk to him. I don't know if I'll be able to get anything out of him, but I'll try. I'll have a better shot at it alone than I would with the two of you looming behind me."

There is was again, that suspicion that Bronmuth was cutting us out of the best parts, and yet what he said made sense. If he had any kind of relationship with Carmine's brother, he might be able to leverage it into knowledge, whereas we certainly wouldn't.

"Okay," I said. "Fair enough. You want us to wait for you in front?"

"Are you kidding?" he said. "You're the homicide cops. Get to the docks. Figure out what the hell happened down there."

"You're okay with that?" asked Steele.

"Right now, I'll take all the help I can get," he said. "Seriously, our town isn't equipped for this sort of thing. If anyone asks, tell them you're supposed to be there. Show them your badges. I'm sure they won't fight you."

It sounded good enough to me. I gave Shay a nod. She nodded back, and we got moving fast.

30

The sun hung low in the sky as we returned to the docks, sending long shadows trailing from the warehouses and casting their backsides into darkness. A crowd of a dozen individuals huddled together at the base of one of the alleys, muttering among themselves in low voices and surrounded by a cloud of fear.

With my badge clutched in one hand, I pushed my way through. "Excuse me. Police business, coming through. Make way."

I punched through the other side, Shay trailing right behind me, only to run into a uniformed guy in his mid thirties with a mustache so big it could've been used by a stage magician to hide a wayward assistant or two. He slammed his forearm into me as I left the crowd, his moustache dancing as he spoke.

"Hey! Who the hell are you? What do you think you're doing? This is an active crime scene."

"Cool it, mop face," I said. "I'm Daggers. This is Steele. We're homicide."

"Yeah?" he said. "Because I've never seen you before in my life. So why don't you turn your butts around—"

"Hang on there, Morris."

The cop stepped to the side—or was pushed to the side, rather. Mines appeared behind him, her face lined with worry.

"Daggers. Steele," she said. "Boy, am I glad to see the two of you. Were you with Silverbrook?"

I glanced at Morris, almost surprised at having found one of Aragosto's other reclusive cops, although there had been four desks at the station, so I knew there'd been others.

"We were," I said. "He's at the clinic. Carmine Abano is alive, but only barely. His brother Orlando is there, too. Silverbrook stayed behind to talk to him. Said he'd fare better alone than with us at his side."

Mines wiped her hand across her face. "This is a disaster. Here. Come on in. Step away from the crowd."

We followed her into the alley, one smelling of fish and intermittently dotted with large wooden crates, iron-banded barrels, and piles of shipping supplies tied down and covered in tarps. The sun couldn't work its way past the warehouse roofs to the alley floor, which probably explained why there were still puddles here and there despite it not having rained in at least a day and a half. All in all, the alley could've been a dead ringer for the one in which we'd found Quinto and his brother, Felix—except for the section with all the blood.

A shallow pool of the dark sticky stuff slicked the stones underfoot, and a few other smears of blood stood out on the wall of the warehouse to my left and on a crate on the same side. Said crate had received a greater indignity than having been bloodied, however, as the front side of it had been crushed, the boards cracked and bent inward. A fishy smell emanated from within, even stronger than what lingered in the air.

"This is where they found him," said Mines. "Laying on the ground, bleeding out. I'm guessing there was a fight. Carmine, or whoever he was fighting with, must've gotten thrown into that crate. The witnesses say he was stabbed, or appeared to have been."

"With something pointed but not sharp," said Steele. "The doctor confirmed it. And these witnesses are?"

Mines pointed up the other side of the alley. "Mickey Smuthers and Don Black. A couple of local fishermen. Said they'd docked and were heading into town, coming down this alley when they found him. Probably hadn't been more than a few minutes since Carmine had been stabbed. Said he was trying to tell them something but kept choking on his own blood. They're the ones who took him to the doctor. Told us he passed out on the way there."

I followed Mines' finger to the pair in question. With their flannel shirts and woolen caps, they looked the part. Another uniformed face that was new to me talked to them and jotted stuff down in a notepad.

"That them?"

Mines nodded. "Returned about twenty minutes ago after dropping Carmine off. Travers is taking their statements."

I assumed that was the cop. "Hard to believe they'd be involved if they came back."

"That's what I thought," said Mines. "I'm assuming they're clean. We'll check with Keonig to make sure they arrived when they said they did."

"And nobody saw anything of the fight itself?" I said. "Or heard anything?"

"Not to my knowledge," said Mines. "The crowd at the front developed recently. I don't think any of them were here when Carmine got assaulted, but who knows? Morris asked, but no one stepped forward."

I grunted. While I'd talked with Mines, Shay had knelt at the crime scene, peering into cracks and crevices and corners that might contain evidence only she'd be able to parcel out, although with the fading light, even her eagle eyes might soon fail her.

I nodded toward the buildings. "Any idea what these are?"

"One of them is an Abano building," said Mines. "A warehouse, nothing special. The other is a cannery. Belongs to someone else."

Steele stood, and joined us, her gaze focused on the cobblestones underneath. "Do you have a lantern?"

"Not on me, no," said Mines. "We'll have to head back to the station to grab one."

"You find something?" I asked.

"Maybe." She walked up the alley, toward the new officer and the two citizens who'd saved Carmine. "Excuse me? Guys? You two found and carried Carmine Abano to the doctor's, right? I'm guessing you took him straight there, heading that way?" She pointed at the crowd at the far end of the alley.

The pair cut off conversation from the officer, looking like they weren't sure if they were supposed to respond.

Mines gave them a nod. "Go ahead, guys."

"Uh, yeah, that's right," said the taller of the pair. "We took him to Doc Pryor's as fast as we could. Headed straight there."

Steele pushed past them to the mouth of the alley. She swiveled her head around, eventually locking eyes on something. "Bingo."

"What is it?" I asked.

She knelt down. "A blood trail, heading the opposite direction our fishermen took Abano. Carmine's assailant must've been injured in the fight. Not badly, given the blood droplets. I'd guess he suffered a minor laceration, maybe to his hand or arm, something that would've dripped as he fled the scene."

I knelt beside her, gazing at the stones underfoot. "Where?"

She pointed it out.

I blinked, leaning closer. Finally I saw it. A tiny pair of spots, barely darker than the surrounding rock. "Seriously? You can see that?"

"I won't be able to for long," she said. "We either need lanterns stat or we need to hurry. Preferably both."

"You never cease to amaze." I stood. "You coming, Mines?"

Her brow furrowed. "Well...I suppose I should, shouldn't I? But what about Travers and Morris? They're not exactly used to dealing with this sort of thing."

"And you are?"

She took a breath and blew it out forcefully through her lips. "Fair point. Travers? You're in charge until I get back, and no, I have no idea when that'll be. Keep the crime scene clear. Don't let anyone in who doesn't need to be here. Clear?"

The officer nodded. "Yes, sergeant."

We headed off as fast as Shay could track the trail, skirting another warehouse and into yet another alley. From there, our path wove snakelike in and around service buildings in a seemingly chaotic manner, but as we paused at an intersection for the fourth or fifth time, Shay scanning the ground with narrowed eyes, I started to understand what was going on. The blood trail led away from Aragosto's center, east toward the lighthouse and the path toward Millionaire's Row, but that wasn't the most important point.

"Carmine's attacker knew what he was doing," I said. "Or at least where he was going."

"What's that?" said Mines.

"The attacker," I said as we rushed down another alley. "Look around. I know it's late, but we haven't bumped into anyone else yet. He deliberately took back roads, knowing where he wasn't likely to be spotted fleeing the scene. He knows the docks."

"It's a small town," said Mines. "That doesn't mean much."

We burst free of the warehouses' embrace and stumbled upon a familiar road, the one we'd taken with Silverbrook in search of Rigger's house. Shay didn't waste any time, heading up it, presumably still following a trail only she could discern. The sky wasn't interested in playing along, however. It had turned from a sea blue to a deep purple.

After jogging a few hundred feet along the path, Shay stopped in the middle of the road. She sighed. "I've lost it."

I didn't blame her. I was having a hard time making out the features of the houses on either side of the street, never mind a miniscule trail of blood that might've seeped into the earth or clotted along the way.

One of the homes stood out clearer than the others, illuminated by a bright lantern hung from a hook on the front porch.

Mines made a beeline for it.

An old guy sat on a porch swing next to it, smoking a pipe and eyeing us suspiciously as we approached. "Hey! What do you think you're—"

Mines hopped up the steps and snagged the lantern. "Sorry. Police business. I'm seizing this due to extraordinary circumstances. We'll return it when we're able."

The old guy sprang up, surprisingly sprightly given his apparent age. Sweet-smelling smoke from his pipe swirled around him, looking as if it might be coming out of his ears. "You can't do that. That's my only good lantern. How am I supposed to—"

"Leer at people as they walk past on the street?" I asked.

The old guy glared at me.

Steele and Mines had already started back toward the street, but I paused at the base of the steps. "You weren't out here smoking say, an hour ago, were you?"

He grunted. "What's it to you?"

"See anybody go by?"

"What? You mean the big guy?"

Steele and Mines both turned.

I suffered a sense of foreboding, hoping I wouldn't have terrible news to share with Quinto when he came back to town. "What big guy?"

"A strapping young lad," said the old guy, still huffing on his pipe. "Tall. Bushy beard. Seemed like he was in a hurry."

I turned to my partner. "It's not much of a description, but I can think of one person who fits the bill. Someone who worked on the docks and would know his way around. Someone who would have a motive to kill Carmine if we're right about him and Bianca and what that could've meant for Johnny."

Shay nodded. "The thought crossed my mind the instant we heard about Carmine. But now we have evidence."

Mines blinked, confused. "Who?"

"Johnny's brother," I said. "Joey Nicchi."

Mines' look didn't budge. "Why would he try to murder Carmine Abano?"

"It's complicated. We'll fill you in on the way. Right now, we don't have any time to lose. Let's go."

31

We trekked up the hill, past the abandoned ranch house and toward Joey's place at the Sea Ridge Preserve, our appropriated lantern bravely fighting the now all-encompassing dark of night. Shay hadn't managed to pick up the blood trail after securing our newfound source of light, but that hadn't stopped us from high-tailing it through town as quickly as we could.

I put a hand on Shay's shoulder and motioned for Mines to stop as we approached the sign. "Hold on. We need to have a quick conversation before we go in there."

"You want to iron out a game plan," said Mines.

"We should tread carefully," said Shay. "If Joey is in there, and he's our guy, he's liable to be in an extremely fragile emotional state. If he attacked Carmine, we have to assume he'd be willing to use violence against us."

Mines wore a heavy truncheon on her belt. She unbuckled it and hefted it in her right hand. "Don't worry. I can take care of myself."

Her attitude and physique both made me think she could. I reached into my jacket, into my secret pocket for my own head smasher, Daisy. I was so used to her presence that I'd learned to ignore her weight, her cold caress, and the way she pressed against my chest from the inside of my coat. I pulled her out and gripped her tightly, the lantern held in my other hand.

"Good to hear, Mines. Still, Joey isn't your typical bruiser. He's a hunter, by trade if not by nature. We saw several blades in his barn when we stopped by with Silverbrook earlier. We should assume he's armed and dangerous. Steele? You know I trust you, but I think it would be best for you to stay behind me, at least until we can get you armed."

She nodded. "Agreed."

"You ready, Mines?"

The sergeant nodded.

"Okay. Let's check the barn first."

We moved in, Mines leading the way, and gosh darn it if the sergeant didn't finally seem in her element. Until now I'd seen her as a small town functionary, not fully qualified for her station but at least more level-headed then those around her, but now, finally, I saw something of value. She walked fluidly, in a partial crouch, her striking arm relaxed but ready and her head constantly moving from side to side, gaining whatever knowledge she could from sight and sound. If I didn't know any better, I'd say she'd been in a military unit in a previous life.

We headed to the barn, making little noise but giving ourselves away nonetheless by our light. Mines paused at the door, still open as it had been in the morning, and glanced inside. I lifted the lantern, spreading the lamp's flickering light over the dusty plows and yokes and other old pieces of farm equipment, all of which looked notably creepier in the dark of night.

"Joey?" called Mines. "You in there?"

"Look," said Steele, pointing.

I followed her finger to the rack on the near wall, the one next to the hoes and rakes and pitchforks. I clicked my tongue. "Damn."

"There a problem?" asked Mines.

"There were two more knives and another bow there this morning," I said. "Armed and dangerous, indeed."

Mines pulled back from the door and started scanning the surroundings, first the ranch house behind us and then the forested areas off on either sides.

"What is it?" asked Shay.

"Nothing," said Mines. "I'm checking the obvious vantage points. I don't see anyone. We should be okay, but if he has a bow, that'll change our strategy. Joey's a good shot. There's a reason he has this gig."

I gulped. I'd never had to deal with a sniper with a grudge before. "Steele, you want to grab one of the remaining knives?"

"Are you serious? I'd be as liable to hurt myself or one of you as I would to defend myself." Shay nodded in the direction we'd came. "Let's check the house."

We retreated to the home, but no light streamed through any of the windows. We skirted around it, heading to the front door, Mines once again leading the way. The sergeant reached out to test the handle, but Shay grabbed her by the arm before she could.

"Wait!" Shay pointed. A dark substance smeared across the brass knob. "That's blood."

Mines nodded and tested the handle anyway, though she tried her best not to touch the portion that had been contaminated. The door didn't budge.

"Damn." Mines knocked. "Joey? You in there? If you are, please come to the door. We can still resolve this peacefully."

"Come on. He's not here. Not anymore. Either that or he's hiding. Either way, he's not coming out, no matter how nice you ask." I shooed her. "Go on. Give me some room."

"What for?"

"So I can kick this door down and we can keep searching for clues."

"What?" said Mines. "You can't do that. We don't have a warrant."

"A warrant? Please. We don't need one when we're in hot pursuit of a dangerous felon. Besides, don't you hear that?"

"Hear what?"

"That woman screaming, coming from within the house. Sounds like Carmine's cousin, Rialta. She could be in danger."

Mines gave Steele a look. "Is this how the two of you normally operate?"

"Not as often as we used to," she said. "But to be fair, he's right about the hot pursuit statute."

"Fine." Mines stepped to the side. "But stick together. If he's armed with a knife, he'll be more dangerous in close quarters than out here."

I did what I do best. My boot slammed into the padlock, sending the door flying inward. We surged through after it, tackling the rooms one by one. Shay found another lantern near the hearth in the living room, which we promptly lit before continuing our search, but the room itself was clear. So was the kitchen.

We moved down a hallway and into the first room on the right. A bedroom. The dresser on the side had its drawers thrown open, with a number of clothes strewn across the floor and bed.

"Think he's just messy?" I said.

"Either that or he was trying to make a hasty exit," said Steele.

We kept moving, pausing at the next open door. A washroom.

"Hold on," said Steele.

She walked inside, her lantern filling the room with light. A white porcelain washbasin stood in the center, filled with water of a decidedly reddish hue. A towel with blood on it hung over the edge of the tub, and shredded pieces of cloth littered the floor.

"Looks like someone was making bandages," I said.

Shay didn't respond. She walked to the other side of the washbasin and knelt. "What the hell...?"

I couldn't see around the edge of the basin, and the washroom wasn't big enough for me to easily scoot around my partner. "What is it?"

Shay stood, holding a wastebasket between her hands. There were more scraps of bloodied cloth at the bottom, but something else stuck out. Literally.

"What the heck is that?" said Mines over my shoulder.

"It's...the murder weapon," said Shay. "It's some sort of horn."

Some sort was right. About a foot and a half long, straight, coming to sharp point at the tip and widening to an inch and a half in diameter at the base. A tight spiral wove along its entire length, and though there was blood both at the tip where it would've punctured Carmine and at the base where Joey would've held it, it was the unbloodied portions that caught my eye. They sparkled, almost as if they were embedded with flecks of quartz.

"You know what that is, don't you?" I said.

"I'd guess some kind of antelope. Maybe a narwhal."

"Stop kidding yourself," I said. "Look at it. It *glitters*. That's a unicorn horn, Shay."

My partner gave me one of her familiar looks of disbelief. "Come on, Jake. A *unicorn?* I'm sure it's just covered in sparkly paint, or if not, perhaps it's petrified. It could've been infused with minerals that give it this appearance."

"Not with that shape, that taper, that spiral. I've seen one in a museum, Shay. That's the only thing it could be. I swear to the gods."

Mines had lost her voice, but she finally managed to locate it. "Wait...*what*? Are you suggesting Joey Nicchi stabbed Carmine Abano with a unicorn horn? That's insane."

"Any more insane than Johnny Nicchi getting stabbed with a trident?" I said.

"Yeah," said Mines, nodding. "A lot more insane, actually."

I hadn't really thought that through. "Okay. Fine. Point taken. But I've learned not to ask questions when evidence is staring you in the face, and this particular piece is making itself self-evident, no pun intended."

"Daggers, I don't understand what's going on," said Shay. "Every time I think I have a handle on this investigation, every time I think it's an open and shut case about debts or affairs or revenge, something like this crops up. I'm good at piecing clues together when they're sensible, but when fate throws *this* crap at us, that's where you come in. Help me out."

"I..." I sucked on my lips and sighed. "I have no idea. Not the slightest. Maybe Joey had one in his possession, but why take it with him to murder Carmine? I mean, he took knives and a bow with him, didn't he? Unless he took those with him after he returned from his assault, but why would he take this with him in the first place? Even if I'm right that Johnny died from a mermaid attack, that doesn't tie Johnny, our victim, together with Joey, a perpetrator, using another odd weapon. It doesn't make any sense."

Mines sighed and wiped her hand across her forehead. "Well, whatever the reasoning behind it, it doesn't matter now, does it? If what you told me on the walk over is right, Joey had probable cause for attacking Carmine, and now we've found a weapon and blood. Furthermore, Joey doesn't appear to be here. Even if he is, we're not going to find him now with night having set in. Not with his survival skills."

"So what do you want to do?" asked Steele.

Mines shrugged. "Let's get the weapon back to the station. I need to spread the word about Joey being armed and dangerous, and in the morning I'll scrape together every officer I have and make a public appeal. We'll start the manhunt. Right now, I'm not sure there's anything else we *can* do."

I opened my mouth to object, but my brain intervened. Despite her inexperience, Mines was right. Everything pointed to Joey, and though Mines seemed concerned about his threat to the general public, he'd only attacked Carmine, who he must've suspected had been having an affair with Bianca. We still didn't know what role, if any, Carmine played in Johnny's death, but Carmine wasn't about to be a threat to anyone else in his condition.

I nodded. "Alright. We'll get started first thing tomorrow. In the meantime, we'll escort you downtown."

32

After accompanying Mines to the police station, we continued to our hotel, ascended the stairs to the third floor, and approached our doors. As I reached into my pocket for my key, I suffered an overwhelming wave of déjà vu.

I looked up. Shay stood outside her door, once again waiting on me, an expectant look on her face.

"Well," she said. "Mines said she'd want to get the manhunt started bright and early. I'd love to be able to wait until Quinto arrives with our overnight bags before we leave, but who knows how long that might take."

I nodded.

"You want me to wake you up? Maybe around seven? That should give us time to eat and still get to the station in time to be involved in whatever efforts Mines enacts."

"Yeah," I said. "Seven should be fine."

"You sure? That's early for you."

"It's early now. I'll have plenty of time to sleep."

Shay nodded. A moment stretched into infinity. "Well. Okay. Good night then."

Shay stuck her key into her lock.

I fingered the key in my own pocket. What was it folks said about the definition of insanity? Doing the exact same thing and expecting different results? Well, I'd been here before, in this exact same situation, mere hours ago in fact.

I might be an idiot, but I wasn't insane.

"Wait," I said.

Shay paused, her hand still on the key. "What is it?"

I let go of my key, pulled my hand from my pocket, and approached her. I looked into her brilliant azure eyes, and she gazed back into mine.

"Shay, I'm not perfect."

"I never said you were."

"I know that. But let me get through this, and I promise I'll listen to anything you have to say when I'm done. Okay?"

She nodded.

"You know about me, about my past. I've never hid what I went through. Losing my mother to those muggers, never finding out who they were, or what their motivations might've been. It changed me. Drove me into detective work. Fostered an unrelenting search for justice in me that hasn't faded to this day and probably never will. But that wasn't the only way losing my mother changed me. It turned me inward, and it did the same to the rest of my family, my father in particular. At the time I didn't understand the degree to which it affected him, but I do now. I've loved. I've lost. I get it. And it changed my brother, made him less willing to embrace compassion and to attach himself emotionally to the rest of us. And of course, it changed me.

"You know I've never been the best at expressing my emotions. I'm just not that kind of guy. I couldn't even tell you the last time I cried. Probably toward the end of my relationship with Nicole, when I realized it was over and there was no going back. Over the years I became quite adept at hiding my emotions even when I had them, usually with comedy, sarcasm, or a tailored tough guy exterior. I became a master of emotional suppression. But it's not simply that I suffer from an inability to *express* my emotions. It's that I've lost the ability to connect with them, period. If I can't understand them, can't face them, listen to them? If I can't take them all in, nod my head, and process them, then they become a problem.

"And that's what happened when I spent time with your family the other night. I sensed they thought I wasn't good enough for you, but that wasn't the root problem when I thought about it. It was merely a trigger. The problem was the love your family has for one another in general, and trust me, I know how crazy that sounds. But over the years, I trained myself to steer away from that love. I didn't have it anymore, and I taught myself I didn't need it. It was a survival skill. That's why when I did have a family of my own, with Nicole and with Tommy, I pushed them away, too. So they wouldn't hurt me. And of course I got hurt anyway, but not as much as I could've been if I'd let them in further. That's why I still struggle with my relationship with Tommy...and with you. Because even though I want you, even though I care for you, hell, even though

I *need* you, there's a part of my brain telling me I could get hurt, *badly,* if I go on and that nothing could be worth that.

"So I'm sorry. Sorry for the way I acted in the presence of your parents and brothers, sorry for the way I've treated you over the past couple days, sorry for the way I've kept myself bottled up. I need to let it out. I know that now. But I have to be honest with you. I don't know how to fix what's wrong with me. I don't even know if I *can* be fixed."

I took a deep breath and let it out slowly. Shay waited, making sure I was done before speaking.

"So...you're saying you might be damaged goods?"

"I know I am."

Shay smiled. "You know I have two older brothers, right? I played with engineering sets all the time growing up, and they'd always come by and break them. I like putting stuff back together."

"Come on. Be serious."

The smile disappeared. "I am, Jake. Look, I'm not trying to minimize what you've gone through. I understand how difficult it is for you to share that with me, and I appreciate it wholeheartedly. But you shouldn't be so hard on yourself, either. You've recognized the problem. That's *huge.* Knowledge is half the battle. You know what problem you need to solve. Now you just need to do it."

"But how?"

"By talking to people. By continuing to explore your emotions. By not forcing them down when they bubble up, and by engaging them in a constructive manner instead of letting them collect into an uncontrollable geyser that knocks you and everyone else over with its force. And I'm not saying you should do it alone. I'll be here for you, but you might need more help than I can give. You might want to consider seeing a counselor."

I mulled it over. "Alright."

"Really?" Shay lifted an eyebrow. "I thought you might reject that out of hand."

I shook my head. "No. I don't want to keep sabotaging my life. If there's a way out, I'll take it. I'm ready for change. The good kind."

Shay smiled again, then she reached her hand into the hair at the back of my head, pulled me in, and kissed me. Her lips were warm and soft, her lavender perfume faint after not having been applied the night before. I could've stayed in her embrace forever, if she'd let me.

When she pulled back, she looked me in the eyes. "I love you, you know that?"

She said it so matter of factly. So easily. Without question or hesitation.

"I love you, too," I said.

Shay unlocked her hotel room door, pushed it open, and stepped inside. She turned and looked at me. "You coming?"

"I would, but the captain's paying for two rooms. Seems like a waste not to use both."

Shay snorted, a smile curling her lips. "And you think I'd tell the Captain?"

I entered after her, closing the door behind me. "You're so fiscally irresponsible. What a minx."

Shay's smile didn't waver. "You're an idiot, you know that?"

"I do. Want to make out again?"

Lucky for me, she did.

33

cracked my eyelids and blinked in the darkness, tendrils of a dream floating away like flower petals on a gust of wind. My mind had been churning through an imagined story, something about a decades long battle between merfolk and unicorns, the rulers of the sea pitted against the kingdom of the forest. There'd been action and adventure, battles with speared unicorns and gored mermen, gratuitous flying as there always was in dreams, and even more gratuitous appearances of half-naked elven lovelies.

Of course, I didn't need the latter. I had one of those next to me already. I craned my neck, making out Shay's outline in the bed against the calm darkness of night. On the far side of the room, our window was cracked open, allowing the cool night breeze in alongside the occasional warble of a nightingale. Beyond that in the sky above, stars twinkled, though faintly against a backdrop more dark purple than black.

I blinked again and yawned, confronting a singular question that assaulted me with its pertinence. *What in the world was I doing up so early?*

Based on the color of the morning sky, I'd wager it was about six in the morning, but I was the last person in the world to make an educated guess on the matter, mostly because I could count on two hands the number of times I'd woken before dawn. Even when I had, I'd rarely glanced at a speck of nature before swilling at least two cups of coffee, at which point my sensory perception and color balance were already wrecked from caffeine.

Shay breathed quietly beside me, so I lifted the blanket off my side of the bed, rolled, and escaped without waking her. I crossed the room slowly so as to not stub my toe on a lurking sofa chair and made my way to the wash closet. There I took some of the cool water in the basin and splashed it on my face.

Somehow I managed not to gasp. It was colder than I'd expected.

I looked into the mirror, barely able to make out my own features in the darkness. Whether by the water I'd doused myself with or some trick of the light, I noticed a reflected sheen over me, like that of a merman's scales.

I shook my head and reached for a towel. Apparently, fragments of my dream still haunted me. *Mermaids versus unicorns...* It was a fairy tale befitting a twelve year old boy, or girl more like. A total implausibility, at least in this day and age of cities and modern armies and progress, and yet something of the sort might've happened in the past before the combined might of humans, elves, dwarves, and others forced them into hiding.

Still...maybe they weren't as extinct as I and everyone else of modern sensibilities thought. Sure, the mermaids might be a stretch. Although that crazy old coot Connors had insisted he'd heard merfolk in the waters off Aragosto on misty nights, we had zero tangible evidence that they'd been seen in decades. We didn't even know for a fact that Johnny Nicchi had been stabbed with a trident, so to tie his murder to a mermaid was speculation even I had a hard time convincing myself of.

But the unicorn? Again, we hadn't seen a live one. Maybe the horn had belonged to a specimen long dead, maybe a corpse someone had happened across in the forest and pilfered. But there was no question in my mind that the bloodied horn we'd found in Joey's ranch home was, in fact, from that most magical of equine species.

The burning question, though, was how the horn had come into Joey's possession? He was a hunter, so maybe he'd found and slain one of the mythical beasts himself, but why in the world would he use a horn to attack Carmine Abano? Wouldn't he stick to a knife or bow, one of the weapons he was used to? And what role did the horn play in Johnny's death, because there was no doubt his demise and Joey's attack were related. Basically, what role would a unicorn play in a murder and subsequent retaliation?

Or, put differently, why would someone murder over a unicorn?

I paused as I wiped my face with the towel, blinking into the mirror.

I threw the towel back over its rack, returned to the bed, and sat down gently, trying not to make a ruckus. I reached out and gently shook Shay by the shoulder.

"Shay? Shay?"

She muttered and rolled over. I tried again.

"Shay? You awake?"

Her eyes fluttered, and she looked about without recognition for a second. Then her eyes flicked toward the window and back at me.

"Jake?" She yawned. "What's the matter? What time is it?"

"I don't really know. I'd guess about six."

"In the morning?"

"Unless winter came a lot fast than expected, it would have to be."

She reached a hand up from under the blanket and rubbed her eyes. "What are you doing up?"

"Something woke me."

"A volcanic eruption?"

I snorted. "I deserved that. Ask a stupid question, or vice versa. Whatever. The point is, do you remember when Mines told us about the last murder in Aragosto?"

"The last murder...?" Shay sat up a little. "Jake, what's going on? What are you talking about?"

"The last murder in Aragosto. Back when they still had a homicide detective on staff. How long ago did she say that was?"

"I don't know. Six years?"

"Yeah. That's what I thought." I stood and started to pace. "When I asked Joey about that abandoned home near Sea Ridge Tours, he said the guy who owned it died five or six years ago. Not that he was murdered, that he died, but still."

"You think it was the same guy?"

"Yeah. Martin something. No. Martinsvale. It was a last name."

Shay sat up all the way. "Martinsvale? Who the heck is that?"

"Connors mentioned him. Said he was the guy who told him about the merfolk, who showed them to him. Silverbrook ignored him, but what if Connors was telling the truth? Martinsvale must've been the guy who lived in that abandoned house. I'm willing to bet that unicorn horn on him being the guy who was murdered six years ago."

Shay swiped a hand through her hair, trying to tame its unruly nighttime behavior. "Since when do you come up with crazy theories at night? I thought that was a daytime pastime?"

"Think about it, Shay," I said. "Joey said the home next door belonged to the head of a nature conservancy. That the guy who'd lived there had been a real pain in the ass, both to guys like him and to the Abanos, who if my mind serves me correctly own the hunting ranch Joey works at. Why would he be a pain in the ass? Because he kept them from hunting and fishing the sorts of creatures they wanted to, I'd bet. If they could eliminate a guy like that? The only person who stood in the way and was willing to make a scene about it?"

"Whoa, there," said Shay. "Are you suggesting all these murders are about—"

"Territory," I said. "Hunting and fishing rights, and not just to the obvious stuff like fish, crabs, turkeys, and deer. I'm talking about hunting merfolk and unicorns. Trophy hunting, perhaps. Or poaching. But I'm willing to bet there were two sides to that business, the Abano's and the Nicchi's. Based on how wealthy the Abanos are, I'll give you one guess as to who won that battle."

"But...you think this has been playing out for the last *six years*? Why would it come to a head now?"

"I don't know," I said. "Maybe it has something to do with Bianca. Either way, we need to get ahold of the files related to the murder from six years ago. If I'm right and it was this conservancy guy Martinsvale who was murdered, then we might not need to prove who murdered Nicchi. We might be able to nab our killer off a six year old crime."

"That's a lot of ifs," said Steele. "And it assumes people are actively hunting merfolk and unicorns. And what about Joey's manhunt?"

I started throwing on my clothing. "Mines will be fine without us for the search. She'll know his haunts better than we would. For all we know, he's off hiding in the forest. We need to focus on the things we can control, and I know for a fact where those case records will be."

"But can't this wait? You know, until dawn at least. Preferably until after Quinto arrives with our clothes and we put some breakfast in our bellies?"

"Good call," I said. "We can grab more of those egg and sausage sandwiches on our way out. But that's going to be a no-go on Quinto and fresh clothes. Don't worry.

I won't throw you back just because you're a little on the ripe side."

Shay snorted. "Oh, I wasn't worried about *me...*"

"Come on, Shay. Chop-chop. We're one connection away from breaking this thing wide open."

Shay grumbled, but she got up and started to get dressed, all while I learned what it felt like to wait on someone else in the wee hours of the morning. It gave me a sense of empowerment, but I somehow doubted I'd be rising early again just for the hell of it.

34

"Come on, come on." I paced in front of the Aragosto police station, my arms crossed tightly. The morning sky resembled a shallow pool, a dark sea green in color flecked with streaks of blue and magenta. "Seriously, where is everyone? Shouldn't someone be here? This is a police station, for crying out loud! What if someone got knifed or assaulted or robbed in the middle of the night? They're supposed to wait until the morning to report it?"

Shay sat on a bench to the right of the locked front doors, finishing the last of her breakfast sandwich. "That's what Bianca did."

"Well, it's a terrible system. Someone should work overnight."

"Aragosto is small," said Shay. "As far as we know, there are only four cops in the entire town, all of whom I'm guessing were working later than we were last night."

I kept pacing. "Mines said she'd be here bright and early to start the manhunt."

"Well, I guess this is a little *too* bright and early."

I snorted and approached a window. Through it, I could see the interior of the station, which stubbornly remained as empty as a minute ago. A clock on the wall ticked rhythmically, the hour hand firmly stuck at six and the minute hand approaching fifty.

"Those doors aren't going to open no matter how hard you scowl," said Shay.

"I'm disappointed with the lack of service here. I'm going to file a complaint."

Shay swallowed the last of her sandwich. "You know, earlier I was thinking I should capture a vivid mental picture of you waking me up before dawn to drag me off to work. You know, to preserve it for posterity. But if this is how you're going to act before seven, I think I'd rather forget it entirely. Heck, I'll never wake you this early again myself."

"Do you think they'd mind if we break in?"

Shay raised an eyebrow in my direction. "That's a joke, right?"

"Sort of. This front window doesn't look like it would stand up to a good pounding. We could always blame the damage on Joey if anyone asks."

"We can't break into a police station, Daggers. We'll just have to wait until someone shows up."

I shook my head. "We can't do that either."

"I'm assuming you mean *you won't,* but okay. Do you have any better suggestions?"

I snapped my fingers a few times. "What if we talked to the homicide cop in charge of the case directly? You said it yourself, it's a small town. If he's still here, I'm sure we can find him."

"We don't even know his name," said Shay.

"No, Mines mentioned it. It started with a 'G'. Grimes or Gimley or—"

"Gentry."

"There you go. See? You do remember. Good job."

Shay stood. "Alright. So we have a name. I'm still not sure trying to find him is a better idea than waiting. Even if he's up—"

I snorted. "Come on. An old retired guy? Of course he'll be up early."

"As I was saying, even if he's up early, how would we find him? Someone else who's up would have to point us his way. You plan on asking Weston at the hotel?"

"Well, I'd rather do *something* than sit here. And no, I wouldn't ask Weston. We need someone we can trust. Someone who won't lead us astray." My eyes widened. "Someone who'd be up at seven in the morning in a spot where we'd know where to find her."

A light flickered behind Shay's eyes. "Fair enough. Race you there."

35

We must've arrived right at the top of the hour, but Norma's word proved true. The door opened upon our touch, the shopkeeper's bell sounding as we pushed into the bait shop. Just as when we'd let ourselves in yesterday, no one manned the counter.

"Norma?" I called out. "It's Daggers and Steele. Quinto's pals, from yesterday? You back there?"

I heard a thump and a groan, and I almost darted into action except for the fact that a deep voice rumbled around the corner from the break room. "Just a sec."

Instead of Norma, it was Felix who lumbered through the doorway, holding a hand against the top of his head.

"Hey, Felix," I said. "You okay?"

"I'm fine," he said, waving. "I was rummaging around in one of the back cabinets when you called. I startled and smacked my head. No biggy."

I remembered his mom saying something about missing gin, but he didn't seem drunk. He'd better not be at seven in the morning.

"Your mom around?" asked Shay.

Felix shook his head. "Said she was going to be a half-hour late. Asked me to cover for her. I didn't have any jobs this morning, so I obliged. Family business and all. Why? Is something going on with Folton?"

"Nothing like that," I said. "Actually, you might be as much of a help as your mother. You've lived in Aragosto for a long time right?"

"Close to two decades. Why?"

"Do you remember a cop who retired a few years back by the name of Gentry?"

Felix rubbed his head, whether in thought or to massage his sore noggin I wasn't sure. "Uh...yeah. An old guy. I remember him."

"Is he still in town? And if so, do you know where we could find him?"

Felix pulled his hand down. "Well, to the first question, yeah, he's around. He comes by the bait shop every now and again. He's got a fishing dinghy that he takes around the bay, just for sport. Got to do something when you're retired, I guess. But I have no idea where he lives, if that's what you're asking. Sorry."

I clicked my tongue. "Dang. You wouldn't happen to have records of bait shop customers somewhere in the back?"

"Not with their addresses, no. Although..."

"Although, what?" asked Steele.

"Well, if he's got a boat, that means he pays to register it with Keonig, the dock super. His address would be on the registration."

"And do you think Keonig would be in at the moment?" asked Steele.

"There's a good chance," said Felix. "Here. Come with me. I'll lock the shop up behind us. Mom'll forgive me."

Felix ushered us out, down to the edge of the wharf, and over to the middle pier numbers, eventually stopping at a small shack situated there. He pushed on in, and we followed, virtually filling the standing space at the front of the shack's interior. What little other space remained was occupied by a collection of bookshelves, filing cabinets, and one lonely, yellowing potted plant that looked like it hadn't been watered in a month.

Keonig sat on a stool behind a slim counter, reading a book with a tattered binding. He looked up as we entered. "Hey. Skillethands. And you guys. The cops. What's up?"

"You've met detectives Daggers and Steele, right?" said Felix. "They're trying to track down that ex-cop. Gentry? He's got a fishing boat at the end of the dock, pier thirty-seven or thirty-eight or something. Any chance you have his address somewhere?"

"Yeah, on his pay slip," said Keonig. "You need it?"

"If you don't mind," said Steele.

"Sure. No problem. Give me a minute."

Keonig stood, squeezed past us to one of the filing cabinets, threw open a drawer, and started flipping through the contents. We waited.

Felix cleared his throat, sounding like a rhino with whooping cough as he did so. "So, um...since we're here. Do you mind if I ask you a question about Folton?"

"Sure," I said. "Shoot."

"I know he's a cop like you are. But he's also my family, even if we've been separated for over fifteen years. And I know he wasn't exactly a saint before he joined up with you, but with all that said..."

We gave him a moment. He didn't finish his thought.

"Yes?" said Shay.

"Well...how upset do you think he'd be if he found out I'd screwed up in the past? I mean...he'd forgive me, right?"

I waved him off. "Come on, Felix. As you said, Folton's past is checkered, too. As long as you didn't murder or rape anyone, I think you'll be fine."

Felix's eyes widened. "*What?* Oh, no. Nothing like that."

"Then you'll be fine. Seriously, he's family. He'll forgive you." I narrowed an eye. "You're not involved in any of *this* though, are you?"

"Any of what?" asked Felix.

"Johnny Nicchi's disappearance. Carmine Abano's stabbing. Whatever Joey Nicchi is up to."

"No," he said. "Absolutely not. I promise. I wasn't even that good of friends with Johnny. We'd talk on the docks sometimes, that was it. I try to be friendly with everyone. Gets me more work, you know?"

Despite being so familiar with Quinto, I couldn't get a good read on the half-troll's face. Nonetheless, I trusted him. Call it the family connection.

Keonig pulled a slip from the cabinet. "Here we go. One twenty-one Hill Avenue. If you go down Main, take a left on Walnut, you'll find it."

"Thanks," I said. "You, too, Felix. We appreciate it. Take care of yourself, will you?"

Shay and I started for the door.

"Wait," said Felix.

I turned. "Yeah?"

"Folton. He'll be back, right?"

Shay put a hand to Felix's arm. "He will. Don't worry. We all want him back."

"Mostly because he has our clothes," I said.

Shay nodded. Felix didn't get it, but he was nice enough to wave goodbye anyway.

36

I knocked on the door for a second time, shifting impatiently on the balls of my feet. A family of baby birds in a nearby tree was chirping up a storm, but as far as noises within the house, I still hadn't heard any.

"Maybe he's not in," said Steele.

"Like I said earlier, he's a retired guy who lives in a small town. Of course he's here. The only other place he might be is at sea, and we checked the pier to make sure his raft was still in before hoofing it over here."

"*Raft?*"

"Even referring to it as a skiff would be generous."

With the morning sun strengthening and warming the back of my neck, I knocked a third time and called out. "Excuse me? Officer Gentry? Are you there?"

Finally I heard something. A creaking, some footsteps, what might've been a groan, and then the door opened, but only halfway. A guy of middling height stared at us through the gap, his gray hair thinning but closely cropped. Whatever care he took in grooming the hair on top of his head didn't apply to the bottom half, however, as a wiry, disheveled beard stuck out from his chin in every direction at once.

He glared at us in the way only old-timers can. "Well? What is it? Who are you and what the hell are you doing on my porch?"

"Officer Gentry?" I said.

"Who's asking?"

"I'm Detective Jake Daggers. This is my partner Detective Shay Steele."

"Never heard of you." He started to close the door.

I stopped it with my hand. "We're not local. We're from New Welwic, the 5th Street Precinct. I'm sorry to bother you, but we'd really like to ask you a few questions."

"And I'd really rather not answer them," he said. "Now get your damn hands off my door. My coffee's going cold."

I didn't flinch. "It's about Martinsvale. I'm right in assuming he's the one who was murdered six years ago, aren't I?"

Gentry squinted at us. "What the hell are you talking about?"

"The guy who ran the nature conservancy. I'm taking a bit of a wild guess, but I'm assuming his name was Martinsvale and he was murdered six years ago. You investigated the case, right?"

Gentry pulled the door open a bit further. I drew my hand back. "Who did you say you were again?"

"Daggers and Steele." I indicated who was who with my thumb. "We work in homicide."

"Alright. That explains things a *little*, but it doesn't tell me why you're here asking about a six year old murder investigation."

"Mr. Gentry," said Steele. "Were you aware that a local man, Johnny Nicchi, had been murdered?"

Gentry pulled the door the rest of the way open. "I'd heard he'd gone missing, not that someone killed him." He shot a glance my way. "I don't get out much."

I didn't doubt him. "Nicchi washed ashore in our jurisdiction, which is why we're here investigating his murder. It's a long story, but we think his death might be related to the murder you worked six years ago. It was Martinsvale, right?"

Gentry nodded. "Yeah. Phillip Martinsvale. Ran a nature conservation society, just like you said, though I'm pretty sure he was the only member."

"And the case into his death," I said. "It was ruled a murder, correct? Was it solved, or is it still cold?"

"Murder, yeah," said Gentry. "But it's not a cold case. It was warm and pink in the center. We found the guy who did it within a few hours."

"You did?"

The old guy nodded. "A local bum by the name of Thimbleton. He was drunk as a skunk when we found him, not more than a few blocks from where Martinsvale got stabbed. Claimed he had no idea what we were talking about, that the last thing he remembered he was walking out of the Blind Pig on 4th, but he had blood on his hands and the murder weapon on him. We matched the entry wound and everything."

I looked at Shay. She gave me a shrug.

Gentry got cagey again. "What? What's that supposed to mean?"

Questioning the guy's investigative chops wouldn't get me anywhere. "Nothing. It's not important at the moment. But maybe you can tell me a little about the Abanos, since we're here."

Gentry lifted a thick eyebrow. "The fishing tycoons?"

I nodded. "When did they start building their fishing and crabbing businesses?"

"I'm not exactly sure. Maybe ten years ago."

"But I'm guessing they didn't take off until after Martinsvale died."

Gentry's brow furrowed. "Well...I don't know. I never kept that close an eye on them. Why?"

"Do the Abanos have a history with the Nicchis?"

"You mean like a family feud?"

"Exactly," I said. "Do you know if they've clashed over hunting or fishing rights? Or gotten into any fights since Martinsvale's death?"

"Look, Detective," said Gentry. "You're barking up the wrong tree. I'm retired. Been retired for over three years. I don't work cases any more, and I'm not plugged into the goings on at the station either. If you think there's a blood feud or gang war going on in Aragosto, I think you might've lost your marbles, but talk to Sergeant Mines or whoever's in charge these days. They'll know far more than I would. I can't help you."

I felt a surge of adrenaline like I always did when I felt close to the end of a case, urging me to push forth and kick down doors and pound heads and shake people until the clues I needed fell out, but I forced it down. I could tell Gentry was telling me what he knew, little as it may be.

I swallowed back my frustration. "Thanks for your assistance, anyway. Hope you enjoy the rest of your morning."

The old guy grunted and closed the door, but at least he didn't slam it. I turned and walked with Steele down his porch steps and back to the street, a quaint stretch of gravel lined with leafy trees and flowers. Apparently, every neighborhood in Aragosto tried to make you gag with its bucolic nature.

"Well, that wasn't as useful as I'd hoped it would be," I said.

"It wasn't exactly a waste of time, either," said Shay. "We confirmed your theory about Martinsvale, for one. You should pat yourself on the back over that alone. And we found out an innocent man might be in jail for murder."

"Yeah, we'll have to bring that to the DA's attention. Assuming we can find proof it wasn't a frame job. All in good time. But discovering I was right about the murder of a local naturalist by itself doesn't put us any closer to discovering the man's killer."

"It doesn't?" said Shay. "What about the Abano and Nicchi brothers?"

"Let me rephrase that. If doesn't put us any closer to *proving* any of the above did it."

"I suppose so," said Shay. "But Joey's attack on Carmine opens up his life to legal scrutiny. We may not have warrants to search the Abanos' various properties yet, but the clues you've put together might be enough to sway a judge into granting the order. Beyond that, there are always witness statements. If Carmine survives, I'll be interested to hear what he has to say. Likewise with Joey, assuming we can find him."

"Right. The manhunt." I paused, blinking. Then I smacked my palm into my forehead. "Oh. *Of course!*"

"What?" said Shay.

I smiled. "I bet I know where Joey Nicchi is hiding. Come on!"

37

As we rounded the edge of town, I noticed a dust cloud approaching from the direction of the city. It could've been anything. A dust devil. A storm. A herd of stampeding mustangs, or even unicorns. But I suspected I knew what caused it. There was a reason Quinto had travelled behind Shay and me during our ride into town.

The rickshaw pulled up beside us, the driver huffing and puffing. Quinto hopped down, a look of surprise on his face. "Hey. What are you two doing out here? I thought I'd find you at the hotel."

"Negative, bud," I said. "We couldn't wait. A lot's changed since last night."

"Such as?"

"Carmine Abano got stabbed," said Shay. "By Joey Nicchi, unless something really weird is going on. There's a manhunt ongoing for him."

Quinto whistled. "Sounds like things got good right as I left. As always…"

"You spent the night with Cairny," I said. "I'm assuming you made out fine."

The big guy smiled. "I did. Oh, and speaking of spending the night..." He reached into the rickshaw and extracted a backpack. "Got a change of clothes for both of you. You want to head back to the hotel?"

"Maybe later. We've got more pressing matters to attend to."

"Suit yourself." He thanked the rickshaw driver and threw the pack over his back. It looked comically small against his massive shoulders, almost as if he was wearing a pack designed for a kindergartener.

Shay chortled.

"What?" said Quinto.

"Nothing," said Shay. "We're glad to have you back. Especially because we might need your help subduing an unhinged huntsman armed with a knife and a bow."

Quinto grunted. "Of course. Why is it you never ask for my help decoding a complex cipher or patching together a web of disparate clues into a cohesive narrative?"

"I ask you to help with paperwork," I said. "Doesn't that count?"

Quinto snorted. We started up the path toward the forest.

"So," I said. "You manage to make it to Taxation and Revenue last night before they closed?"

"By the skin of my teeth," said Quinto. "But yeah. Good thing, too. Your instincts were right. I wasn't able to delve into the files as thoroughly as I wanted—I left them at the precinct for safekeeping—but an initial perusal showed what I would say are abnormally large gross revenues for both Doc Fowler's flying horse show and the Abano brother's fishing enterprise."

"Right. Fowler," I said. "I'd almost forgotten about that guy."

"What about for Nicchi Fishing and Crabbing?" asked Steele.

"Those records actually looked pretty normal," said Quinto. "As a matter of fact, they showed severe financial trouble. Just what Bianca and Joey hinted at."

"Hmm." I scratched my chin. "So we weren't lied to about that. Unless Johnny was hiding some of his income. But that wouldn't make sense. His company would be an ideal way to launder funds. Odd... What about Joey Nicchi?"

"I didn't look into him," said Quinto. "You didn't ask me to."

"That okay," said Shay. "We didn't consider him a suspect until last night, after you left. And he still isn't, in his brother's murder. We're just trying to figure out how his family and the Abanos tie together."

Quinto shot his finger up the hilly forest path. "Speaking of Joey, are we heading to Sea Ridge Tours? If there's a manhunt going on, I have to imagine that would be the first place you'd look."

"It was," I said. "But we're heading to that abandoned shack next door, instead."

"Hmm." Quinto shrugged. "I guess it would put him in close proximity to his stuff."

"It's more than that." I explained the situation with Martinsvale as we walked.

Quinto nodded. "That makes sense. But how in the world did you figure it out?"

"I had a dream about mermaids fighting unicorns."

"*Right.*"

The dilapidated farmhouse came into view, the field of yellow flowers in front of it still a hive of animal activity.

I extracted Daisy from my jacket and gripped her tight. "Well. Here we are. Let's treat this like we would any other breach and enter scenario. Assume Joey is in there, still armed and dangerous. I'll take the lead. Steele, you're in the middle. Quinto, you've got the rear. Anyone want to secure a weapon from the barn before we go in?"

Quinto shook his head. "I'm better with my fists in close quarters. Besides, I can use your backpack as a shield if need be."

"And risk having all our clothes get slashed?" said Shay.

"Better than my arm. Or something more vital to my health."

None of us could argue with that. With a plan settled upon, we headed up the hill. I approached the hovel's front door, knowing from the growth of ivy over it that Joey hadn't used it to gain entry. Nonetheless, the 'breach' part of our breach and entry turned out to be exceedingly easy. The door fell inward, crashing to the floor with the slightest of pushes. I think the ivy stuck to its face provided more resistance than the hinges had.

"There goes the element of surprise," I said.

I moved in carefully, Daisy at the ready. A rich earthy scent worked into my nose, that of moss and damp wood and mold. A greenish light filtered through the house, tinted by lichens and the leaves of creepers that covered what remained of the home's windows. I heard a crunch and spun, only to see a gray, squirrel-shaped blur dive into a rotten hole through the base of one of the outward-facing walls.

It only took us a couple minutes to secure the house. I shook my head as we left the bedroom and its collection of mushrooms growing from the mattress, heading back into what must've been the living room once upon a time.

"I don't get it," I said. "I was sure Joey would be here."

"It would be a good place to hide," said Quinto. "Except for the fact that you'd actually have to spend an extended period of time here."

"It might be a good hiding place in general," said Shay, eyeing a lumpy, moss-covered sofa with unease. "But I'm not sure I buy that it would've necessarily made sense for Joey to come here."

"How so?" I asked.

"It's your theory," said Steele. "I think you've got it wrong."

"I'm listening."

"Well, since the start of this case, you've focused on the fact that Johnny was stabbed with a trident, namely because you associated the weapon with merfolk and you always latch onto the supernatural elements of any case we're assigned to. I've always thought this had far more to do with something mundane, Johnny's finances or Bianca's infidelities perhaps. I think the truth lies somewhere in the middle.

"Since you made the connection about Martinsvale this morning, you've seemed convinced the Abanos and Nicchis were both involved in the same illegal enterprise, but the evidence suggests otherwise. Only the Abanos are wealthy, as evidenced by their mansion and the records Quinto found at Taxation and Revenue. If someone is running a poaching operation, it's probably them and them alone."

"So how does Johnny get dragged into this, then?" I asked. "He needs a loan and goes to the Abanos?"

"That's a possibility," said Shay, "but another is that it all happened organically. Let's assume Johnny was tight on funds, that he fired his brother for the reasons he claimed. The money problems put stress on his already souring relationship with his wife, Bianca. Bianca saw the tide coming in, so she decided to get out in front of it. She needed someone to take care of her, so she went after Carmine. Her personality may leave something to be desired, but there's no question she's attractive. She could've easily seduced Carmine."

"Then Johnny somehow finds out she's cheating on him, does a little digging, figures out who it is, and confronts him."

"Something like that," said Shay. "Maybe there's an argument. For whatever reason, Carmine, or perhaps he and his brother, kill Johnny and dump him at sea. They steal his boat and either sell it or scuttle it to defer suspicion. No one's the wiser until we show up a week and a half later with proof of his murder. At that point, thanks to Bianca or Keonig at the dock, the word spreads, including to Joey."

"He implied he hadn't heard when we first talked to him," said Quinto.

"And he was probably lying," said Shay. "Because I suspect he'd also heard the rumor about Bianca's infidelity, and he didn't mention that either. If I'm right, he's the one who broke into her home. Being Johnny's brother, he almost certainly would've had a key. Remember, it was their parent's home. That explains why Bianca reported the break in, because it really happened. Maybe at Johnny's home, Joey found evidence not of financial distress but of who Bianca was seeing. That's why he attacked Carmine."

"Okay," I said. "I think I could be willing to believe all that. But where did the unicorn horn come from? We looked inside the barn and in the Sea Ridge ranch home. There didn't appear to be more contraband."

"I get what you're implying," said Shay. "It threw me for a loop that the Abanos own Sea Ridge Tours. It made me think that for sure Joey was involved. But what if he was a patsy? Just someone to run the front of the house, someone with plausible deniability for any illegal activity. It's entirely possible the Abanos were running poaching operations in the woods without Joey's knowledge."

"Which would mean the unicorn horn didn't come with him," I said. "But that he found it elsewhere. Probably at one of the Abanos' warehouses near where he confronted him. Maybe he was lying in wait for Carmine and happened upon the contraband unintentionally."

"That's what I was thinking, too," said Shay.

"Which would mean there might be more to the crime scene than we originally thought," I said. "More clues. Who knows if they'll tell us anything about where Joey is now, but it might be worth checking out."

Shay nodded. "Perhaps."

"You think our efforts would be better served elsewhere?" said Quinto.

Shay bobbed her head from side to side. "Well, the way I see it, Joey's probably done one of two things. Either he's fled the scene, knowing we'll be coming after him for murder, or he's gone into hiding. Unless he's been framed, which I *highly* doubt, there's only one reason he would do the latter."

"Because he wants to finish the job," I said. "Or perhaps go after Orlando, too."

"Exactly," said Shay. "We should get people to the hospital, his home, and his businesses at the docks."

"We're going to need more people."

"Maybe Mines will be at the station by now."

I nodded. "Let's go."

38

Luckily, Mines was at the station, along with Officers Morris, Travers, and a new one I hadn't yet seen, a guy with a fuzzy upper lip who looked like he hadn't even graduated from the academy yet. Silverbrook was oddly absent, but Mines explained that she thought he'd spent the night at the medical clinic keeping an eye on Carmine and Orlando.

That caused me to sigh in relief. Although my sympathy toward Carmine and his brother could be measured with a pipette, that didn't mean I supported vigilante justice. After sharing our theories with Mines, she agreed with us wholeheartedly about the danger to the Abanos. She ordered Travers and the new guy to check on the Abanos' hillside home, sent Morris packing to the clinic to join Silverbrook, and decided to accompany us to the docks to check on what remained of the crime scene and expand the search, if necessary.

When we arrived, we found the scene largely unchanged from the night before. The crowd had dispersed, and no others had shown up to take their places, but no one had bothered to clean up the alley. The cracked crate still sat there, stinking of old fish, and the pool of blood upon the cobblestones had dried into a dark stain.

"So let me get this straight," said Mines. "You suspect Joey Nicchi found the unicorn horn he used to attack Carmine with while he was poking around one of the Abanos' warehouses?"

"That's the theory," I said. "You said one of these was owned by the brothers, right?"

"This one." Mines indicated the one on the left. "It's one of three seaside warehouses they own, if memory serves me right."

"Seeing as the fight occurred right outside this one, I'm guessing we should start here," said Shay.

"Well, sure," said Mines. "But unless the door's unlocked, we can't barge in. Last night we were in hot pursuit of a fugitive. We're not anymore. We don't have any clue where Nicchi might be. If we were to break into any of the Abanos' properties without a warrant, any evidence we found to corroborate your theory about poaching or smuggling would be forfeit."

I rubbed the bristles protruding from my chin. In my rush, I hadn't shaved. "Not if we find evidence of forced entry. Nicchi is still on the loose."

"But Nicchi would've entered the premises last night."

I smiled. "Who's to say that? Criminals often return to the scene of the crime."

Mines shot me a wary look. "Does every cop in the city work by the same methodology you do?"

"Some are a lot worse," I said. "At least we're bending the rules to make sure justice is done and not vice versa."

The sergeant sighed. "Fine. But it's got to be legit. I'm not going to kick down the door to the warehouse unless we find verifiable evidence that someone forced their way in last night."

"Fair enough."

We skirted the edge of the building, looking for clues. I trained my eyes upward, about fifteen feet off the ground where windows had been intermittently set in the side of the warehouse to let in light. After exiting the alley, crossing behind it, and entering the alley on the other side, I stopped in my tracks.

"There."

I pointed. I honestly wasn't sure if we'd find anything—I was simply looking for an excuse to get into the warehouse—but there it was. The lower left hand corner of one of the windows had been punched out. Glass shards sparkled atop a stack of crates underneath it.

"Well, I'll be," said Mines.

I climbed atop the crates, reached up, and tested the bottom corner of the window. It swung open on hinges attached at the top—soundlessly, I might add, as if they'd been greased.

"This is almost too good to be true," I said.

Quinto tested the crates to make sure they'd support him, then hopped up beside me. "Here. I'll give you a boost."

He cupped his hands. I stepped on them, grasped the edge of the window, and pulled myself through.

When I dropped down on the other side, it was onto another stack of crates, one covered with a tarp that muffled the sound of my fall. Though sun streamed through the high-set windows, it wasn't enough to bring the warehouse to life. Shadows stretched across the interior, crosshatching patterns of light and dark created by the tall shelves inside and the trusses holding up the roof. The fishy smell that surrounded the building intensified by an order of magnitude.

I heard Shay's voice, then a grunt, and she rolled over the lip of the window above and landed beside me.

Quinto's voice followed her. "Mines and I will stay out here. Take a look around. If you find anything, report back and we'll meet you at the front door."

"Gotcha," I said.

I hopped down and turned back to catch Shay as she followed me. I looked around, trying to make sense of the maze of crates, barrels, and containers around me.

"Maybe we should've brought a crow bar," said Shay.

"Perhaps. Let's look for anything that's already been forced open. The Abanos' wouldn't have left unicorn horns lying around, not if they have half a brain cell between them."

I headed off along the edge of one of the tall racks, keeping my eyes peeled for broken boards, discarded lids, or rumpled tarps.

A creaking sound stopped me in my tracks.

I turned toward the front of the warehouse to find an entrance set inside the larger, barn-sized door at the front opening. Two figures entered, the latter closing the door behind him, but not just any two figures. Bronmuth Silverbrook and Orlando Abano.

I shrunk behind the nearest crate, my mind racing. What the heck were the pair of them doing here, and *together?* I'd questioned Bronmuth's motives, but he couldn't possibly be on Abano's side. He wouldn't be complicit in murder, would he?

I forced my heart to slow as I listened, Shay silent as a mouse behind me.

"This is inexcusable, Bronmuth," said Orlando. "To think that *my brother* was brutally assaulted, in my town, outside my own place of business! *Explain that to me!*"

"Look, Orlando," said Bronmuth. "We're doing everything we can, I promise. It's not as if—"

Something whistled and thwacked. Orlando spun, crying out, as an arrow sprouted from his shoulder.

Bronmuth cursed as a figure dropped from the trusses at the ceiling, bounding off a crate and rolling as he hit the floor. Bronmuth reached for his nightstick, but he was too slow. Joey Nicchi ditched his bow and crossed the space between them in two loping bounds. He jumped and kicked, striking the dwarf in the face and knocking him to the ground.

I could barely believe it. I'd been kidding when I'd suggested Nicchi might've returned to the scene of the crime, and yet here he was, a knife strapped to his belt and his body coiled like a spring. He'd been lying in waiting for his chance at Orlando, just as we'd predicted.

Bronmuth groaned and rolled, but Joey planted another boot in his gut to silence him.

He turned toward Orlando, drawing his knife with a bandaged hand. "Well, well, Orlando. Fancy seeing you here."

Orlando groaned and grabbed his shoulder, stumbling to his feet. "What...? What the *hell* is wrong with you? You...you *animal!*"

Nicchi spun the knife. "Me? You're calling *me* the animal? After everything you've done? After what you did to my *brother?* You're a sick, twisted monster. A gods-damned sadist. You don't deserve as good an end as I'm about to give you."

He hefted his knife and stepped forward.

I jumped from the shadows. "Joey, stop!"

Joey spun, evaluating us with a cool gaze, almost as if he'd known we were there. Hell, he probably had. We hadn't exactly been quiet. A good twenty paces separated us from him, and for a split second I wasn't sure what was going to happen. He could've just as easily rushed us as plunged the knife into Orlando's heart.

He chose a different path. He yanked Orlando to his feet, secured him with one arm and pressed the edge of his knife to his neck with the other.

"Don't come any closer," said Joey. "I'll open him up from ear to ear. Don't think I won't."

"I don't doubt you, Joey," I said. "I know you will. But you don't have to do this. You don't have to kill anyone."

"*Bullshit,*" said Joey. "This bastard murdered my brother. Him as that scumbag Carmine, both. And I'm going to make damned sure he pays for it."

"And he will, Joey. I promise you. But not like this. It's not right. We can put him away for life. Trust me."

"*Trust you?*" Joey laughed and pressed the edge of his knife further into Orlando's throat, producing a croak from the captive. "You're not putting anyone away for life, not on poaching charges. And something tells me you're never going to prove he killed my brother either. I've looked around. They didn't leave any evidence behind. This bastard and his brother were *thorough*."

I heard more noises. The front door yanked open again, and Quinto and Mines poured through, the latter with truncheon in hand.

Joey took a couple steps back, Orlando still firmly gripped and the knife held in a vice-like grip. "Stay back! Don't even think about it!"

"Help me!" croaked Orlando.

"Shut it," threatened Joey, pushing the edge of the blade further into his throat.

I took a couple steps forward, my hands outstretched. "You're wrong, Joey. Orlando and Carmine are going down, not just for your brother's murder, but Phillip Martinsvale's, too. I can prove it."

Joey's eyes flicked in my direction. "What?"

"The man who ran the nature conservancy," I said. "Orlando and Carmine killed him so they could expand their poaching operation. We were at his abandoned home this morning. I found hard evidence it was them."

Out of my peripheral vision, I could tell Shay was looking at me, but she didn't say a word.

"That's impossible," said Joey.

"It's not impossible," I said. "They framed a poor idiot to make it look like a mugging. I can prove it. Listen to me, Joey. Carmine and Orlando are going away for life. You don't need to kill him. I met you. I talked to you. I could see it in your eyes. That's not who you are. You're not like them."

"You're damned right I'm not," he spat. "This isn't murder. This is justice!"

I took another step forward. I needed a new approach.

"You can't bring him back, Joey."

Nicchi stared at me, his jaw set and his eyes hard.

"I know you don't want to hear that," I said, "but it's true. Joey, my own mother was murdered when I was a teen. I've dealt with that loss my whole life. Don't you think I wanted to kill the men responsible at first? String them up and beat them before cutting them open? You're damned right I did. But it got easier. That anger faded over time. And life went on. It didn't seem like it would at first, but it did.

"Now you, Joey? You have a decision to make. If you kill Orlando, you'll go to jail for good, with today's choice weighing on you every day for the rest of your life. But it doesn't have to be that way. Carmine is still alive. If he pulls through, all you'll go to prison for is assault. You'll be out in a few years, and maybe it doesn't seem like you have anything to live for right now, but trust me, you do. You still have your mother, your sister. There's a woman out there who you haven't even met yet. A life with love and children. It's there for the taking if you want it. It's worth giving it a shot. For crying out loud, my friend Quinto found his missing family right here in Aragosto after two decades of searching, and I was a miserable wretch until my partner saved me.

"Trust me, Joey, your life is worth living. You just have to put the knife down and let me do my job."

The younger of the Nicchi brothers hadn't taken his eyes off me the entire speech, and I couldn't tell at my distance, but there might've been a hint of a tear in one of them.

His knife hand didn't move, and his teeth grated as he spoke. "You promise me both of them are going away for life? Carmine *and* Orlando?"

"I promise you, Joey."

Joey's arm fell. The knife clattered to the floor as he pushed Orlando to the ground. The elder Abano brother stumbled to his knees, grasping his throat.

Shay patted me on the back, and I heard her whisper, "Nice work."

I walked forward. Joey stood there, unflinching. I gave him a nod. "I won't disappoint you, Joey. Now, come with me. Peacefully."

39

I stepped out of the men's restroom at the Aragosto police station, feeling dapper or at the very least clean. After washing my face and de-funking my armpits, I'd donned the change of clothes Quinto had brought with him from Shay's apartment. With warm weather upon us, two days was more or less the respectable limit for how long a set of clothes could conceivably be continuously worn.

I found Shay in the center of the station, seated at one of a half dozen chairs that had been pulled together. She'd already changed into her new garb, now wearing dark jeans and an airy purple blouse under her yellow blazer. The smile on her face indicated she was also glad to be out of the attire she'd worn for the past fifty hours.

Bronmuth sat in one of the chairs beside her, holding a wet cloth to the side of his face. It couldn't completely hide the ugly welt that had sprouted over his cheek. Looked like it would leave him with a nice black eye, too.

"Hey, Silverbrook," I said, taking a seat in one of the chairs. "The doctor cleared you already?"

He grunted. "He poked and prodded me. Hurt like a mother, but he said there wasn't any structural damage underneath. Said it's somewhere between a grade three and four contusion, which apparently means it's a wicked bad bruise."

"Well, I'm glad it's not worse."

After the incident with Joey at the warehouse, Silverbrook had left for the medical clinic to have Pryor or one of the other physicians look at him, and I have to admit, I hadn't been sure if we should've let him go. Not that I had any legal authority to stop him, but his interaction with Orlando had me concerned. Of course, in the aftermath, I'd reevaluated the little I'd heard of their interaction, and there wasn't anything incendiary in what either of them had said. Sure, Bronmuth's personal relationship with the man was disconcerting, but he'd acted chummy with everyone we'd come across in town, even old crazy Connors.

I tried to approach the topic from the edge. "So...hard to believe Joey skewered Orlando. Though I have to think he could've hit him right in the heart if he'd wanted to. I guess he wanted to get in the last word."

Bronmuth grunted again. "I guess I didn't get the worst of it, did I?"

"You worried about Orlando?"

"Why would I be? He'll be fine. And if he did what Joey accused him of, he deserved worse. I'm surprised you talked him down."

"What? Why?"

"Hard to say. I got the impression you two don't play by the rules."

I looked at Shay.

She shrugged. "He's not wrong. Except about his insinuation that we'd let someone get murdered for kicks."

"Honestly, I thought you'd be more upset about the ordeal," I said. "You seemed chummy enough with Orlando."

The dwarf snorted. "I knew the guy. I never said I liked him."

I didn't get a chance to press the issue, which was probably for the best. The front door opened, and Quinto and Mines walked in.

"Hey," said Shay. "That didn't take long."

"Mostly because Orlando didn't have much to say," said Quinto.

"How is he?" I asked.

"He'll be fine," said Mines. "Doctor Pryor patched him up. The arrow hit soft muscle tissue, so he'll be up and running in a week or two. I left Morris and Travers at the clinic to keep an eye on him. If anything, Detective Quinto oversold our discussion with him."

"That bad, huh?" said Shay.

Mines nodded. "He maintained complete and total innocence in both the deaths of Johnny Nicchi and Phillip Martinsvale. Hell, he even claimed innocence regarding his poaching enterprise, and that was after we confronted him with the collection of powdered unicorn horn aphrodisiacs and mermaid scale handbags we found at the warehouse. Said if we had any evidence against him to present it in court and then asked for his lawyer. Wouldn't say a word after that."

I shook my head. "He's not stupid. He knows we have him dead to rights on the poaching charges, but he also knows that'll only get him a few years in jail, maybe less depending on the quality of his lawyer. He's hoping we don't have any way to pin the murders on him or his brother."

"The latter of whom is now in a coma," said Quinto. "Doctor Pryor gave him about a fifty-fifty shot of making it. If he does, it'll be good news for Joey, but even so, I can't imagine he'll talk any more than Orlando has."

"Speaking of Joey," said Shay. "How did you know your bluff was going to work, Daggers?"

"What bluff?" I said.

"Back at the warehouse. You told him we'd found evidence at Martinsvale's abandoned home that incriminated the Abanos. Obviously, we didn't."

"Oh. That," I said. "I didn't know it would work, honestly, but I was trying anything I could to talk Joey down."

Shay lifted a brow. "Seems kinda ballsy."

I shrugged. "That's how I roll. Also, I don't have a lot of experience in hostage situations. Good thing it worked, right?"

"Well, regardless," said Shay. "Joey's given us his testimony, and while it's nice to know we were right about him looking into his brother's death, finding the unicorn horn at the warehouse, and subsequently getting into a fight with Carmine, I'm not sure how much that's worth. He tried to kill both Carmine and Orlando, which kind of ruins his credibility as a witness, and all his suspicions about what they did to Johnny are just that. Suspicions. We can't count on him to bolster our case in any way."

"Good thing we won't need to," I said. "Not with the ace in the hole he gave us."

"You seem overly confident your plan is going to work," said Shay.

"It'll work," I said. "Trust me, I know her type. Mines? You want to come with us?"

"Might as well," she said. "But I'll let you two do the talking, if that's okay."

"Fine by me."

I stood and headed toward the back, going into the hallway that led to the restrooms. Before I got there, I took a detour, cranking on a door handle and letting myself into a small room.

Bianca sat at the table in the center. She looked up, her jaw tight and her brow creased in anger. "There you are! You still haven't told me what I'm doing here, you know. This is no way to treat someone who's had her life turned upside down in the last couple weeks. You realize I'm the victim, right? That *I'm* the one with the dead husband?"

I took a seat before her, and Shay joined me. Mines closed the door and stood in a corner, watching.

"Look, Bianca," I said. "I don't want to drag this out, so I'm going to cut to the chase. We know about you and Carmine Abano, okay? We know you were having an affair."

The young woman took a sharp breath and exhaled it just as sharply. "I don't know what you're talking about."

"Are you sure you want to try that strategy?" said Shay. "Joey told us what he found. We're going to recover it from his home as soon as we can get an officer there."

"Recover what from his home?" said Bianca.

"The broach," I said. "The one Joey stole from your home when he broke into it the night before last. The one with the inscription on the back stating, and I quote, 'To my dearest Bianca. Love, C.'"

"That doesn't prove anything," said Bianca. "Even if it does exist."

"Come on," said Shay. "There've been rumors about you circling for a while now. You met him for drinks two nights ago, for crying out loud. You may have been careful, but do you really think someone in town hasn't seen you sneak a kiss or hold hands at some point? Once we start pushing, how long do you think it'll take until a few witnesses step forth?"

Bianca didn't say anything, but I noticed a bit of a waver in her gaze.

"Let me lay it out for you, Bianca," I said. "You have two choices. Either you tell us everything you know, or we charge you with accessory to murder. I don't know how familiar you are with the law, but the sentence for that isn't much less than murder itself."

Bianca broke, and she broke *hard*. A deluge of tears poured forth, the dam holding them back suddenly broken. "Oh, *gods!* Fine! I admit it. I was seeing Carmine, okay? Is that what you wanted to hear? I'd been seeing him for months. My relationship with Johnny was a mess. If there was any love left between us, you sure as hell could've fooled me. But I swear, I didn't have anything to do with his death! I'd never wish that on any-one, especially Johnny! I just... I just wanted what every girl wants. Some love in my life, and not to have to worry about where I'd get my next meal or if the roof over my head would disappear. And now that's gone! You want to talk about Johnny? What about *me*? What was I supposed to do, huh? With my husband's business failing? Our marriage on the rocks? But that's all ruined now. Johnny's dead. His debts are going to fall onto me. He already mortgaged the house to keep his business afloat. He thought I didn't know, but I did! And now Carmine's in a coma. Even if he does survive, he'll be going to jail, right? But what about me? What about *me*? Gods, maybe I'd be better off in jail. At least there I wouldn't have to worry about starving or freezing to death in the winter."

"Hold your horses, Bianca," I said. "You're not think-ing this through."

The young woman wiped tears from her cheeks. "I'm not thinking things *through*? *How dare you*? My life is in tatters, and here you have the gall to—"

I put up a hand to silence her. "If Carmine and Or-lando Abano murdered your husband, they won't just go to jail. You can sue them in civil court for damages. Their fortune may have been gained partially through illegal means, but they're still loaded. It would be a slam dunk case for you. You'd be set for life."

The tears magically ceased, almost as if they'd all been for show. "*What?*"

"It only works if you tell us what you know, Bianca," said Steele. "If they both go down for murder. So start talking."

Bianca wiped her cheeks again, her demeanor worlds away from what it had been moments ago. "Um. Okay. So...here's what happened. The honest truth. I'd been seeing Carmine for months, just like I'd said. Johnny suspected, or at least I think he did. That night when he went missing? I suspected he'd gone out to confront Carmine. I didn't know for sure. It was a gut feeling. Or I thought he might've been leaving me. Either way, I found out for good the following morning."

"How?" I asked.

"Orlando and Carmine came to my house," she said. "They sat me down and told me what happened. That Johnny had been investigating Carmine, trying to make sure he was the one. He broke into one of their warehouses and found evidence of what they were doing. The poaching. You know about that, right? But it turns out Johnny wasn't that angry about *me*. Not after he found out something that gave him leverage. He tried to blackmail Carmine for a cut of the profits. That's why he went out the night he went missing. He'd already known for a while, they said. But Orlando and Carmine weren't interested in that. So they killed him, chopped his boat into pieces, and dropped his body in the ocean."

"Hold on," said Shay. "They *told you*? Why would they tell you that?"

"Carmine said I needed to know everything if I was to be brought into the family."

"You mean...?"

"He was going to marry me," said Bianca. "After the heat died down, he said. A few months from now. Once it was obvious Johnny wasn't coming back and no one would suspect anything."

I turned to Shay. She cocked an eyebrow, tilted her head, and mouthed what I thought were the words 'sole witness.' I think we were on the same page.

"Bianca," I said. "I believe that you and Johnny had grown apart, even to the point where you didn't care for each other. I also believe you never would've hurt him, not physically, not to kill him. So when Carmine told you what happened to Johnny, how did that make you feel?"

"Scared," she said. "Really scared. I didn't know what to think."

I nodded. "Good. And surely you must've been scared because Carmine threatened you? Told you he'd come after you if you went to the police, or if you refused to marry him?"

"Well, no, he never—"

"Bianca, think about this," I said. "He must've *threatened you* into *not telling,* otherwise that would mean you were aiding and abetting a known murderer, which would make you an accessory after the fact."

The young woman blinked. "Oh... Right. He did threaten me to keep quiet. I remember now."

"Of course you do," I said. "Now what can you tell us about Phillip Martinsvale."

"Who?"

"Local guy, head of the nature conservation society," I said. "Carmine and Orlando probably killed him, too."

Bianca's eyes widened. "Seriously? I...I don't know anything about that. Carmine never mentioned him."

I looked to Shay again. She nodded.

"That's alright," I said. "Just figured I would ask. Thankfully, one life sentence for murder should be enough. You stay right here. Let me a grab a notepad for you to write down your statement."

40

Steele, Mines, and I left the interrogation room, closing the door behind us. I hefted the legal pad with Bianca's confession, feeling pretty good about how everything turned out.

Mines hadn't said a word the entire time, but she finally spoke. "Um, Daggers? As I said, I'm not terribly experienced when it comes to these sorts of things, but...why did you lead Bianca into telling you Carmine had threatened her into keeping quiet?"

"You want to take this one, Shay?"

My partner nodded. "It was a twofold decision. For one thing, Bianca may be a cold, heartless, gold-digger, but that doesn't make her a murderer. Daggers and I both believed her on that. It seemed cruel to send her to prison on accessory charges simply because she was too stupid to understand what she was getting herself into. And second and perhaps more importantly, she's our only witness. We don't have a murder weapon. Without her testimony, the case against the Abano brothers falls apart. If we threatened her with serious jail time, she might wise up and realize she's the link that holds the chain together. If I were in her shoes in that scenario, I'd take my chances with Carmine's injury, hold my tongue, and marry him anyway, knowing he was only going away on poaching charges. We couldn't risk it."

"And there you have it," I said.

Mines shook her head. "Wow... I never would've thought of that. Guess it's a good thing I don't have to deal with murderers often."

"You'd gain the experience if you did," I said. "That's all it is. Experience. And some learn quicker than others." I shot a finger in Steele's direction.

She smiled. "Thanks, though you're the one who deserves the praise. You knew Bianca would crack, and she did."

"Honestly, I didn't expect the waterworks," I said. "But I knew the bit about filing a civil suit against the Abanos would work. I've seen her type before. Carmine might've been in love with her, wanting to marry her, but to her, Carmine was a paycheck, nothing more. Suing the Abano estate for their money solves her problems and does so without the chore of marrying Carmine. Bianca saw her opportunity and took it, just as I knew she would."

Mines sighed, looking defeated. "She's...really not a good person, is she?"

"Sometimes we have to let small stuff slide to make sure the really bad guys get the fate they deserve," I said. "The good news is, now you know. You can keep an eye on her. If she tries anything that crosses the line from skeezy to illegal, you'll be all over her like barnacles on a hull."

"Sure. Of course."

I held the notebook out. "Well. Here you go. I think you can take it from here, but if you need any help navigating the obstacles between here and the finish line, I think you know where to find us."

She accepted my offering. "Thank you, Detective Daggers. You too, Detective Steele. I'm not sure we could've solved this without you."

"Not a problem. Take care."

I turned to leave, motioning for Shay to follow me, but I paused after a couple steps. "Oh, one more thing, Sergeant."

"Yes?"

"You might want to take a look at Doc Fowler," I said. "We have reason to believe he's laundering large amounts of money through his flying horse show business."

"What?" Mines blinked, her eyes widening. "What makes you say that?"

"Our fellow detective, Quinto, pulled his financial records when he returned to town. I spotted gambling equipment when we stopped by his home to talk. Combine that with the fact that the bartender at the Muddled Merman sent a kid packing into the back at the sight of us like we were part of a sting operation. I put two and two together, and let's just say there's a good chance Fowler is running an illegal gambling ring out of the back of his bars."

Mines blinked again, her mouth agape. It took her a second to respond. "Um. Right. Thanks for the tip. I'll be sure to check into that."

I regarded Mines carefully, squinting as I looked at her. "You already know, don't you?"

"*What?*" said Mines. "No. Of course not. I mean…"

She sighed, hung her head, and gazed at her shoes. She rubbed a hand across her forehead, filled her lungs with air, pulled herself back up to full height, and closed the distance between us.

She spoke in a low voice. "Look, Detective, I never lied to you two. Aragosto is a small town, and it's safe for the most part. Take out Nicchi's and Martinsvale's murders, and this place would be darn near perfect. Given both of those might've been committed by the same two guys, I'd say our town is safer than it's ever been. But that doesn't mean it's stronger than ever. With the Abanos out of the picture, jobs'll be lost. All we have around here is fishing, crabbing, and tourism, and when it comes to the latter? Yeah, maybe there's a segment of people who aren't coming here for the horse show and the carnival attractions. But it keeps our town running. As long as they behave themselves, what's the harm?"

Shay and I exchanged glanced. "That's for you to decide. This isn't our jurisdiction."

Mines eyed us warily. "So you're not going to say anything?"

Shay shrugged. "We're in homicide. As long as no more of your residents wash up dead on our shores, you probably won't be hearing from us anymore. So try to avoid that."

Mines nodded. Shay and I turned and left.

When we reached the central portion of the station, Silverbrook was the only one left.

"Where's Quinto?" I asked.

Bronmuth pointed toward the front. Through the windows I spotted our oversized detective friend. Next to him was his brother. They gave each other a hug. Felix separated, waved, and walked away.

"Huh," I said.

Shay gave Bronmuth a wave, too. "Well, Silverbrook, we're on our way out. Nice working with you. Let us know if you need anything going forward."

The dwarf grunted, the cool compress still held against his face. "Right. Later."

"I'll miss that sunny disposition," I said. "Don't ever stop being you."

We left and joined Quinto at the mouth of the station. The big guy gave us a nod but kept his eyes on his brother, who receded into the distance.

"What was that about?" asked Shay.

"Oh, nothing," said Quinto. "He popped by while you were in the interrogation room with Bianca. Said he wanted to get something off his chest."

"Oh, right," said Shay. "He helped us get an address this morning with the aid of that superintendent, Keonig. He was acting a little cagey about something."

"Hopefully nothing bad," I said.

Quinto shook his head. "No. Not really. He actually...he told me he sometimes works for Doc Fowler. Moving stuff around, mostly. But the interesting part is that he wanted to let me know that Fowler—"

"Is running an illegal gambling operation out of his bars?"

Quinto nodded. "Yeah. And that he plays on occasion, cards mostly. I mean, the gambling makes sense given what I found in the financial documents and what you've said about the popularity of that horse show. But how did you know that?"

"You were distracted with other matters when we visited the bar," I said. "That and we stopped by Fowler's yesterday evening. Don't kick yourself over it."

"I wasn't about to."

"So," said Shay. "Are you going to forgive him for not mentioning it sooner?"

"What's there to forgive?" said Quinto. "What do I care if he gambles on the side every now and then? As long as it doesn't get in the way of his work, or comes down on Mother. Besides, he's family. He forgave me for being gone from his life for the past two decades. I think I can cut him a little slack."

"That sounds like sage advice, big guy," I said. "Probably some I should take to heart myself."

"To reach out to your brother?"

"It's one of the many relationship building exercises on my to do list. But I meant it in general. Don't sweat the small stuff, right?"

Quinto clapped me on the shoulder and showered me with his awkward, bucktoothed grin. "Exactly."

Shay smiled, too. "You know what? I'm glad this case brought us here. Not just because we were able to reunite Quinto with his folks and solve a murder, but because I think we all learned something."

"That small towns are never as idyllic as they seem?" I offered.

"I meant about the value of family."

Wasn't that the truth. It may not have been easy to endure at times, but with a little help on Shay's part, I'd faced a part of myself that I hadn't ever wanted to unearth. And even though the digging had been tough, it felt better to have it out in the open where I could address it. The thought of repairing my relationships with my brother and father was enticing. My renewed energy for strengthening my relationship with my son was invigorating. But it was the growing desire to build a new family with Shay that was most surprising.

But I was getting ahead of myself.

I gazed into the bright blue sky, trying to gauge the time. "Well, if I'm not mistaken, it's getting close to lunch. By the time we eat and head back home, the day'll be shot. Anyone else up for some fun and games on the boardwalk and a few Catch-a-Purries before we head back?"

"Catch a *what?*" said Quinto.

"We'll show you," said Shay. "They'll be right up your alley."

Shay took my hand, which I accepted happily, and we all headed in the direction of the ocean breeze.

ABOUT THE AUTHOR

Alex P. Berg is a mystery, fantasy, and science fiction author, a scientist, and a heavy metal aficionado. Connect with him at www.alexpberg.com. If you'd like to be notified when new books are released, please sign up for his mailing list on his website. You will only be contacted when new books come out, your address will never be shared, and you can unsubscribe at any time.

Word of mouth is critical to author success. If you enjoyed this novel, please consider leaving a positive review on Amazon. Even if it's only a line or two, it would be a *huge* help. Thanks!

www.ingramcontent.com/pod-product-compliance
Lightning Source LLC
Chambersburg PA
CBHW021216250626
47155CB00008B/2835